Where is Jason Rayner?

By
K.J.RABANE

Where is Jason Rayner

Copyright © 2013 K.J.Rabane
All rights reserved.

Where is Jason Rayner

Dedication.
To Rhys, Jack, Taylor and Zahra

Where is Jason Rayner

Acknowlegements

My thanks go to Nona and Glyn Evans for their help and continued support, retired Police Sergeant Alan Lloyd MBE for answering my repeated questions, Warren Pegley, Forensic Scientist, Sue Mort, Integrative Counsellor, Jan Marsh of Coleridge Press for her expertise and to Frank for listening.

Where is Jason Rayner

Table of Contents

Beginning
Chapter 1	Chapter 2
Chapter 3	Chapter 4
Chapter 5	Chapter 6
Chapter 7	Chapter 8
Chapter 9	Chapter10
Chapter11	Chapter 12
Chapter 13	Chapter 14
Chapter 15	Chapter 16
Chapter 17	Chapter 18
Chapter 19	Chapter 20
Chapter 21	Chapter 22
Chapter 23	Chapter 24
Chapter 25	Chapter 26
Chapter 27	Chapter 28
Chapter 29	Chapter 30
Chapter 31	Chapter 32
Chapter 33	Chapter 34
Chapter 35	Chapter 36
Chapter 37	Chapter 38
Chapter 39	Chapter 40
Chapter 41	Chapter 42
Chapter 43	Chapter 44
Chapter 45	Chapter 46
Chapter 47	Chapter 48
Chapter 49	Chapter 50
Chapter 51	Chapter 52
Chapter 53	Chapter 54
Chapter 55	Chapter 56
Chapter 57	Chapter 58
Chapter 59	Chapter 60

Where is Jason Rayner

Chapter 61	Chapter 62
Chapter 63	Chapter 64
Chapter 65	Chapter 66
Chapter 67	The End

Where is Jason Rayner

Where is Jason Rayner

Catherine's story

Chapter 1

He is a short man with kind eyes. "I'm glad you decided to come," he says, as I shake his hand. "You might be more comfortable on the couch or if you prefer there's always the chair."

I sit opposite him in the chair; I'm not ready for the couch.

"I want you to feel perfectly relaxed during these sessions," he says, switching on a small recording machine. "You don't mind? I always find it easier than writing notes."

I shake my head and look out of the window. Although it's still early afternoon, the sky is grey, a nothing colour, which leaches light from the room. He presses the button on a desk lamp then disappears behind it leaving me bathed in a yellow glow.

"Very well," his tone is cheerful, upbeat, "when you're ready, let's start at the beginning, shall we?"

Beginnings are always difficult. Where should I begin, especially now, after all that has happened? He's waiting, there's no pressure and the decision is mine. Taking a deep breath, I start my story.

Where is Jason Rayner

I suppose it began when I moved away from home. University wasn't an option I wished to consider so I enrolled on a crash three-month office management course at a college of Further Education in Bristol. After I qualified, I rang my aunt, with whom I lived, who said it was up to me what I decided to do. Financially in a comfortable position, thanks to the inheritance from my parents, I relished the freedom of being able to go wherever I wished, so I stuck a pin in a map of the British Isles and it landed on Lockford, a town on the south coast. Yes, you could say that was the beginning.

I remember it was raining; it was Mason Trent's birthday and I was hurrying back from the bakery with a tray full of doughnuts when I tripped over a raised paving stone and fell headlong into the arms of Jason Rayner.

"Steady," he said, rescuing the doughnuts with one hand and me with the other.

I thought he had the bluest eyes I'd ever seen, although perhaps even those were a fantasy too.

"Let me give you a hand," he offered. "Where are you going?"

"Arbuthnot and Trent, just over there."

He carried the tray across the road, dodging the puddles, then handed it back to me. In the office doorway, he leaned against the door to open it and stood back as I edged past him.

"Can I give you a ring sometime?" he asked.

I nodded and he made a note of the telephone number, which he took from the sign on the window. "By the way, what's your name?"

"Kate Newson," I answered, without turning around.

Where is Jason Rayner

I didn't think anymore about the encounter. No, that's not quite right. I dreamed about him that night. But in the morning his face vanished like breath on a mirror and I wondered if I'd imagined those blue eyes.

The next day, I was in the middle of filing a pile of court reports when the telephone rang. "Arbuthnot and Trent, Kate Newson speaking, how may I help you?"

"You can start by letting me take you out to dinner," he said.

I pretended not to know who was speaking and I heard him sigh, " How many dinner invitations do you get at ten past ten on a Wednesday morning, Miss Newson?"

"I'm not sure that's any of your business," I replied firmly.

"Well then, if you've decided that the answer is 'yes, I'd be delighted to have dinner with you on Saturday night, Jason', then I'll see you at eight in the Bell on the corner of High Street and Manor Road."

The telephone line clicked and I was left listening to the dialling tone.

He wasn't uppermost in my mind throughout that day or the next but when Friday arrived, I couldn't stop thinking about him. Would I go or would I leave him sitting at the bar of the Bell, wondering?

After work I walked to my flat, which took about fifteen minutes. I didn't get the bus - I wanted to think clearly about Jason Rayner. Opening my front door, I smelled a faint odour of disinfectant and smiled, everything was clean, orderly and 'spick and span' as my aunt would have said. Then the telephone rang and Rita's voice filtered into my ear. "Hello, just wondered how you are getting along - OK are you?"

"Yes, I'm fine. How are you, aunt?"

"Not so good, I've been missing you, especially after Bill...."

I listened without really listening. You could do that with Rita, she didn't require any input except the odd yes or no at appropriate gaps in the conversation. Finally she said 'goodbye'; I didn't mention Jason Rayner or our date for Saturday night.

I suppose I'd always known I'd go – why else would I have bought the emerald green dress? He was, as I'd imagined him - sitting at the bar - waiting. I was ten minutes late. He was looking at his watch as I stood behind him and put my hand lightly on his shoulder.

"Did you think I wasn't coming?"

"Not for a minute, I knew you'd come, just wasn't sure when."

One of the things I liked about him from the start was his self-confidence; he never had any misgivings about the decisions he made. The second was his sense of humour.

"Didn't bother to get dressed up then?" He gave me an appreciative glance that slid from my shiny black bob to the tips of my killer heels. "I've booked a table at La Maison for half eight. Shall we go?"

As I said, he was so sure of himself; sure I wouldn't stand him up.

Where is Jason Rayner

La Maison was situated in a side street a five-minute walk away from the Bell. It was small and intimate, a total of ten tables at the most, which were waited upon in an efficient but unobtrusive manner. I knew it was expensive and had often wanted to sample the menu but didn't fancy dining alone in such a place, without a companion to talk to, someone to share the experience.

We were seated at a table overlooking the street. Candlelight spread across the crisp white tablecloth and lit his face with a soft radiance. He wasn't handsome in the accepted sense, but there was something that drew me to him, sex appeal - animal magnetism, words that mean nothing unless experienced, but which might explain why I was so captivated by Jason Rayner.

During a lull in the conversation, I asked, "Where do you work?"

"Lockford Juniors, I've been teaching there since I qualified. I suppose, it's time I moved on but the kids are great and I like living in Lockford," he said, "even more so now I've met you."

I ignored his last remark and asked, "So you enjoy teaching?"

"It's swings and roundabouts. Some days the kids are angels, some days they're devils. It could be worse, I might be working in an office."

It was said tongue-in-cheek, a throw away remark, but I felt the hairs on the back of my neck stand up as I bristled with indignation. "I *like* working in an office," I said.

"Horses for courses – get down off your high one, love – I didn't mean anything by it – it was a joke."

Where is Jason Rayner

Then the meal arrived. A waiter spread a crisp linen napkin on my lap with a flourish and another poured an inch of wine into Jason's glass and waited for his approval. I've forgotten what we ate, but there were no more uncomfortable exchanges between us and I enjoyed the evening, up until we arrived at my flat.

For a start, I wasn't sure whether I liked the idea of him knowing where I lived. It did occur to me to lead him in the opposite direction, wait until he'd got in his taxi and then retrace my steps. However, I found his conversation entertaining and before I knew it, we were outside the block of flats where I lived.

"Aren't you going to invite me up for a nightcap?" he asked as we reached the lift.

In hindsight that was the turning point. If I'd only said no, the rest might never have happened.

Where is Jason Rayner

Chapter 2

The recording machine clicks and whirrs in the background. He smiles at me encouragingly and waits for me to continue. This is not easy, my future depends on how I reply, and authenticity is the key I will use to unlock the past.

The following day, I awoke, with the cold light of dawn creeping in through the gap in my bedroom curtains. Spreading my arms wide, I screwed my eyes tightly shut fearing my fingers would touch flesh but felt the empty space at my side. I was alone.

The events of last night crowded into my mind. Jason Rayner had come up for a nightcap, at least that's what he called it. I'd poured red wine into two of the glasses I'd bought when I moved in.

I remember watching him drink the wine then he leaned towards me and kissed me. I kissed him back and one thing led to another. How we ended up in bed together is not important but why probably is. I suppose I was lonely, although I wouldn't admit it. I hadn't had a boyfriend since I was fifteen, and that had ended badly. I'd sworn to keep away from boys from that moment on. Jason wasn't a boy of course. He was at least ten years older than me and I suppose I was flattered that he'd wanted to spend the night. It's not much of an explanation but it's the only one I have.

Where is Jason Rayner

Yawning, and annoyed for putting myself in such a situation, I slid out of bed and walked towards the window. It was still early; the re-cycling lorry was crawling down the street as pigeons strutted the pavements waiting for scraps. The paperboy, the one with red hair, was cycling down the middle of the road. He was whistling. I opened the window wider and felt the chill of a spring morning.

The note was propped up on my dressing table. *Thanks for the nightcap – I enjoyed every minute of it – I'll be in touch – J xx*

I shivered. Did I want him to ring me? I wasn't sure, only time would tell. In the bathroom, I stepped into the shower and let it wash away the night then watched the soapy water trickling away with something akin to regret. Did he realise it was my first time? I'd tried to hide it, there were no obvious signs but then there wouldn't be of course – as far as *I* was concerned last night *was* my first time. I was Kate Newson and I didn't want to think about - before.

After breakfast, I dressed and walked to the bus stop. I relished the anonymity of being cocooned inside the bus during rush hour. Squashed up against an overweight man wearing the yellow fluorescent jacket of a school-crossing warden, I began to wonder where he'd managed to put his lollipop and how he could possibly continue without it. An insane need to laugh out loud hit me as I turned away and looked out of the window to avoid his gaze.

As soon as I opened the office door, I knew something was up. Mason Trent raised an eyebrow and gave me the lecherous look he usually gave Tracy, Larry Arbuthnot's secretary, when she wore the red dress that just covered her backside. Tracy smiled knowingly and Oliver Watts the legal clerk looked downcast.

Tracy followed me into the washroom as I hung my jacket on a hook and took a quick look in the mirror to comb my hair. In the sink was a large bouquet of flowers wrapped in cellophane with a bright yellow ribbon around the stems, the lower half of which were immersed in water.

"OK spill the beans," Tracy said, nodding in the direction of the flowers. "Who are they from?"

"I'm sorry? I don't know what you're talking about."

"The flowers. Who are they from?"

"You mean those are for me?" I stared at the bouquet.

"Open the envelope, for goodness sake - put me out of my misery." Tracy gave me a nudge in the direction of the sink.

The card inside the small envelope read. *"Thanks again, hope we can continue what we started. J x"*

"Well?" Tracy was waiting for an answer.

"Er, they are a thank-you from a friend," I said, hoping my reply would satisfy her.

"Don't give me that. Who is he?"

"A friend, that's all, just a friend," I replied, walking away from the washroom.

It wasn't my imagination - Mason Trent did rub his leg up against mine as he dictated the routine morning letters – the ones for which there was a template on the computer – the ones I couldn't cock-up, as he was so fond of telling me.

Where is Jason Rayner

At lunchtime Oliver asked if I'd like to join him. "Nothing much, just a bite in the Sweet Pea café," he said, waiting for my customary refusal.

"Thanks Ollie, I'd like that very much." I smiled, and even I was shocked by my reply.

The café was pretty busy for a Monday and we had to wait for a seat. Eventually we sat at a small table overlooking the High Street.

"It's nice in here, good food, cheap too," Ollie rambled on but my thoughts kept returning to Jason Rayner and the flowers. Were they a 'thank you very much but that's that' or could I take the message at face value? I should explain here that from an early age I've been sceptical where men are concerned, and in view of what happened, I think, rightly so.

"So what d'you say?" Ollie was waiting for a reply.

"Pardon me?"

"The film at the UCA tomorrow night. It's Meryl Streep – you did say you liked her? We could go to the first showing and have a meal afterwards, if you like?"

I came down to earth with a bump. "I, um, can I think about it, Ollie? I'll let you know by the end of the day."

Ollie was OK; I could handle Ollie. It might be nice to go out no strings attached - at least no strings on my part. I knew he fancied me but as I said, I could handle Ollie.

He beamed, lifted his knife and fork and attacked his steak and chips with delight.

I really should have gone to see Meryl Streep.

Where is Jason Rayner

Chapter 3

Jason Rayner rang just after three o'clock. I told Oliver that the cinema was not an option and said sorry. He looked so downhearted that I felt bad and added, "Perhaps another time, Ollie."

I didn't leave work until five past six, in fact I was almost the last to leave; Mason Trent wanted a letter completed and Tracy had a date. He hung around my desk, his three-piece suit emitting an indiscernible odour, dark hair flopping over his forehead in a style once favoured by the actor Hugh Grant. Mason Trent was no Hugh Grant - a man in his late thirties who looked as if he'd escaped from the nineteen-fifties and who liked young girls - he made my flesh creep.

"Got a date tonight, Kate?" he asked, edging forwards, his breath inches away from my face.

"Not tonight, Mr Trent."

"At a loose end, are you?"

"Not at all, Mr Trent, I have plenty to do and plenty of friends to meet should I require company."

"Yes, quite, I'm sure you have, pretty girl like you."

"There, if that's the last, I'll be off." I handed him the letter together with an addressed envelope. "Have a nice weekend, Mr Trent."

"You can call me Mason when we're on our own you know, Kate."

"I'm afraid I couldn't do that, Mr Trent, but thanks anyway."

Where is Jason Rayner

Rushing out of the office to get the scent of him out of my nostrils, I hurried in the direction of the bus stop just in time to see the number 92 pulling away. I looked at my watch, half an hour before the next one and it was starting to rain. The Café Noir was opposite the bus stop; one quick cup at a table near the window where I could see the bus coming, I decided.

It was whilst I was watching the passage of a raindrop sliding down the steamed up windowpane that I felt a hand on my shoulder. "We'll have to stop meeting like this," Jason Rayner said, as I turned around.

He pulled a chair away from the table and sat down. "Looks like fate has thrown us together yet again. I'm a great believer in fate, aren't you, Kate?"

I didn't say a word. There was nothing I could say.

"Well now, in view of the fact I'll be seeing you tomorrow night, I suppose I should say, 'nice to see you once more and see you at seven tomorrow'. But that would be flying in the face of fate wouldn't it?"

His questions, for which there were no answers, were making me dizzy. "Would it?" I managed to splutter through a mouth full of coffee.

"I think so. Do you have any plans for this evening?"

"Just a night in."

"Then I suggest I join you."

Why didn't I make an excuse? Perhaps I didn't want yet another night spent on my own. Perhaps I was hoping this night would end up like the last. In hindsight I should have spoken, not smiled like a

Where is Jason Rayner

fool, nodded, and effectively invited him in. I should have known better, I'd seen enough vampire films to know it was the worst possible thing you could do.

That night was to set a pattern for what was to follow; he was amusing company and as before we ended up spending the night in the same bed. Even when he took me to dinner, the cinema, theatre, it always ended the same way and gradually I began to think he loved me. It was a warm, comforting feeling and slowly my guard began to slip.

I expect you want to know a bit about his personality? There's not much to tell but
I never heard him raise his voice to me. If he was angry he would breathe deeply through his nose, his lips drawn into a tight line but he never shouted, never lifted a hand to strike me, not like Bill did to Rita. He had his moods though, but then most of us do, we can't be happy all the time. I began to recognise the signs. Sometimes it would be a slight droop of his shoulders or one-word answers when I spoke to him but his moods didn't last long and summer was approaching.

There was nothing remarkable about our first summer together. We hired bikes and cycled along the new dedicated paths that Lockford Town Council had created. Our favourite route skirted the river and ran into Bluestock Woods. We would take a picnic and a ground sheet and lie together in the sunshine on the banks of the river, cooling off in the shade during our ride home.

Throughout the long summer holiday from school, he cleaned my flat, shopped for food and more often than not cooked a meal for me when I

Where is Jason Rayner

returned home from work. We were like a married couple and I began to imagine what it would be like if we were married. Bill would have had a fit if he'd known in which direction my thoughts were taking me. I was eighteen, and in his eyes, still a child. But then Bill was dead so I had only myself to consider - myself and Rita, of course.

When summer ended abruptly with cold September winds, evenings drawing in and the start of a new school term, I saw yet another side of Jason Rayner. He approached the autumn term with enthusiasm. We didn't see so much of each other; he had lessons to prepare, his books were at his flat. It made sense, he said.

"I haven't mentioned his flat before?" I hesitate and behind the light I see him shake his head.

The reason for this omission is because I never liked it. Situated on the second floor of a terraced house overlooking a row of empty shops, I found it dismal and depressing. It was perfectly clean and tidy but there was something about it that made me want to hurry outside for a breath of fresh air. That's the reason we spent more time at my place during that first summer.

I think I've satisfied his curiosity. Only I know the true reason why I disliked the flat at first sight. It was a premonition of what was to come - a warning lingering in the walls – a sign. I know there are such things, otherwise why did I want to run from there as if the hounds of hell were snapping at my heels?

Where is Jason Rayner

Chapter 4

It's another day. There will be no more, if I can convince him.

"Would you care for a drink of water? The central heating can be very drying, especially as we have so much ground to cover today."

I can see his outline but not his face. The light is bright and shining into my eyes. I wonder why they do that? I've seen it on TV; they all do it, therapists, psychiatrists, interrogators.

"I would. Thank you." I have to appear normal. There must be no doubt in his mind at this late stage.

"Right." He waits until I've finished drinking. "Then let's continue."

A year passed; it was spring again, the hottest on record.

"How d'you fancy a holiday?" Jason Rayner asked, whilst flicking through the pages of the holiday supplement of our daily newspaper. "We could go on a last minute deal. I've two more weeks off from school before the summer term begins. Ask Trent if you can take ten days off."

"I don't know. I could try, I suppose."

"Don't sound so enthusiastic, darling. I thought you'd jump at the chance." His shoulders drooped. "Amsterdam looks reasonable - we could hire some bikes."

"I'll ask in work on Monday and let you know," I said.

Where is Jason Rayner

Mason Trent had phoned in sick, Tracy told me with a smirk. I didn't ask, I knew there would be a long tale focusing on Trent's love life, his affairs, his long suffering wife – it would follow a pattern and I was bored by the subject.

I knocked on the door of Arbuthnot's office. Larry Arbuthnot had white hair. He was still only in his late forties but his hair was as white as his newly bleached teeth. I liked him better than Trent. He was a married man who seemed to know how to make his marriage work. He had no time to spend leering at girls who were young enough to be his daughter.

"Mr Arbuthnot, would it be possible for me to take a ten-day holiday break starting on Wednesday? I realise this is short notice but my boyfriend and I have a chance to book a bargain holiday…" I began.

"I don't see why not, Kate. There's nothing outstanding is there?"

I shook my head.

"Well then, have a word with Oliver, he'll mark you off on the holiday rota. Where are you planning to visit, by the way?"

"Amsterdam."

"Very nice, enjoy yourself and watch out for the cannabis and happy pills," he smiled. It was a joke.

Jason had done his homework. We travelled up to London and caught the Eurostar to Brussels then a High Speed train to Amsterdam. The journey was stress free, short and enjoyable, as he said it would be. His mood was upbeat, he made jokes, told me entertaining stories about the places we would visit

Where is Jason Rayner

and I sat back and began to let work and day to day problems drift away.

Our hotel overlooked a canal not far from Dam Square. It was clean and comfortable without being luxurious and well within our budget. We were used to sharing the cost of everything and he'd worked it all out before we left, including spending money and the cost of hiring the bikes. I told him I didn't mind paying, I was comfortably off due to my inheritance, but he wouldn't hear of it.

The weather was warm but not uncomfortably hot; most days there was a breeze and it only rained on the last day, when we were coming home. During the day following our arrival, we hired bikes for the duration of our stay and rode them through the narrow streets and alongside the canals, getting the feel of the place. We drank ice-cold beer sitting outside in the sunshine and watched the steady progression of sightseers drifting down the canals, cameras stuck like Velcro to their fingers.

"Glad you came?" he asked.

"Of course."

"When you were in the shower this morning, I went shopping." He slipped his hand into his pocket and removed a packet of cigarettes. " Take one," he offered.

"No thanks, you know I don't smoke."

"You'll like these, I promise," he said, tapping the side of his nose conspiratorially.

The penny dropped and I felt my cheeks go red.

"The answer's still the same," I replied.

"Your loss, lighten up a bit, love." He lit one of the thin cigarettes and blew the smoke in my direction. I inhaled the sweet-smelling tobacco in spite of myself. "When in Rome," he grinned.

I stood up and walked toward my bicycle, which was chained to a bike stand. "I think I'll take a ride along the canal. I'll see you in the hotel later."

He nodded and continued puffing away at the weed. Feeling annoyed that he would think I'd just go along with it, I pedalled furiously over the cobbles. It might sound prudish but I thought he should have discussed it with me first. Whatever anyone says, cannabis is a mind altering drug, recreational or not and I prefer to keep my mind free from contamination. I cycled onwards trying to put things into perspective and break free from my anger.

When I returned sometime later, he was sitting outside the hotel drinking beer.

"Join me, Kate? You must be ready for a cool drink." His smile was genuine and my anger had long since dissipated.

Locking my bicycle into the rack, I walked across the cobbles and sat down opposite him. I noticed he had a paper carrier bag resting on his lap. "Have you been shopping?" I asked.

"Just a few cakes. I couldn't resist them. I thought we could take them up to our room when we have our afternoon nap, have a cup of coffee and indulge ourselves."

It was my turn to smile 'afternoon nap' was a euphemism for sex. "Fine," I agreed.

Our room was bathed in sunlight. I stood at the window and watched the dappled surface of the canal shimmering like oil on a puddle. Behind me, I could hear him putting on the kettle and making the coffee. I sat at the small table near the window and sighed, it was a beautiful day and I was in love, at least what passed for love in my limited experience.

"Here you are, try one of these."

He handed me a plate on which was a round cake not dissimilar to a cupcake. It looked delicious. I had no idea then that, like my lover, it was a mistake to put my trust in face value alone.

I'd never had any inhibitions where our sex life was concerned, I was a healthy young girl, with normal appetites, but after we'd drunk the coffee and eaten the cakes every sense seemed heightened. The bed was softer, his body more sensual, our kisses more intense. I wanted the afternoon to go on forever and relished the fact that we had many more such afternoons left before we returned to normality.

The next day we decided to cycle to the Rijksmuseum, a popular tourist destination. I was so looking forward to it even though the day had started with a pounding headache which I couldn't shift until I'd downed a couple of painkillers.

It was when we were cycling past a café, Jason Rayner a couple of metres in front of me, that I noticed a sign in English hanging above the front door. *Sample our 'special' cakes for an experience you won't forget. Non- smokers especially welcome.*

The pleasure of the day evaporated. Why hadn't he told me? I started to wonder what else was he hiding or was I becoming paranoid? I was very naïve where he was concerned and it was beginning to look as if he had counted on the fact.

Where is Jason Rayner

My forehead is wet, beads of sweat trickle into my eyes. I bend down and pick up my handbag, remove a tissue and pat my forehead dry.

Chapter 5

"Something bothering you?" he asks.

I take another sip of water, hesitate, then say, "Recounting the episode of the cakes, I realise how immature it makes me sound and I would have to admit to a certain degree of naivety. Trust is fragile and in view of what happened to me it's something I value beyond most things. To know that he tried to trick me, albeit in such an insignificant manner, ate away at the foundations of my faith in him and made me wonder at the veracity of any of his statements. Remembering makes me feel uncomfortable that's all. Especially as we now know why I'm telling you this. It makes sense - now that I know."

"Would you like to stop here? Finish it later in the week perhaps?"

"Yes, maybe I could come again on Friday? I hoped we could finish it today, the sooner I the better, but it's getting late." I glance at the clock on the wall.

"Well, if you're sure, Friday then. There is no hurry, take your time."

The rest of the week passes slowly – too slowly for my liking. This has to be done, otherwise it's all been for nothing. I stay in my flat, read, or try to, and watch television; I don't have to go back to work until Monday. Larry Arbuthnot has been very kind; he wants me to take as much time as I need, but I think it's better if I go back on Monday.

Where is Jason Rayner

When Friday arrives, I'm more than ready to put an end to this. As I brush my hair, I try to see if it shows. But the same face looks back at me, amber eyes, dark hair and pale skin, no trace of the woman, who has lived through my life, shows in the mirror.

He is waiting for me, and smiles reassuringly as I enter his consulting room.

"Ready?" he asks, switching on the recording machine.

The incident with the cakes put a dampener on the rest of our holiday. When he suggested we visit the Red Light District, I began to wonder if more deceit lay in wait but had no real choice in the matter. We reached the infamous district as darkness descended. Couples walking hand in hand, and groups of young men eying what was on display in the windows, ambled slowly along in the warm night air. Hen parties, wafting a wave of hair-spray in their wake, ran giggling and pointing as they passed the scantily clad prostitutes plying their trade up and down the street, each one attempting to be more appealing than their neighbour.

"You're quiet tonight," he said, sliding his arm around my shoulders.

"I'm OK, just taking it all in."

"They don't hold a candle to you, love." He bent his head and kissed my cheek.

"I should hope not." I tried to smile but my heart wasn't in it.

"If you've had enough, we could stop at a bar," he suggested.

Where is Jason Rayner

"I'm fine, let's follow the rest of the sightseers. Don't worry about me."

Women of every nationality showed what was on offer in red-fringed windows or standing in doorways. I wondered what it would be like to change places with them – what part of their brains did they employ in order to turn off their emotions? What were they thinking when a client, perhaps drunk or under the influence of drugs, attempted that most intimate of actions?

"Penny for them?"

"Nothing, just wondering what it would feel like to be in their position."

He held me at arm's length, "You want to find out?" He was laughing at me but part of me wondered if there was more to his question than met the eye. Did the thought excite him?

"I think it's time we found that bar," I replied.

If I'm honest, our holiday in Amsterdam unsettled me for a while, but not to any great extent. For the most part we enjoyed the break from work. I tried not to show how badly the affair of the cannabis cakes had affected me and I'm sure he had no idea. At the end of the ten days, we were tanned, rested and had decided that once we were home we'd continue with the cycle rides. It was not only good exercise but we enjoyed getting out in the fresh air, in addition to which summer was approaching.

The journey home was not quite as stress free as the outgoing one had been. The High-Speed train, connecting us to the Eurostar terminal, was late – something to do with a fatality on the line – we were never quite sure what – it was most unusual for it to be late, apparently. We then had a protracted delay as we'd missed our connection. Eventually, travel weary, we reached my flat.

"You're sure you don't mind if I don't stay the night?" He kissed me lightly on the cheek, after carrying my bag inside.

"No, of course not, school tomorrow, I understand. Besides, I'm bushed and the thought of seeing Mason Trent, in the morning, requires a good night's sleep."

When he left, I made a cup of coffee, sat down and switched on the television news. A reporter was standing outside a terraced house. I turned up the volume and caught the end of his report.

The whole area has been cordoned off and police forensic team are inside looking for clues as to why a seemingly sane father butchered his family, whilst they slept. Gerald Dayton for BBC News.

The coffee hit the back of my throat and I coughed. My heart was pounding, my hands shaking. My handbag was on the floor alongside my case and I grabbed it like a drowning man reaching for a life raft, opened a side pocket, removed a thin card then pressed the pearl-like pill through the silver paper, swallowing it with the remains of my coffee.

Gradually the room stopped spinning and I could watch the amiable weatherman smiling in the face of a projected forecast of rain for the coming week. I closed my eyes and sat back in the chair, as the world righted itself once more.

Everyone was talking about it in the office the next day and my holiday slipped into old news.

Where is Jason Rayner

"How could a father do that to his family. He must have been off his rocker?" Tracy asked in between applying yet another coat of red lipstick to an already perfect pout.

"Dreadful," I agreed, picking up a large pile of filing that had accumulated whilst I'd been away.

Mechanically glued to the filing cabinet for most of the morning, I escaped most of the office discussions about the breaking news. I did hear that the house I'd seen on the TV was situated in the town of Nettleby upon the Marsh, an hour or so away from Lockford. I suppose that's why I couldn't get away from it – everyone seemed to be talking about it. I even half-welcomed Mason Trent's comment as he passed me, as it had nothing to do with death.

"Bring any mind altering substances back in you luggage, did you Kate?"

"Of course not, Mr Trent," I replied primly.

"You don't fool me. You and that boyfriend of yours took full advantage of the perks of visiting Amsterdam, I'm sure."

"If by that you mean did we enjoy visiting the sights, I'd have to agree."

He grinned, a sleazy expression at the best of times. "I believe you, Kate, though thousands wouldn't."

As usual, whenever in close proximity to Mason Trent, I wanted to take a long hot shower but had to make do with a quick trip to the washroom to scrub my hands until they were red raw.

I'll have to be more careful; I'd been about to tell him about my childhood. It would have been a big mistake. I don't intend to go back beyond meeting Jason Rayner for the first time it's not relevant and who knows, once I start, I might not be able to stop.

Where is Jason Rayner

Chapter 6

It's almost the beginning of May, the room is hot and I wonder why the central heating is still on. I remove my cardigan and place it on the back of my chair. He doesn't seem to notice and waits for me to continue.

The weekend, following our holiday in Amsterdam, Jason Rayner suggested we drive to the outskirts of town where there was a large store selling bicycles, outdoor activity equipment and clothing.

"If you buy a bike from the Internet, it might be a bit cheaper but there's no after service," he said as we drove out of Lockford.

It was a reasonable day, not as warm as it had been in Amsterdam but at least the sun was shining. His car was a four by four, with a personalised number plate A1 JR, not large but suitable for cross-country driving. I suppose he could be said to have an athletic build, although it hadn't been apparent when I'd first met him. In fact I thought he was rather fragile looking; he'd looked as if a good puff of wind would blow him over, as my aunt would have said.

He was a good driver but insisted on sounding the horn at every motorist whom he considered was a 'crap' driver; they were usually women, in his estimation. I found my shoulders tightening at every symptom of his frustration – the drawing in of his breath followed by its slow release – the short sharp

Where is Jason Rayner

expletives – finally the unrelenting 'barp, barp' of the horn. By the time we reached the store, it was a relief to step out of the car.

The building was in fact a converted warehouse, large and stocked full of goods. We made our way to the section where the cycles were displayed and spent time deciding which would suit our purposes. At last, we left the store with two hybrid bikes, which would be equally suitable for riding on the road or along rough country lanes. In addition to the cycles, we purchased all-weather jackets and over-trousers, panniers and maintenance gear. He seemed to know what he was doing; I didn't have a clue but insisted on paying for the equipment and this time he didn't argue.

"That should do us," he said, closing the door of the boot, the cycles resting on the rack outside. "I'm glad to see you're serious about this and not just going to be a fair weather cyclist."

"It will be good exercise and a change to get away from the busy road traffic. There are so many cycle paths and routes in and around Lockford, it makes perfect sense to me," I replied closing the passenger side door. I didn't mention that it would be a pleasure to get away from his constant frustration with other motorists. There were no ugly premonitions of the disaster that would follow the purchase of our cycles. It was an ordinary day.

The start of the summer term found Jason Rayner responsible for taking the year six pupils away for a week which would be spent in a residential centre for outdoor pursuits – rock climbing, canoeing and hill walking were on the agenda, he said. He would be jointly in charge of thirty-five pupils along with Vivien Richards a tall, athletic woman in her mid twenties with thick fair hair tied back in a ponytail. I'd seen her photograph but never met her. I offered to go to the school to wave them off on the morning of their departure but he said there was no need and besides he would be far too busy keeping an eye on the kids.

"I'll miss you, Kate," he said kissing my cheek, "and remember, don't do anything I wouldn't do!"

Did I miss him? Difficult to say; I supposed I missed his company but it was only a week. He did ring once, just to say that the mobile signal was ineffectual and it was awkward to find a landline. In some respects I felt free to do just as I liked. I was young. Besides it was ridiculous to become too reliant on a man.

I know I read a lot that week and on the Friday evening went to the cinema with Ollie. It wasn't to see Meryl Streep - I can't remember which film it was. He was pleasant company, couldn't do enough to please me, and afterwards there was no suggestion that we should share a nightcap. When I left him standing on the doorstep saying, "See you on Monday then, Kate. I did enjoy tonight; perhaps we could go out to dinner one evening when you're free?" I felt callous, as I replied, "Yes, perhaps, I'll see what my boyfriend's got planned and let you know."

From the window of my flat I watched Ollie walking down the street. He kicked a can on the pavement and I heard it bounce into the gutter with a clang. It was obvious he was disappointed by my reply to his offer and I felt really bad about it. I turned away as the phone rang.

"Kate?" It was Jason. His voice was indistinct, and there was some sort of background music and chatter going on. It sounded as if he was in a pub. "I'll be back tomorrow evening about six." The rest of his words were cut off as the dialling tone cut in.

Before he'd left, a week ago, I'd offered to pick him up from the school but he said not to bother, he'd get a taxi. I was in the middle of making a pot of tea the next day when I heard the buzzer. Clicking on the intercom screen, I saw him standing on the step outside the main entrance. I pressed the door release.

"God, am I glad to see you," he said, throwing his backpack on to the floor. He leant across to kiss me and I smelled *J'aime* perfume on his clothes; Vivien's presumable, I thought, trying to muster up some jealousy but failing miserably. Was that odd? Perhaps, but I'm trying my best to be honest.

"You don't mind if I stay over tonight?" he asked as I pulled into the traffic.

"Of course not."

"Did you miss me?"

"Of course."

"I could do with a long hot soak in the bath, care to join me?" He smiled and I was hooked once more.

As it turned out, the shared bath was not a precursor to sex, as I'm sure was his intention – he fell asleep on the couch and I covered him with the duvet from the spare bedroom before making my way to bed to sleep alone. I had no idea then that it would be the last night I would sleep without Jason Rayner for

Where is Jason Rayner

some time. Hindsight is a blessing or a curse depending on which way you look at it. For me it was the latter.

Where is Jason Rayner

Chapter 7

Thankfully the room is getting colder. I take a deep breath, my mouth is dry but I won't stop now – not until I've told him everything. I don't want to draw out the agony a minute longer than is necessary. There are times when I'm sure I've dreamt it but reality soon steps in and I know I mustn't fail now; it's the final stage of our plan.

As I mentioned, Jason Rayner and I spent every night together from that moment on, mostly at my flat but sometimes at his place. The summer was the hottest on record and we rode our bikes nearly every weekend until I felt more at ease with the gears and could steer without veering towards an object like a magnet.

Throughout the autumn and winter of that year we cycled as often as we could, I lost weight, my leg muscles tightened and I felt quite pleased with the result. It didn't go unnoticed in work either.

"You look fit these days," Mason Trent sleazed. "It suits you, Kate. I bet you and that boyfriend of yours….," he stopped short of what he'd been going to say, hesitated, and repeated, "Yes, it certainly suits you."

Ollie was the same as always. He still asked me out occasionally but they were half-hearted attempts, he knew what the answer would be. And Tracy had become unaccountably spiteful, "If there's one thing I can't stand, it's a woman with muscles. Have you

Where is Jason Rayner

seen those pictures of female body-builders? It's enough to make you vomit."

I didn't rise to the bait, knowing that she'd soon get fed up and move on to someone else.

When the year turned full circle and summer arrived once more, it was a far cry from the previous one, it rained throughout June and July and to my sorrow August began in much the same manner. We still cycled in the lanes around Lockford, although now it was over mud and wet grass and we wore light raincapes over our shorts. So it was no surprise when he suggested we spend a weekend in London at the end of August.

"It will be good to have a few days away before school starts," he said.

I had absolutely no idea what he had in mind and wonder now, if I had known, would it have made any difference?

He proposed in Hyde Park in the middle of a thunderstorm. He'd bought the ring in a jewellers' shop, whilst I was ambling around the market stalls in Covent Garden; it was a solitaire diamond set in white gold.

If I close my eyes, I can see him now, in the little wooden park shelter, bending down on one knee. "Kate Newson, will you do me the honour of becoming my wife?" he asked.

I couldn't see why not. We'd been inseparable for almost two years; there was no reason why I shouldn't accept his rather archaic proposal. "Of course," I replied, as he drew me into his arms in a

Where is Jason Rayner

bear hug. The rain pelting down on the roof of the wooden shelter sounded like applause.

Afterwards, he started school in the September and we planned to get married during half-term at the end of October. I can't quite remember who suggested that we didn't mention it to our families; I don't think I did. Anyway, we decided we'd have a registry office wedding and induce some passers-by to be our witnesses. At least that was the first idea we came up with.

I didn't tell Rita, not at first; in fact I don't believe I ever did tell her. The police informed her. I suppose it must have come as a bit of a shock, especially in view of what happened.

As half-term approached we changed out minds. At least Jason decided it might be a better idea and I went along with it. So we married in Las Vegas. I know it sounds excessive but, as I said before, money was not a problem for me. Jason Rayner had seen a wedding package in a holiday brochure. He'd put it aside saying it was too expensive but I managed to persuade him that I would pay and, after a while, he agreed. It seemed the answer to both of us – I didn't want to get married in Lockford, where no doubt Tracy and the rest of the office staff would come to watch. He liked the idea of Las Vegas and this way we could do it with as little fuss as possible.

We booked into a hotel we'd seen in the brochure. It was on the strip but not one of the new themed hotels, which had sprung up like a rash spreading into the desert. Nevertheless, it boasted a casino, pool, various restaurants catering for most tastes and a security guard on duty near the lifts

Where is Jason Rayner

leading to an accommodation area. The first thing I noticed about him was his gun, which was slung in an over the shoulder holster, the butt of which rested under his arm. Jason said it was for effect but I had my doubts.

Our wedding day arrived in the middle of a heat wave, which swept over the west coast of America. Las Vegas was used to such temperatures and the hotels and casinos were all air-conditioned. I wore a cream suit with a yellow rose pinned to the lapel of my jacket; he wore the beige linen suit I'd bought him in a department store in Lockford during the summer. After the short ceremony, we drank champagne in the bar of a Venetian - themed hotel and spent the evening walking down 'the strip' in the warm night air. At one point I looked up at a gigantic thermometer, which was floodlit and studded with flashing lights. The temperature read 98 degrees and it was nearly midnight.

Afterwards, we considered selling his flat and living in mine, whilst we looked for something more suitable in which to start our married life. But as it turned out we did neither. Christmas arrived, Rita developed a chest infection and said not to bother to drive all that way to see her, she'd let me know when her health improved and perhaps we could get together later in the spring. Jason Rayner's parents were dead. And still I hadn't told Rita about my marriage.

It snowed in January; he said the school was closed due to frozen pipes and the offices of Arbuthnot and Trent were similarly affected. So we stayed in my flat, watched the snowflakes fall, read,

Where is Jason Rayner

and made love – it was the happiest time of my life. A time which I saved in my memory to resurrect when things turned bad.

When the thaw set in, life returned to normal. But at the beginning of March I found the letter.

I try to measure how my story is affecting him. But he shows no emotion; there are just the background noises in the room to accompany my tale.

Where is Jason Rayner

Chapter 8

The whirring of the tape machine and the ticking of the wall clock are the only sounds that break the silence in the room. There's an occasional plop from the water cooler but it fades, becoming lost amongst the mechanical components. Outside the room there is a gentle tap, tap of a branch stroking the windowpane like a lover's touch and the muted sound of traffic in the distance. The atmosphere in the room is one of relaxation but my mind is like a coiled spring, quickly unfurling to get to the end as I reveal the twists and turns of my life with Jason Rayner. There is no time to relax.

The reason I was alone in the flat in the middle of the day was because I'd caught a heavy cold and was taking a few days off work. The first day, I spent in bed and on the second I felt well enough to do a spot of housework. I changed the bedclothes, dusted the furniture and was tidying his desk in the spare room when I noticed a piece of paper trapped between the top drawer and the desktop. I tugged at it but the drawer was jammed – locked. My curiosity was aroused as we didn't have secrets from each other and a locked drawer was unusual.

In the kitchen, I found a flat-bladed knife and slid it into the space between the drawer and the desktop then gradually eased out the sheet of paper. It was part of a letter, the last page I presumed. It read;-

Where is Jason Rayner

Every minute we are apart tears at my heart. How could you be so cruel? You know how I feel about you. We've spent so much time together so we know how we feel by now. I've always understood things are difficult and there are others involved but you must sort things out. Promise me you will? I love you so much R.

I peered at the neat handwriting, unable to believe what I was reading. Jason Rayner had been unfaithful to me. My legs began to buckle, my heart pounded uncomfortably and I sat down on the edge of the single bed. If I'd never felt jealousy before, I felt it now; it swept over me like a gigantic wave, robbing me of rational thought, I wanted to tear his clothes, his skin, his hair. For a while I was like a mad thing. Then I began to cry, until my eyes puffed, my nose ran and my chest ached. It was later that afternoon, before he returned from school, that I realised who R was.

The image of the athletically built games mistress with her long fair hair filled my thoughts. Vivien Richards had been having an affair with my husband. I was still sitting on the spare room bed, my cheeks stained with tears, when I heard him open the front door and call out his usual greeting, "Get rid of the milkman, Kate, I'm home."

"Kate?" he called, walking into the spare room. "Kate? What on earth's happened?"

I was still holding the sheet of paper in my hand. I was past being angry; I held it out to him. He took it from my shaking fingers, read it, then started to laugh.

"You think it's funny?" I spat at him like an angry cat.

Where is Jason Rayner

"Kate, my little Kitty, calm down. It's not what you think." He walked over to the drawer, took a key from his pocket, unlocked the drawer and removed a volume of *Romeo and Juliet.*

He said he was now teaching a simplified version of Shakespeare to the year six pupils preparing them for their upcoming entrance into the Comprehensive school system. They had been reading *Romeo and Juliet*. Apparently he'd shown them a short film and they'd enjoyed the cut and thrust of the warring Montagues and Capulets but had joked about the love affair between the youngsters. So he'd set them a task of composing a love letter from Romeo. By way of explanation he offered to show me the other part of the letter that had jammed in the desk drawer. I shook my head - I felt a fool.

It was during the spring bank holiday of the year I was twenty-one that we decided to take our bikes down to Devon for the week. The weather was behaving itself and the first couple of days we spent discovering cycle routes that wound through beautiful country lanes and alongside riverbanks. On the fourth day, the sun was shining from the minute we awoke so, anticipating a day of settled weather, we decided to take a picnic and ride along the river until we reached the estuary.

The route we took was relatively free from cyclists. We did see a family unloading cycles from the back of a large off-roader when we started off - three young children, a mother, father, and woman in her twenties. They were preoccupied, they had their backs to us as we passed them but I saw Jason Rayner give the young woman an appreciative

Where is Jason Rayner

glance. She was certainly pretty and wearing a pair of shorts that I thought far too revealing for such an event.

We'd been cycling for about half an hour and had seen no one else; the family we'd seen earlier, no doubt having matched their pace to that of their children. Boats of all shapes and sizes sailed down the river to the sea, sunlight glinting on their painted hulls and bouncing off their metal masts. I noticed the track beginning to narrow and slowed down.

"You go on ahead, I'll take up the rear," my husband said falling back behind me.

I remember that the hedges to either side of the track were overgrown and we could no longer see the river just the occasional mast drifting by. I rode for a while then turned around in order for him to give me a reassuring wave. "Still here," he said.

The sun was hot on my back, dragonflies hovered in the bushes at the side of the river and the scent of wild flowers filled my nostrils. If I close my eyes, I can still smell and feel exactly what it was like, every second and every minute before I turned around to see he was no longer behind me.

"Jason?"

No answer.

"Jason, stop teasing me." I called out.

Still no answer.

"Jason you're scaring me now." I dismounted and waited.

I heard the sound of a bicycle bell tinkling a short way off, then the unmistakeable shift of gears as someone approached. He must have been delayed. It wasn't like him not to shout out, to let me know. I clicked the stand rest on my bike and waited.

Where is Jason Rayner

"Oh, hello." It was the pretty young woman whom I'd seen wearing the brief shorts, earlier. " I thought I'd ride on, stretch my legs a bit. My brother's children are great but far too slow for pleasure cycling." She was passing me now but turned around. "Are you OK?"

"Er, not really. I wonder - did you see my husband back there?"

"No." She looked back along the path. "There was no one between my brother Dan and his family and you."

I put my hands up to my face. "You're sure?"

"Certain."

By this time she had dismounted and was bringing her bike over to mine.

"He was there, right behind me, the last time I looked, he waved and spoke. Where on earth can he be?" I was beginning to panic. "Perhaps he's taken another track without realising." I was frantic.

The woman looked doubtful. "Er, I don't think so. You see I know this stretch of track really well. We've been holidaying here for years. There is no way he could have ridden off the path in the other direction, I'm afraid. By the way, my name's Sandy. Look, I'll ride back with you, if you like. Maybe he's injured and lying in a hedge along on the way."

I knew it was highly unlikely but was grateful for the suggestion.

"Thanks, I appreciate your help. I'm Kate Rayner by the way and my husband's name is Jason."

"Don't worry, Kate. I'm sure there's a simple explanation. We'll find him," Sandy said as we mounted our bikes and rode back along the way we'd come.

If only it had been that simple – Sandy's words filled my head as we slowly scanned the path bordering the river and found no sight of my missing husband.

"And that's how you believe it happened?" The question is there and he's waiting for my answer. The room is warm and I take a sip of water. I know that my reply is important; it will shape the rest of my life.

Where is Jason Rayner

The Investigation

Chapter 9

The offices of Richard Stevens, Private Investigator, on the second floor of Hastings Buildings, smelled musty. A fortnight's holiday, during which Richie had visited his old mate DCI Norman Freeman and his wife Cheryl at their home in West Brompton, had contributed to the general air of abandonment. The Freemans lived on a tree-lined street in a large semi-detached built in the nineteen thirties. They were good friends, who knew about Lucy and the kids but didn't make a song and dance about what happened. He'd enjoyed his time in London, which was something he would never have thought possible a few years back.

Nevertheless, Lockford was his home now and returning to his office after his holiday was like sliding his arms into a well-worn and much loved cardigan. Walking over to the window, Richie opened it wide letting in a gust of cool fresh air then picking up the post from the mat, placed the envelopes firmly on Sandy's desk, and put the kettle on. He looked at his watch. She'd arrive about now, and it was anyone's guess what colour her hair would be or what persona she would have adopted. Of late it had been the athletic cyclist, all shining hair and bronzed limbs. Richie smiled; it suited her.

The door flew open and his PA arrived bringing with her the smell of the morning.

"Did you have a good holiday?" Sandy asked, slipping her arms out of her cycling jacket.

Where is Jason Rayner

"I did."

"No unpleasant flashbacks?"

"Not one. Fancy a coffee before we start, Miss Smith?"

"Do you have to ask?" She grinned, sat behind her desk, and began to open the mail.

Richie, pouring the coffee into two mugs, thought, not for the first time, how fortunate he was that she'd not moved on. She was too well qualified to bury herself away in his office, however much she protested. With a first class honours degree in psychology and being fluent in three languages, she could do much better than the type of work he could offer, in spite of her insistence to the contrary. The Miss Smith business was a joke but one, which was on going and they saw no reason to change it.

Handing her the mug of coffee, Richie asked, "How did the holiday in Devon go then?"

"Great as usual. Dan, Jane and the kids are good company. Rob wasn't too happy that he couldn't join us but he's working in Sweden for the next two months."

Rob and Sandy had been going out together for nearly a year and Richie thought he was good for her, a decent, solid, type in his estimation. Sandy put her mug down on the desk.

"Actually, something very odd happened just a couple of days ago. We parked up near a cycling route we often use and set off. I'd left the family behind on the river path, as Chloe was performing and holding us up by making a fuss about wearing her helmet, and cycled on ahead. After a while, I suddenly came across a woman who looked

Where is Jason Rayner

distressed. She'd parked her bike on its stand and was looking anxiously down the path. Apparently, she'd been with her husband, who was cycling a short distance behind her, when he just disappeared."

Richie said, "Did he turn up later?"

"Well, no. That's what was odd. I walked back along the path with her, inspecting every inch of the way but there was no sign of him. By this time she was getting really worried as you can imagine."

"He hadn't fallen off, injured himself?"

"No. We eventually reached Dan and his family who were further back down the route and they hadn't seen him either."

"Well now, that is surprising. Any ideas?"

"I knew you'd want to investigate," Sandy said.

"Now hold on a minute, Miss Smith. Firstly, I'm sure I've enough work to be getting on with at present and secondly, no one has approached me to investigate on their behalf."

Sandy raised the mug to her lips and looked over the rim at him. Her arched eyebrows said it all.

"OK, I admit that things are quiet here at the moment and it would be good to get our teeth into something worthwhile but I'm sure the Devon police will have it all in hand," he said.

Sandy frowned.

"What is it?" Richie asked, recognising the signs.

"The woman lives and works in Lockford."

"Does she indeed?"

"She works in Arbuthnot and Trent, the solicitors' office just down the High Street."

Tucking a strand of sun-bleached hair behind her ears, Sandy continued opening the rest of the post

Where is Jason Rayner

whilst Richie walked into the small office that was his inner sanctum. He sat down behind his desk, switched on his laptop and scanned the papers until he found a report in a local newssheet called the Kingslea Echo.

Two days ago, Mrs Kate Rayner reported the disappearance of her husband, whilst the couple were on a cycling holiday in the area. Mrs Rayner said her husband Jason went missing whilst they were both riding along a narrow track, which borders the river Lea. It appears that one minute he was behind her and the next, he was gone. The local police force are in the process of investigating the matter but a spokesman said, after considering the facts, they are of the opinion that Mr Rayner left of his own accord and have advised his wife to return home and wait for him to contact her.

"Miss Smith, when you have a moment."

Sandy opened his office door.

"What's up?"

"Take a look at this." Richie turned his laptop screen to face her.

"I see."

"You do?"

Sandy frowned. "What I mean is, I didn't get the impression that Mrs Rayner believed for one minute that he'd taken off on his own. I saw the expression on her face and she was certain he was behind her and shocked he was missing. The whole thing is very odd."

Richie closed his laptop and leaned back in his chair. "Explain," he said.

"As I told you, we were all riding along the same track. Dan, Jane and the kids were way behind but they were following me, albeit at a slower pace. If Rayner had returned the way he'd come, they would have seen him. He would have passed them. When I came across his wife, she and I retraced our steps until we met up with Dan. There was no way Rayner travelled back along that track – no way at all."

"So where do we begin?"

Sandy's face was wreathed in smiles.

"You'll do it?"

"We'll do it, Miss Smith and as you have already established contact with Mrs Rayner, I suggest you arrange a meeting."

"Contrived? OK, then I'll try and bump into her by accident?"

"Precisely. See how you get on. You'll know when the right time comes to tell her where you work and maybe by then we'll have some idea of what's actually going on here." Richie walked over to the window. " Of course you do realise that until we are instructed to act on her behalf, we can't spend too much time on this – our paying clients come first."

"Of course," Sandy said, "but divorces and fraud cases are nowhere near as interesting as this, you have to admit."

At the window, Richie looked down to the street until his eyes rested on the offices of Arbuthnot and Trent. It was nearly on his doorstep, it couldn't hurt to let Sandy loose on Mrs Rayner. If anyone could encourage confidentialities, she could.

Where is Jason Rayner

Chapter 10

It was lunchtime. Sandy waited inside the bookshop, supposedly browsing their table display near the window, until she saw the woman leaving the offices of Arbuthnot and Trent.

"Hullo, it's Mrs Rayner, isn't it?" Sandy said, timing her exit from the bookshop to coincide with the woman's approach.

"Er, yes."

"I met you in Kingslea, when your husband…"

Recognition dawned. "Of course, Sandy isn't it? What a surprise to see you in Lockford."

"I work here actually."

"Really? What a coincidence." She screwed up her eyes in the sunshine.

"It is." Sandy could see any advantage she had slipping away. "Look, I'm on my way to the Sweet Pea cafe for some lunch; why don't you join me? I've often wondered how things turned out for you."

The woman hesitated then came to a decision. "OK. Yes, I'd like that."

They were at the coffee stage, having finished their lunch and discussing Lockford's limited attractions, when Sandy broached the subject of Jason Rayner.

"Did you ever discover what actually happened to your husband that day on the river path?"

Her question was greeted with silence.

"Sorry, I didn't mean to pry."

Where is Jason Rayner

"It's alright, I suppose I do owe you some sort of explanation, especially as you were kind enough to try and help me." Sandy noticed her gaze focusing on the tablecloth, as she continued. "The police think he left me. I tried to tell them he wouldn't – not without leaving me a note – a phone call – at least letting me know somehow. He wouldn't just disappear."

"And you've not heard anything since?"

"Not a word. I don't know what to do."

"There's no one who can help you find him?"

"My aunt is my closest relative and she doesn't live near. She's elderly and I don't want to worry her."

"I see."

Sandy watched as she toyed with the corner of the tablecloth. "Mrs Rayner, I think there's something I should tell you."

"There is?"

"Don't look so worried." Sandy wasn't sure how to explain without making their chance meeting appear contrived. "I work for Richard Stevens, a Private Investigator, his office is in Hastings Buildings." She removed a business card from her purse. "If you feel in need of his services, please give him a ring. He's the best and is very discreet." Feeling she was beginning to sound like an advert, she handed the woman the card.

"I don't understand, is this just another coincidence?"

"It's perfectly reasonable for you to be sceptical but I can assure you, it is – and it's one that might just be to your advantage. If the police don't wish to pursue the investigation, maybe it's time to look elsewhere. "

Sandy continued to explain how successful her boss had been in the past. It wasn't difficult for her to sing his praises; she genuinely respected Richie Stevens and admired his judgement. It was one of the reasons she'd stayed and not looked for a more financially profitable job elsewhere.

"You think he might be able to find Jason Rayner?" she asked, when Sandy had finished.

"I think he'll do his utmost to discover what happened." Sandy wondered why the woman constantly referred to her husband using both Christian and surnames. It seemed a little odd. "But, of course, it's up to you, Mrs Rayner. I don't want you to feel pressurised in any way."

"I understand." She thought for a moment then seemed to come to a decision. "Perhaps you should start by calling me Kate and showing me the way to your boss's office."

Sandy looked at her watch. "Are you on your lunch hour?"

"I am."

"Maybe it would be better if I made an appointment for you. Let's say after work tomorrow. How does that suit you?"

"Fine. I usually finish at five. I have your card – if I'm going to be any later, I'll ring."

Richie had his feet up on his desk when Sandy arrived back from lunch. "I bought you a corned beef pasty, all the steak and onion were gone. Oh and I've got us a new client!"

Where is Jason Rayner

"Thanks on both counts, Miss Smith." He unwrapped the pasty. "Right, let's have it."

After Sandy told him about her meeting with their new client, he said, " Could be interesting."

"It's a while since we've had anything come close, I think," Sandy replied.

With pastry crumbs still clinging to his shirtfront, Richie asked, "What impression did you get of her?"

"Difficult to say really, I only talked to her for a short while over lunch. But she is adamant that her husband didn't leave her and naturally fearful of the alternative. She was a little on edge, which was understandable but I think she's plausible."

"OK." Richie slid his feet to the floor. "So I suggest you make up a file and after I've seen her, we'll decide what to do next." He turned around and looked at the clock on the wall behind his desk. "Time for a quick half in the Bell, I think. See you later, Miss Smith."

When Sandy was alone, she began to think in more detail about her lunch with Kate Rayner. She hadn't mentioned to Richie that there was something bothering her about the woman. She hadn't mentioned it because she wasn't exactly sure what that something was. But if she'd learned anything during her time working for him, she knew that it was a mistake to ignore the little things; they had a habit of growing.

Chapter 11

She arrived the following day, just after five. Richie heard her talking to Sandy in the outer office, followed, soon after, by the sound of his internal phone ringing.

"Thank you, Miss Smith," he said, when his client was shown into the small room that was his office. "Please sit down, Mrs Rayner."

She was a pretty young woman in her early twenties with dark hair, cut in a bob, which swung to her shoulders. Her skin was pale and she wore little make-up. She was wearing a grey jacket and skirt with a crisp white blouse. She looked smart and without the usual flash of leg or breast that he saw every morning whilst driving to work. She looked old fashioned, as if she'd escaped from the last century at a time when neat little skirt suits and smart shoes were de rigueur for secretaries; the sight of Sandy's ever-changing image, as she appeared for work each morning, reinforcing his assumption.

"Miss Smith has filled me in with the details of why you wish to hire me. I gather it's to find your missing husband?" he began.

At first she didn't meet his eyes but kept them glued to her hands resting in her lap. Then as if arriving at a decision, she raised her head. "It is, Mr Stevens. Although how you are going to do it is beyond me, as the police have refused to take this seriously. You see, I really have no alternative but to seek additional help."

Where is Jason Rayner

"They've listed him as a missing person, I presume?"

"Eventually, but with some reluctance I might add, but that's all. I'm certain they think we had some sort of row and that he's taken off to get away from me or maybe left to be with another woman. But I assure you, that is definitely not the case."

Richie nodded. "I understand, so I'll make a start by visiting the place where your husband disappeared; Miss Smith will accompany me as she was on the scene when it happened. I'll also have a word with the local police and get back to you once I have anything to report. Do you have a photograph of your husband?"

"No, I'm afraid not. We had a flood in my flat and an album was destroyed. I'll get back to you if I come across anything that will be of help."

"Perhaps you could leave your address and telephone number with Miss Smith on your way out?"

"I will, and thank you for taking this seriously, Mr Stevens."

Through the open doorway, he watched her talking to Sandy in the outer office and after she'd gone, left his desk, stopped at the water cooler, and said, "Fancy one?"

"No thanks. Well? What did you think?" Sandy asked.

"She seems plausible enough but has an odd way of talking – very precise."

"Old fashioned?"

"You thought so too? Was it just the clothes?"

Sandy hesitated then replied, "I don't think so. I'm sure you're right. It's the way she speaks.

Where is Jason Rayner

Young women don't talk like that today. It makes me wonder where she grew up and what her parents were like."

"Older, do you think?"

"Possibly, yes, maybe controlling. She did marry young and to a much older man."

"To get away?" Richie bounced questions towards her and as usual got a quick fire response. Once again he thanked his lucky stars for Sandy Smith.

"Could be. There may be any number of reasons. I'll arrange a few casual lunchtime meetings and let you know what I discover. Do you want me to ring and make an overnight booking for two at a cheap hotel in Kingslea, for starters?"

"Excellent, Miss Smith but be sure to book single rooms, won't you?"

He could hear her laughter drifting towards him as he walked to the washroom in the corridor outside the office, and smiled.

The Hollybush Guest House was situated in a side street off the main thoroughfare leading through the village of Kingslea. From his attic bedroom Richie had a view of the river Lea wending its way through lush green countryside. He guessed that Sandy wouldn't be as fortunate, as her room, although larger, was situated on the floor below. Mrs Trevethick, the owner of the guesthouse, had informed them upon arrival that dinner was to be served at seven sharp. He glanced at his watch; it was nearly that now.

Where is Jason Rayner

He met Sandy in the hallway outside the dining room. She had changed her clothes and now wore a dress in place of her denim jeans and tee shirt.

"Very nice," he commented.

"Wish I could say the same," she said but her smile took the sting out of her words.

Dinner was an unremarkable affair, tasteless, but filling and conducted in an atmosphere more suitable to a library, conversation amongst the small group of residents being conducted in hushed whispers.

Afterwards, Richie suggested they walk to a pub at the end of the road where they could discuss their plans for the following day.

"Hang on, I'll just fetch my fleece and join you outside," Sandy said, taking the stairs at her usual speed of two at a time.

The evening air held a distinct chill; Richie turned up his jacket collar and wished, not for the first time, that he hadn't given up smoking.

"Right, lead on," Sandy appeared and, perceptive as ever, noted, " It does get better you know."

"The voice of experience?"

"That's me, Boss."

The Boat and Compass was typical of any small riverside pub, which survived mainly on the tourist trade during the summer season. Attached to the wall above the bar was a large fish in a glass case, casting a lifeless eye over the clientele. Against one wall stood a cabinet displaying the landlord's angling trophies, or ones, which he'd purchased to add to the general ambiance of the place.

"Tomorrow, I thought we could check out the river path, " Richie said, "then take a look at the Kingslea Heights Hotel."

Where is Jason Rayner

Sandy picked up her glass of red wine and frowned.

"What is it?" Richie asked.

"The Kingslea Heights is expensive. Dan says it's the sort of place retired people, willing to splash the cash, stay. Needless to say, we've never stayed there. But I did wonder whether it would necessarily be the kind of hotel a couple like the Rayners would favour."

Richie looked out of the window to the river, which shone in the moonlight. "Interesting," he said. "I think we've already established that Mrs Rayner is not your typical young woman, maybe, as we said, she was brought up by elderly relatives, or is simply one of those people who are old before their time. I wonder what *he* was like? Maybe someone on the staff of the Kingslea Heights remembers him."

"Mmm, or failing that, I can see my job, once we return to Lockford, will be to infiltrate Lockford Juniors." Sandy grinned.

"You make it sound like an SAS assignment."

"And, I'm sure it will turn out to be such." Sandy finished her drink. "Do you fancy another? I'm paying."

"In that case, how can I refuse?" Richie handed her his glass. "Another pint of the landlord's finest please, Miss Smith. I can see I'll have to think about cutting your salary."

Richie watched her walking to the bar. She was a good kid and, under the circumstances, had been a lifesaver at a time when he'd needed one. She was invaluable, had an excellent brain and spot on intuition, a rare combination in his estimation. In addition to which, she knew all about Lucy and the twins, so he didn't have to explain. The night his family was wiped out by a drunk driver, when Lucy was driving the twins home from a disco in London, would haunt him forever but Sandy somehow helped to keep the ghosts at bay. He hoped that boyfriend of hers appreciated what a catch he'd found.

"Penny for them?" Sandy asked, putting two glasses down on the table.

"You wouldn't believe me if I told you," he said. "Now tell me again about the conversation you had with Kate Rayner, when she first discovered her husband was missing - every detail, leave nothing out."

Sandy sighed, "No peace for the wicked then?"

"Not a chance."

Where is Jason Rayner

Chapter 12

There was a cool wind blowing in from the coast. It swept through the grasses bordering the riverbank rippling the surface of the water as it came. Sandy shivered and closed the zip of her parka.

"So, show me exactly where you started your bike ride," Richie said, as they left the car parked in a small communal parking area.

"We parked Dan's off-roader just here, unloaded the bikes and set off down the path."

Richie stepped over a rough patch of ground on to a tar-macadam path, about two metres wide. "Did you see the Rayner's car?"

"There were a couple of cars in the car park. Mostly four by fours; it could have been any one of them."

"Then what?"

"It was hot. Chloe started to complain about having to wear her cycling helmet so I left them to it and started off on my own. I suppose I'd been cycling for about five minutes at the most when I saw Mrs Rayner."

Richie looked around. To one side of the path was the river and on the other grew a high hedgerow beyond which the ground rose steeply into a small hill.

"And you saw nothing of the husband?"

"I passed no one until I saw her."

The hedge was well-established and high enough to make it impossible to lift a bike over the top of it

Where is Jason Rayner

and climb over with any degree of speed, Richie walked towards the edge of the path and the river bank.

"The only possible way he could have gone is by the river – but how?" He bent down and craned his neck to right and left before standing up and stroking his chin. "It's impossible; firstly there is his bicycle to consider and secondly, surely his wife would have heard the splash? The bank is steep, I don't see how he could have done it." He glanced again in the direction of the hill and frowned. "And you are sure this is the place you stopped to talk to the wife?"

Sandy nodded. "Positive; if you look up to the top of the hill, you'll see it."

"What?"

"The oak tree. It's where we used to sit when we had picnics with the kids. If we walk on roughly a hundred metres or so you'll see a gap in the hedge and a path leading up to the summit of the hill. I remember talking to Kate Rayner, looking up and seeing a young couple sitting in the exact spot where I'd sat with the family the day before."

Richie sighed, "Right then, let's find that path leading to the tree. How do you feel about a climb?"

"No problem, although you might like to hold on to your hair, it's going to be windy up there today." Sandy chuckled striding ahead of him.

She hadn't been kidding, Richie thought, as they reached the summit and looked down to the cycle path. The wind was behind them as they'd walked up to the top but at the top it swirled around them like water in a boiling cauldron. The view was of the river winding towards the estuary to one side and

Where is Jason Rayner

behind and below them lay the village and the bypass.

"Now tell me where the young couple, you saw, were sitting. Were they with their backs to the river or facing it?"

Sandy thought for a bit. " Facing the river?"

"Are you sure?"

"Absolutely. I remember thinking that the woman looked a little like my sister-in-law."

"You could see that far?" Richie was doubtful.

"Not initially, not until they walked down to the path but it was the way she wore her hair in the same style and was of the same build."

Richie sat down and patted the grass at his side. When Sandy was sitting alongside him, he said, "So they would have had a clear view of the river path from here. They must have seen Jason Rayner at some point."

"Not necessarily," Sandy said, pulling up the hood of her parka.

"Why?"

"They were young and in love; it was obvious, they couldn't keep their hands off each other. Even when they walked down to the path and I asked them if they'd seen Mr Rayner they looked a bit confused and shook their heads."

"Perhaps it might be worthwhile trying to find them."

"Needle in a haystack springs to mind," Sandy jumped up. "Where do we start?"

"The pub restaurant, on River Street. Let's see if the landlord knows of anyone local fitting their description. It's nearly lunchtime and we could do with a bite to eat. Then we could try the shops on the main street. Someone might know them." Richie held out his hand for her to help him up and she grinned.

"Not a chance, you're on your own," she said, turning her back to him and walking down to the path.

The Duck and Drake had been taken over by a fast food chain, which had refurbished the premises so that the public bar was now an eating area with seats overlooking the river. Richie and Sandy were shown to a table with a view of the main street.

"This do?" A waitress, who was past her best, tucked a lock of bright red hair behind her ear, handed them two, foot-high, menu cards, took their order for drinks and disappeared behind a door to the right of the one marked **Toilets**. Richie sat in the chair facing the charity shop and peered over the top of the menu at Sandy. " What d'you think? I know she's not exactly young but she might know the pair."

"I can't see it myself," Sandy replied. "I think I'll have the trout. What about you?"

"Yeah, trout's fine."

"Take you orders, shall I?" The waitress reappeared with a pad and a pen.

"Yes, two trout and baked potatoes, please. Oh and I wonder if you could help me," Richie asked.

It was as Sandy had suggested, she wasn't in the least bit helpful. He doubted whether she even gave the question a moment's consideration before replying in the negative and hurrying back through the door into the kitchen. He knew that the odds

Where is Jason Rayner

against finding the couple were slim, especially as they might not have been locals but holidaymakers.

"I'll be back in a mo, just off to the ladies," Sandy explained leaving him to watch the ever-changing scene outside the window. An open-topped car drew up and two couples emerged, the women hastily running their fingers through their wind-swept hair before entering the pub. On the opposite side of the road a elderly man wearing a thick tweed jacket and carrying a newspaper under his arm, walked slowly along the pavement, his stick tap-tapping on the paving stones. Richie glanced away from the old man towards a terraced house facing the pub where a woman, wearing a floral apron, was cleaning the inside of an upstairs' window with a piece of rolled up newspaper.

"Sorry to be so long," Sandy apologised as she sat down. "You'll never believe who I've been talking to? Never in a million years."

"Go on."

"I just saw the woman, who was on the hilltop that day. Don't turn around, she's standing at the bar with some friends."

"And she's wearing a blue and white dress," Richie added.

"How…..?"

"Good guess, I saw them arriving and as the other woman was wearing trousers, I made a lucky guess, especially as she and her boyfriend looked as if they were joined at the hip. But I can hardly believe this is just coincidence – an impossibility I would have thought."

Where is Jason Rayner

"Just luck. She and her friends live in Kingslea and this is their local. Sometimes it's a mistake to look a gift horse in the mouth, don't you think?"

Sandy smiled then told him how she'd asked the woman again about Jason Rayner and at first she didn't know what she was talking about. Then she seemed to remember the day because it was where and when her boyfriend proposed to her.

"If that was the case you'd think she'd have known the date as soon as you asked her," Richie said.

"Maybe. But I think she was genuinely a bit confused. And after all, I did sort of spring it on her." Sandy looked over his shoulder. "They're going into the restaurant now. I didn't want to make it look too obvious, as if I couldn't wait to spill the beans."

"Very sensitive, I'm sure, Miss Smith."

Sandy sipped her lemonade through a straw and looked out of window then said, "Anyway, she was absolutely certain she had not seen him."

"How was she so certain, especially as it took her a while to remember she'd been there in the first place?"

"It was her boyfriend, actually. He interrupted our conversation to say they had been joking about the woman who was cycling down the path on her own because she kept wobbling from side to side and was wearing a helmet that looked as if it could have been worn by a soldier in the Second World War."

"I see."

"I expect they missed him – probably too much in love to notice," Richie commented.

Where is Jason Rayner

"Cynicism doesn't suit you, you know. Anyway you are quite wrong."

"I am?"

"They noticed the woman getting out of her car, putting on her cycling helmet and starting off down the path. They even noticed us arriving, and Chloe arguing about wearing her headgear. AND they saw me stop and talk to the woman and remembered speaking to me later."

"But no Jason Rayner?"

"No Jason Rayner."

Richie stroked his chin. "I think the waters look decidedly muddy from where we're standing, Miss Smith. I suggest we take a walk down to the police station and see what they've got to say."

Where is Jason Rayner

Chapter 13

Sergeant Ian Trevelyan was drinking coffee from a mug with the words *'ello, 'ello. 'ello* printed around the side in red letters. He looked at them over the rim of his mug, as if surprised to see anyone having the temerity to come into the station voluntarily. Putting down the ginger biscuit he'd been about to dunk into the thick brown liquid, he cleared his throat.

"Yes? And what can I do for you two then?" he asked in a broad Devonshire accent.

Richie handed him his card.

"Private Investigator?" the sergeant read then looking up said, "Don't get many of them down our way."

Richie proceeded to explain why they were making their enquiries and if the police could shed any light on what happened on the river path nearly a month ago. Sergeant Trevelyan ran his fingers through his sparse brown hair and frowned. "Funny affair that; he took off, in my opinion, only she couldn't accept it. Made up some cock and bull story about him disappearing. I reckon he left her earlier that day, before she rode down the path."

"What makes you think that?" Sandy asked.

"Well stands to reason – people don't just disappear in broad daylight now do they? Anyway she was an odd kettle of fish, if ever I saw one. Pretty, I grant you, but the way she talked; she was like - well I don't rightly know how to describe her - sort of precise, is the best I can come up with."

"In what way?" Richie leaned forward.

"Well now, let me see. If I remember rightly, she asked if we could deploy men to comb the undergrowth bordering the river. And she insisted that she be informed of every effort made to discover what had happened to her husband."

"What's odd about that?" Sandy commented. "That would be standard procedure, surely?"

'It would, Miss. And I grant you the words alone don't sound odd – it was the way she said them, like she was in charge of the investigation. Reminded me a bit of my boss, if the truth were told. Not the sort of reaction I would have expected, under the circumstances – kind of emotionless, if you know what I mean?"

Sandy bit her lip. "I do. It was one of the things I first noticed when I spoke to her. Although she appeared anxious, she hadn't lost any self-control, which would have been understandable, considering her husband had just disappeared."

"Aye, very odd, if you ask me. We investigated at the time but as far as we are concerned the husband did a runner, and until we hear anything to the contrary, that's that."

They left the police station and walked back towards the Hollybush in time for what was known by Mrs Trevethick as 'afternoon tea', which Richie had hoped would at least contain some scones and fine Devonshire clotted cream but in reality consisted of a pot of lukewarm tea and a plate of Rich Tea biscuits.

Where is Jason Rayner

"We need to find out more about our client's past, before we can get to the bottom of this," Richie said, following Sandy through the gate as the guesthouse's sign blew disconcertingly in the wind.

"You want to go on with the case then?"

"Certainly, it gets more intriguing by the minute, don't you think?"

"I do, but was afraid you might want to dismiss Kate Rayner as some kind of nutcase and leave her to her own devices." Sandy squeezed past him into the hallway as he held the door open for her.

"Not at all; it's a challenge. How to find a possibly non-existent husband? Not something I've come across before," Richie said, following Sandy into the front room where the teapot and plate of dry biscuits were waiting.

The next day, they were sitting on a bench in the sunshine outside the Hollybush Guesthouse. It was early; the postman wobbled down the cobbled street on his bike and the grocer was setting up a table of fruit and veg under the awning outside his shop.

"Next stop the Kingslea Heights hotel," Richie said. "Maybe they can provide us with a more detailed picture of the elusive Mr Rayner."

Sandy followed him down the path and into the street. "It's not far," she said, "in terms of distance, that is, but in terms of accommodation it's a million miles away from the Hollybush."

At the end of the road, they turned a corner where the road began to slope towards the river. As they walked, they passed a couple of pretentious looking small hotels, with awnings, garden ornaments and what looked like plastic flowers arranged as window

Where is Jason Rayner

displays, until they reached the driveway of the Kingslea Heights Hotel. It was an impressive building, solid and uncompromising where luxury was concerned. The gardens were immaculate. The lawn, which was cut within an inch of its life, was bordered by plants and was carefully arranged to display them to their best effect.

In the foyer Richie felt his feet sink into the pile on the carpet, as his eyes travelled to the information desk behind which stood a young woman dressed in a navy suit and white blouse with a nameplate pinned to her jacket pocket.

"Hello, Susan," he said with a smile. "My name is Richard Stevens and this is my associate Miss Smith. We are investigating the disappearance of Mr Jason Rayner who, I believe, booked into your hotel with his wife on the 15th of last month." Richie handed her his card.

"Yes?" Susan was tight lipped, he could see there was an uphill struggle facing him."

"We've spoken to Sergeant Trevelyan at the police station and he knows we are working on behalf of our client," Sandy interjected, professionalism dripping from her tongue like honey. "You are the chief receptionist, I presume?" Sandy was all smiles. "We do need to speak to someone in charge, you see."

Richie had to admire the way she was handling Susan, whose chest had suddenly swelled with pride at the mention of the words, 'chief' and 'in charge'.

"Certainly, only too pleased to assist," Susan replied stiffly.

Where is Jason Rayner

"Right then," Richie said. "First, perhaps you could confirm the booking and that both parties arrived on the 15th?"

Susan focused on the computer screen in front of her. "Oh yes, now I remember them. I booked them in, at least....."

"Yes?" Richie asked, seeing her hesitate.

"I mean, I did book them in, but I only saw Mrs Rayner, her husband was unloading the car."

"Is there anyone who might remember seeing Mr Rayner – a waitress, the room maid?"

"I'll have a word and let you know." She held up Richie's card.

"That's very kind of you," Richie replied.

"And very efficient," added Sandy.

Susan smiled. "My pleasure, I should have an answer by this afternoon."

Outside, it had begun to rain. Sandy hurried down the drive and sheltered beneath a large tree outside the main gates. "The plot thickens," she said as Richie caught up with her

"The invisible man couldn't be more undetectable," Richie said, as Sandy removed a small umbrella from her shoulder bag and followed him back to the Hollybush.

The call came through to Richie's mobile as he was waiting for Sandy to come down for afternoon tea. He was alone in the small lounge.

"Mr Stevens, it's Susan from the Kingslea Heights. I've asked around and it's most odd, no one seems to remember seeing Mr Rayner. They remember his wife but the maid said he was usually in the shower or out jogging when she arrived with their breakfast tray and the dining room staff said they assumed the couple dined in town in the evening. I've even asked the window cleaner – no one remembers him."

"I see, many thanks for your help, Susan, I appreciate it."

"My pleasure."

When Sandy arrived a moment later, Richie was pacing the floor.

"What is it?"

"I'm beginning to think this Jason Rayner doesn't exist." He was standing at the window looking into the street. " I think it's time to go home."

"Now?"

"I know the lure of afternoon tea is overwhelming but I suggest we stop off for a decent meal on the way home.

"Sounds a good idea to me, " Sandy said, "I'll get my things."

Where is Jason Rayner

Chapter 14

He'd had a bad night. Dreams of the car accident that robbed him of his family six years ago still recurred at intervals. Waking in a bath of sweat, the dream still vivid, Richie got up and walked to his bedroom window. His flat was on the third floor and he had a view of the river bordered by trees and in the distance Lockford Common, which had initially been the reason he'd bought it. The distant hum of traffic from the by-pas, rather than being a distraction, was faintly reassuring, as having lived in a London suburb for many years the thought of being too far away from civilisation unnerved him.

After he had showered and eaten breakfast, he decided to go into the office. It was early, barely six o'clock. The street cleaners were finishing their night's work as he arrived at Hastings Buildings, parked his car and let himself into his office on the first floor.

The office smelled of paper, Sandy's lemon air-freshener and ink from the printer she had re-filled the previous afternoon. He opened the window a fraction. The early mornings were still chilly and he shivered before switching on the kettle and making a mug of strong black coffee.

His mind was clear, and without any distractions he began to consider the events surrounding the Rayner case. He had yet to discover anyone who could give him a clear picture of Jason Rayner and it disturbed him. His wife seemed genuine enough, as far as he could tell. He was sure she believed her husband had disappeared and certain Sergeant Trevelyan believed the man had done no such thing and that it was a domestic tangle, which he didn't intend to unravel without further evidence. The conclusion of the Kingslea police force's investigation was that her husband had probably absconded with his lover and in time would contact his wife for a divorce. But Richie wasn't willing to accept that assumption too readily. The whole scenario was odd – the woman too – nothing he could put his finger on as yet, but intuition was telling him there was more to this case than met the eye.

A week after they returned from Devon, Richie rang Lockford Junior School and asked if he could make an appointment to see the headmaster for the following day. The school secretary suggested he make it for four o'clock, after school had finished for the day. "Mr Hobbs will see you then," she said.

Sandy's initial visit to the school had proved unfruitful. Taking an unofficial approach, she had talked to a young woman teacher who ended up by saying she'd only been working at the school for three weeks, as a supply teacher, and didn't know anyone called Jason Rayner. So Richie suggested she approach the landlord of the flat, the address of which he'd been given, rather reluctantly, by his client whilst he attended his appointment with Mr Hobbs.

Richie left his office in Hastings Buildings and drove in the direction of the common. The school was situated on the edge of town with a view of the

Where is Jason Rayner

woods and common ground in front of it. As he approached, he threaded his way through the mêlée of cars driven by parents who considered their children required a lift rather than using their legs. A sign of the times, Richie thought, as he parked in the school grounds and walked towards the entrance where he was met by a cleaner who was manoeuvring her bucket and mop through the door leading into the corridor.

"Here, let me help," he said, holding the door open for her. "Perhaps you could point me in the direction of the headmaster's study?"

The woman was in her sixties; she narrowed her eyes and looked at him with suspicion.

"It's alright, Mr Hobbs is expecting me, " Richie said, giving her the smile he kept to instil confidence in his clients.

"Turn right at the end of the passage and his door's facing you," she replied pushing the bucket along the floor with her foot.

Martin Hobbs was in his early forties with thick brown hair that stood up in spikes. He was dressed casually and Richie thought how different he looked from the headmasters he'd known in his youth. "Come in, Mr Stevens," he said, getting up from his desk and reaching across to shake Richie's hand. "Please, take a seat. Now, what can I do for you?"

"My client is married to one of your teachers and I require a little background information about him, if it's no trouble. Obviously you are aware of Mr Rayner's disappearance and the circumstances surrounding it."

"I'm sorry, I don't follow you."

Where is Jason Rayner

"Jason Rayner – the man who disappeared on holiday with his wife, in Devon."

"I'm afraid, I'm still not with you," Martin Hobbs leaned forward, a frown creasing his forehead.

Richie hesitated, "He does work here? I mean did, before he disappeared."

"I think you must be mistaken, Mr Stevens. Perhaps you've got the wrong school. There is no one of that name teaching here and, as far as I am aware, there never has been during the five years that I've been headmaster."

Where is Jason Rayner

Catherine's story

Chapter 15

"Is the light bothering you?"

I've almost forgotten he is there, hidden by the glow from the lamp. "No. Thank you."

"We'll continue then. You are sure you don't want a cup of coffee?"

"I'm fine. The sooner this is finished the better, don't you agree?"

He doesn't answer so I continue.

It was soon after I returned from Devon that I bumped into the woman who had been so kind to me, when Jason Rayner disappeared on the river path. Her name was Sandy Smith and she worked for a Private Investigator whose offices were in Hastings Buildings, just across the road from Arbuthnot and Trent. She wondered if her boss could help me find my husband.

I was so relieved that at last someone was willing to listen. I knew the police didn't believe my account of what had occurred that day and I didn't know what to do. From the start, I felt Richard Stevens was a man I could trust, as he sat back in his chair and didn't comment until I'd finished telling him what happened that day.

Afterwards, I returned to work and even Mason Trent running his finger down my bare arm as I did the filing couldn't lower my mood. I hadn't told anyone in the office about Jason Rayner. They didn't even know we'd got married, until they saw the ring on my finger. I liked to keep my private life, private.

Without him, my flat seemed empty. Every night, when I returned home from work, I expected to see him waiting for me. I saw his smile in every mirror, heard his voice when I woke up and felt the heat of his body at my side in bed at night. It was only in daylight that his image disappeared and I felt his loss so acutely.

Richard Stevens rang to tell me that he and Sandy were going to Kingslea for a couple of days to see what they could discover. I was thrilled; it felt good to be believed at last. There was every possibility that he'd find out something that would lead me to understand what had happened to Jason Rayner.

Whilst they were working on my behalf in Devon, I decided to have a good clear out of the flat. I was a tidy person by nature, Tracy in work thought I was borderline OCD. I wasn't sure what she meant at first until she explained the nature of Obsessive Compulsive Disorder.

"Don't be so ridiculous," I told her.

"I'm not. You are. I mean, well, just a little bit. Take a look at your desk then look at all the others in this place."

I looked down. "Yes, well, a place for everything and everything in its place," I said, faithfully repeating one of Rita's platitudes.

Tracy laughed, "You're so funny, Kate and the thing is, you don't even know it." She giggled and I wasn't sure whether to be pleased or annoyed.

Anyway, I was in the middle of tidying our bedroom when I found the Estate Agents' brochures that we'd been looking at before we went on our

Where is Jason Rayner

holiday to Devon. I would show them to Richard Stevens when he returned. It would surely prove to him that Jason Rayner hadn't been about to run off to start a new life with another woman. We were planning to move to a semi on the outskirts of Lockford. We'd seen one we liked in the brochure. He'd even ringed the page with the red pen he used for marking the schoolchildren's homework.

Putting the brochure on the side table in the lounge, I continued tidying the flat, trying to keep my mind occupied, trying to forget what had happened to my husband on the cycle path in Kingslea.

We had been in the process of transferring his belongings from his flat to mine as his place was being sold. In fact there was only a pair of jeans, a shirt and one old tee-shirt in our wardrobe. I kept telling him to get a move on but he kept saying – there's plenty of time – besides your place is so small there's not much point cluttering it up with my stuff, until we have to.

I picked up his favourite shirt, the blue one with the button-down collar, he'd worn it the day before we left for Devon and it was still on the chair at the bottom of our bed. Placing the fabric to my cheek, I inhaled the scent of him and without warning a thousand tears began to fall. The bed creaked as I fell back, the shirt still clutched to my chest, and closing my eyes tried to picture him. The image was fading and I was desperate to keep it alive, desperate not to lose sight of him altogether.

Later, I washed his clothes on a high heat, dried them and placed them back in the wardrobe then went into the kitchen and poured a large measure of

Where is Jason Rayner

red wine into a glass. Sitting at the table, I drank every drop until the edges of my sorrow were softened, every memory cutting through me with less force than the one before. When I was feeling better, I stood up, put on my coat and walked out into the fading afternoon sunshine.

Somehow my footsteps led me to the school. I stood outside the gate watching the children in the playground as the bell rang and they filtered back inside the building. A well-built woman wearing shorts and a tee shirt appeared in the doorway, blew her whistle and the ragged line of stragglers went inside. I turned away - I wouldn't find him here, however long I waited.

A feeling of impotence swept over me. Although Richard Stevens was working on my case, I felt at a loss to know what to do to help. There was nothing I could do, nowhere I could go, the parameters of my search had begun and ended on a river path and it seemed as though my husband had disappeared into thin air.

I missed him. I felt more alone than I had in my entire life. Did he know that? Where was he? He must know I would worry. My head was full of questions for which I had no answers as I walked disconsolately back to my flat. The police car was parked in the road outside the entrance to my block. The lift wasn't working again and as I walked up the stairs to the first floor I wondered how long it would take the maintenance men to fix it. It was OK for me but there was an elderly lady living on the floor above who had difficulty with the stairs.

Where is Jason Rayner

As I turned the corner of the staircase leading to my flat, it was a huge surprise to see a police constable and woman P.C. ringing my doorbell.

"Mrs Rayner?" the constable asked, as I approached, my key already in my hand.

"Yes, is there any news of my husband?"

The woman looked uncomfortable as she took my arm, "Perhaps we should go inside?"

I opened the door my heart pounding against my ribs. In the living room the constable said, "I would take a seat if I were you, Mrs Rayner. I'm afraid our colleagues have informed us that a body has been found washed up on the coast near the Kingslea estuary."

Where is Jason Rayner

Chapter 16

I take a deep breath and he waits without speaking. I wonder if he really thinks he's making a difference or if he's bored by it all? I wonder if he believes any of it? I've been attending these sessions long enough to know the answer and it's like a wake up call rousing me to be more inventive, whilst sticking to our plan.

I should have been prepared for an event of this kind. But to hear the words 'a body has been found' made my knees buckle and I sank into a chair as I waited to hear the rest.

"Fetch Mrs Rayner some water, Constable Watkins." He was young and awkward, not used to imparting bad news of this kind. I almost felt sorry for him as he continued, "I must stress, at this point, the body hasn't been positively identified but there are signs that foul play has been involved."

His words reminded me of countless television dramas I'd sat through with Jason Rayner. He loved watching detective programmes. I searched for a tissue to blow my nose then took the glass the WPC had filled from the kitchen tap gulping at its contents, "It might not be him then?" I asked. "Do they want me to ……?" I choked unable to continue.

"Not at this stage, immersion in water means there …." his words like mine petered out into nothing but their meaning was plain to see. "The

Where is Jason Rayner

pathologist will want to do a full autopsy before a positive identification is made but we thought it right to warn you that your husband is the only person reported as missing, in the area, who fits the initial description." He stood up, hovered over me for a while then said, "Is there anyone we can contact to sit with you for a bit?"

I shook my head, as I followed him and the WPC into the hallway.

"No, thank you, I'll ring my aunt in a short while but I'll be OK."

It was a tremendous shock, more than I could have imagined possible. The thought that Jason Rayner was dead was something so horrible to contemplate that I started to shake in earnest, once I'd closed the door behind them. What could I do? I picked up the phone.

"Richard Stevens, Private Investigator's office, how may I help you?" It was Sandy's voice.

"It's Kate Rayner, I have to go away for a while. I'll be in touch via my mobile, if there is any news."

When I put the phone down, I realised I hadn't mentioned the visit from the police. Then I dialled Rita's number.

I couldn't drive; I wouldn't be able to concentrate on the road, all I'd see before me would be his lifeless bloated body. I hadn't been to see my aunt since Bill's funeral and she still didn't know about my husband.

I printed a train ticket from my computer and left early the next morning.

Reading, Oxford, Coventry, Birmingham, Derby, the stations passed in a dream, I could think of

Where is Jason Rayner

nothing but my husband, see nothing but his face staring back at me merging with my own reflection in the window as the fields and towns flashed past. My book, face down, on the table top, was still unread as I heard the metallic voice, issuing from the train's intercom announcing that Sheffield was the next stop.

There was no one to meet me. I told her not to come but knew she wouldn't offer anyway. The smell of the city was unfamiliar. It had changed so much since my last visit. It had been 'tarted up' as Bill, no doubt, would have said. Standing in line at the taxi rank, I wondered if my aunt would have changed as much as the city. Everything and everybody did, it seemed.

I needn't have worried. She was more or less the same but the house looked different; the large, rambling, trees which had previously been left to grow wild had been cut down to a reasonable size, the hedges were trimmed and the riot of colour in the front garden was no longer from the flowering weeds but from flower pots full of begonias. It reminded me of a time, which I could barely remember, when the lawn was always trimmed, the hedges cut and my mother's flower borders in full bloom. I felt a lump in my throat as I placed my key in the lock.

Rita welcomed me as if I'd just stepped out for a pint of milk and not been living away for years. At first I didn't tell her about Jason Rayner, our marriage, or his disappearance, enjoying the warmth of my welcome and the sight of the woman with whom I had lived since my parents' accident.

Where is Jason Rayner

"I've kept your room just the same as when you last came," Rita said, giving me the benefit of my mother's barely remembered smile. "I've been cooking your favourite, it's nearly ready then we can sit around the table as always and you can tell me what you've been getting up to down south."

Rita cooking, I thought? That would be a first.

"Roast lamb, mint sauce and the best roast potatoes in the world," she said as my stomach did a somersault in rebellion.

"Great."

How could I tell her? I didn't want to spoil her joy at having me home again. I decided it could wait – the following day would be soon enough.

After dinner, Rita and I sat in the dusty lounge, the French doors were open, letting in the warm night air and I began to let the horror of yesterday drift away by refusing to think about it.

"It's like I've never been away," I said, with a sigh.

"It's good to see you again, Catherine, I've missed you," she replied picking up a bag of knitting from the floor at her side.

"I would have come sooner, but I've been busy at work and getting the flat redecorated." It was an excuse but neither of us acknowledged the fact.

"Well you're here now, that's the important thing."

I watched her pick up her needles and thought how little she'd changed. She was like a small bird. I noticed that her grey hair, which had always been a bit untidy, was now a warm brown colour and her dress looked new. I think I'd expected her to have put on weight, but there were no unwanted rolls of

Where is Jason Rayner

fat, she looked as if a good puff of wind would scatter her to the four corners of the earth. I was pleased to see that apart from superficial differences she was much as she'd always been.

"How are you? Is this place getting you down? It's a big house to manage on your own."

"I'm fine," she replied, her needles clicking like the wings of a cricket as I wondered was she really? The house was much quieter without Bill who had been the stuff of my childhood nightmares with his bedtime stories lifted from the pages of The Brothers Grimm and his large hands tucking me into bed just a little too tightly.

Later, in my single bed, the sheets smelling of faded lily of the valley and mildew, I closed my eyes and remembered my childhood, allowing the memories to wipe away all thoughts of Jason Rayner. I didn't want to face having to tell Rita about it. If I didn't face it then I could pretend it had never happened and perhaps that I'd never met him.

I awoke with a start and the sound of Rita cursing. Dimly aware that it had been preceded by the sound of a crash from the kitchen, I slid my arms into my dressing gown and hurried downstairs. She was struggling to get up from the kitchen floor, where she'd fallen.

"Careful, your arm looks as if it's broken to me," I said, rushing to help. Her arm was twisted at an odd angle and her face was white with pain.

"I'm sorry, love, I slipped," she said.

I managed to lift her into a sitting position and made a cup of hot sweet tea and handed it to her before I attempted to get her to stand. She was

Where is Jason Rayner

obviously in a lot of pain. Ringing the out of hours NHS helpline, I was told my best bet was to get her to the Accident and Emergency Department of the Northern General.

"I'll get dressed and ring for a taxi to take us to the hospital," I told Rita who had begun to shake. "Don't worry, I'll see to things."

She looked relieved.

The day went downhill rapidly from then on. Eventually, we were seen by an impossibly young hospital doctor who told us Rita would require an operation to set her arm, as there was a bone at the elbow that had sheered off. 'It was a bit more complicated than a simple break,' he said.

I explained to my aunt about the operation and told her I would wait until it was over. She didn't want me to stay but there was no way I was going to leave her. So, with all that was going on, there was no way I was going to tell her about my problems, she obviously had enough of her own.

I feel he requires an explanation at this point. My aunt's accident was pure genius on my part I decided, it explains why I disappeared. He's still waiting in silence and the air in the room is suddenly oppressive. I take a deep breath, feel my pulse rate steadying, the flutter in my chest subsiding.

"You see, that explains why I didn't have a clue the police were looking for me," I say.

Where is Jason Rayner

Chapter 17

I'm getting used to this now. I want to continue, to hurry the story along. The elements of the truth are begging to be told but I have to take care; there's too much at stake so I continue.

Rita was home, her arm encased in plaster and a sling and I was in the middle of helping her to dress when the television news came on. There was an item about a body that had been found washed up on the Devon coast. The police were looking for Mrs Jason Rayner – if anyone knew of her whereabouts, please ring this number.

Rita was too preoccupied and fortunately didn't take any notice but I changed channels to Sky Gold just in case.

"You like watching *Only Fools and Horses*, don't you?" I said by way of an explanation.

Rita smiled and said, "Thanks".

What could I do? I couldn't leave her to fend for herself. Then it occurred to me, as she didn't know my married name, she wouldn't know I was the one the police were looking for and so I could stay for a while longer, without causing her further distress. I'd removed my wedding ring in the train on the way to Sheffield, giving myself time to approach the subject without being forced into it by the sight of a ring. I knew there were no photos of me lying around my flat, should the police get the caretaker to let them in. I hated having my photograph taken and

Where is Jason Rayner

as far as I could tell the description of me on the television news could apply to almost anyone with black hair.

"You OK, Catherine?" Rita asked, concerned.

"Of course, just worried about you."

She looked up at me, "No need to be, my dear girl. But I must say, it's good to have you around for a bit longer."

So there was nothing I could do about the police, it would all have to wait until Rita was more mobile and I believed she could cope without me. I did wonder whether I should contact Richard Stevens but he had my mobile number and no doubt would ring if there were any new developments.

"Should I do some shopping this morning, aunt?" I asked sometime later, after I'd made her a cuppa and filled the washing machine.

"If you don't mind collecting some dry cleaning for me and picking up a large sliced loaf on the way, I'd be grateful."

"Anything else?"

"I don't think so, love. I did the big shop once I knew you were coming, so the cupboards and fridge are well stocked. Jennifer used to help me with the computer until I got the hang of shopping online. But it's so easy once you know how and I don't have to carry it all the way home on the supermarket bus."

I nodded in all the right places. It was shock to start thinking about Jennifer in the past tense. Her parents must be devastated. Rita told me last night about the reporters and the fuss that was made at the time. She said they still hadn't found the murderer. I didn't want to risk bumping into her parents so left the house by the side door, just in case, slipped over

Where is Jason Rayner

the style into the field and followed the trodden down pathway through the grass to the road.

Sheffield had changed. I caught the free bus at the end of the road, which soon filled up with shoppers. I hadn't used it since I was in school and was pleased to see it in operation and that it was efficient. The chatter of voices and gentle rocking of the bus as it drove towards the city centre shops was comforting. It wasn't until we passed the school where I spent my youth that a wave of panic swept over me. I pressed the bell and left the bus at the next stop. Once on the pavement, I took a deep breath, filling my lungs in an attempt to steady my nerves – breathe deeply, I thought, – and after a few minutes, it worked.

The school was as I'd remembered it, only the gates were now painted black instead of green. I didn't know why I got off the bus. It was as if I was drawn to the threads of my past life like a fish on a hook. The playground was empty, the children and staff closeted behind the stout stone walls that had kept me imprisoned for five years, most of which I'd enjoyed.

I pressed my hand against the railings feeling the chill of the metal and closed my eyes. Jason Rayner had disappeared but he was still with me, every glance, every scent and every sound of him. My mobile rang and by the time I'd removed it from the depths of my handbag, the caller had rung off. I saw someone had left a voice message so I clicked on the call and listened.

"Hello, Kate? It's Sandy. Could you give the office a call when you have a minute?"

Where is Jason Rayner

I was certain it would be about the television news broadcast but didn't feel up to explaining why I couldn't see the police at the moment. Rita came first as far as I was concerned; there was nothing that wouldn't wait anyhow. So slipping the phone back into my bag, I started to walk the mile or so towards the centre of town.

I passed the pub and felt my heart race. I'd never drunk alcohol before that day when I was still only fifteen, and could still remember the taste of it on my tongue and feel the tingling sensation as it entered my bloodstream. It was after a visit to the museum, lots of year eleven were at the pub, and although most of us were still well under eighteen, no one turned a hair or asked our ages.

Afterwards, I bought a packet of mints at the corner shop, so that Bill wouldn't smell it on my breath. I knew he would go mad. Breaking the law, however small the incident, would be shocking to my uncle, who thought everyone should play by the rules, everyone that was except him.

I've always liked big cities. You can get lost in them. No one wants to know why you're there; no one is interested in you. Department stores, in particular, are places where anonymity is expected – it's possible to wander from department to department, stop off for a coffee or lunch without ever having to speak to anyone, other than to pay for your goods. Being inconspicuous suited me, I needed time to heal; it had been such a shock, just when everything seemed to be working out so well for us both.

Where is Jason Rayner

I was still in the coffee shop at John Lewis's when my mobile rang. This time it was Richard Stevens.

"Mrs Rayner? Where are you?"

"Having coffee, in a department store – why?" I felt indignant – I was explaining again.

"No, I mean - look – the police want you to contact them – it's about the body that was washed up. It's rather urgent."

"It's him?"

"They aren't sure, that's why they need to see you urgently."

"I can't leave here at present, it's impossible. Tell them I will ring them, once things improve." The signal fell away and I was left with a bleep followed by nothing. I looked at the display – no bars – no signal. Fate had intervened it would seem. Taking the escalator to the floor where they sold mobile phones and pay as you go Sim cards, I smiled. I'd seen enough detective series on TV to know that they could trace a mobile phone's signal. All I had to do was cut through the old one and insert the new Sim. It was as easy as winking.

Where is Jason Rayner

The investigation

Chapter 18

"So how did you get on with the landlord?" Richie asked, as Sandy handed him a mug containing his second coffee of the day.

"Like you, I drew a blank. Someone called John Rice, who the landlord had only seen on the day he arrived, paid the rent but there was no question of any missing payments. On the day he'd left the flat, he'd written a note saying he was moving on and enclosing the final rental payment.

"No chance he still had the note?"

"No, I asked him about it and he said it was type written and after he'd counted the money, he'd put the note in the bin."

"I see. I don't suppose he was able to describe him?"

Sandy frowned. "He said he was tallish, brown hair cut very short and that was all he could think of. He said he wasn't taking much notice because the money was all he was interested in, as he'd been caught before with students running off without paying and leaving the flats in a terrible mess. He said, John Rice had never given him any cause to complain."

"It's this JR business all over again; far too many coincidences for my liking."

Later that afternoon, Richie put down the phone and raised his eyebrows at the detective sitting opposite him.

Where is Jason Rayner

"No luck?" DI Flintlock from the North Devon constabulary asked.

"She put the phone down."

Flintlock was in his late twenties and had climbed the ladder to DI principally because he was intuitive and had a good degree but also because he was the nephew of the Chief Constable. The latter was an unfair burden in his estimation. He stroked his chin. "We need to find her and fast. We are trying to trace her mobile's GPS signal and we've spoken to her work colleagues but the only contact details they have are for her flat and mobile telephone number. Her next of kin is named as her husband Jason Rayner – address, the same as hers."

"You said the body shows signs of foul play?"

"That's why it is so important that we find Mrs Rayner – the body has not been identified. There are no missing persons on the list fitting the description, other than her husband."

"Right, well, all I can do is keep trying her mobile and once I make contact I'll be in touch." Richie frowned and followed the detective to the door. "You have no objection to my continuing with my own investigation?"

"None, we're hitting a brick wall and if you can break it down, please - be my guest. Needless to say, if you do….."

"As I said, I'll be in touch."

"Fine. Goodbye, and goodbye to you, Miss Smith." The young detective smiled at Sandy who nodded in acknowledgement.

When the sound of footsteps on the stairs receded, Richie said, "I see you've made a conquest there, Miss Smith."

Where is Jason Rayner

Ignoring his remark, she replied, "Where do we go from here?"

"Arbuthnot and Trent; ring and ask whether I can make an appointment to see either of the partners in the morning, please. Then we'll look into Jason Rayner's history. But I have a strong feeling it won't be easy."

The offices of Arbuthnot and Trent were typical of a kind – large plate-glass windows bearing the firm's office logo and details of opening hours etc., inscribed across them, and inside was a reception desk behind which sat a woman in her mid-thirties dressed in a grey suit and white blouse.

"How may, I help you?" she enquired as Richie approached.

"I have an appointment to see one of the partners."

"Yes, sir, name?"

"Richard Stevens."

She glanced briefly at a computer screen. " Ah, yes, Mr Stevens; Mr Arbuthnot is out of the office at the moment but Mr Trent will see you. If you'd like to follow me."

She was a large woman, which hadn't been immediately apparent when she was sitting down. Richie followed her swaying hips towards Trent's office. Mason Trent looked up from the newspaper spread across his desk, as the receptionist introduced Richie.

"Sit down, Mr Stevens. I understand that you wish to talk to us about Kate?"

"Mrs Rayner, yes."

"Now then, what do you want to know?"

Where is Jason Rayner

Richie explained the reason for his visit and waited until Trent, replied, "Very little I can tell you, actually. Kate started work with us a year or so back. She came to us from Bristol, I understand, she'd been studying at a further education college – I told her she could have gone to Uni., but she said she preferred to learn in the work place, as she'd had enough of studying. She's a bright girl, bit unusual, but good at her job."

"Unusual? In what way?"

"Old fashioned – not to look at, more her way of looking at the world. It's difficult to explain. She didn't mix with the rest of the girls, wouldn't go clubbing with them, never joined them for drinks after work, for example."

"She didn't get on with them?" Richie suggested.

"On the contrary, they liked her well enough." Richie noticed a lecherous expression briefly flitting across the man's face, as he said, "We all did."

"So, she was single when she began working for you? What was her surname?"

"Newson."

"What did you think of Jason Rayner, her husband?"

"Never met the man."

"I see. Is there anyone here who might be able to fill me in on some background details – you know the type of thing – girl talk – how they met etc.,"

Trent thought for a moment. "Tracy Golding would be the one most likely. Tracy knows everything that goes on in this office. I'll show you to our restroom, she should be on her break. Sorry it can't be in here." He looked at his watch. "I have a client due any minute."

Where is Jason Rayner

Richie had taken an instant dislike to Mason Trent. He recognised his type, the photograph on his desk showing him with his arm around his wife and smiling at his children didn't fool him. He thought maybe Kate Newson had been a scalp Trent had failed to add to his collection.

Tracy Golding was waiting for him in the restroom. She was a tall girl with a figure that Richie guessed had been enhanced by surgery. Her grey skirt and jacket fitted where it touched and her rich auburn hair was pulled back into a knot on the top of her head. His immediate impression was of someone who could handle the Mason Trents of this world and turn most situations to her advantage. She was alone and was sitting on a sofa flicking through a fashion magazine; she looked up as he closed the door behind him.

"Good morning. My name is Richard Stevens, I'm a Private Investigator and I'd like to speak to you about your colleague Mrs Kate Rayner," he explained walking over to one of the hard backed chairs and sitting opposite her.

She smiled and he could see a gleam of excitement in her eyes when he'd mentioned the reason for his visit.

"Anything I can do to help, of course." She closed the magazine and leaned forward giving Richie an ample view of her enhancement through the thin cotton of her blouse.

"How well did you get on with her? Did you like her?"

"Yeah, she was OK – bit odd but that's all." There it was again, the word that seems to trip so lightly from the lips when describing his client. He'd thought so himself and now in a short space of time two people had used the same word.

"In what way?"

She bit her lip. "Can't say really, except she didn't mix very well, kept herself to herself. The only one she ever met for lunch, for example, was Ollie."

"Ollie?"

"Oliver Watts, he's a clerk working here. She seemed to feel comfortable with him. He's a bit old fashioned himself, perhaps that's why they got on and he's mad about her, of course."

Richie made a mental note to have a word with Oliver Watts but not in the office environment. "Did she tell you anything about her husband?"

"If you knew her you'd know the answer to that one. She never talked about herself. I've worked with her longer than any of the girls and I'm still in the dark."

"You never met him?"

"No. I think she met him by chance somewhere but that's all I know. He sent her some flowers once but she just said they were from a friend. We didn't know she was planning on getting married, either. She just arrived back from her holiday break with a ring on her finger, I didn't even know they were engaged."

Richie frowned. "He never picked her up from work, never called in at the office?"

"Not that I know of and I think I would know – it would have been the talk of the office, after all."

"Did she ever say where he worked?"

"No. We all tried to get her to open up, especially when we found out she was married but she'd just

Where is Jason Rayner

smile and say nothing. All I know is he was from somewhere up north, Scotland I think or somewhere."

Richie stood up. "Well thank you Miss Golding, you've been a great help."

She was nearly as tall as he when standing and as he shook her hand, she said, "No problem anytime, and it's Tracy by the way."

It was nearly lunchtime. Richie found a window seat in the Sweet Pea café directly opposite the offices of Arbuthnot and Trent. He ordered a ham and cheese baguette and chips and waited. He was just finishing eating when he saw a young man leaving the office and walking in the direction of the café, which was beginning to fill up with customers; Oliver Watts hesitated in the doorway and looked around for a seat.

Richie stood up and raised his hand. "Oliver, over here," he called.

As it turned out there were no introductions necessary.

"You're the Private Investigator who was asking about Kate – Mr Stevens, isn't it?"

He hovered in front of Richie.

"That's right. Why don't you take a seat, Mr Watts, I was hoping to have a word with you."

Making an instant appraisal of the young man, Richie speculated that he was a nervous individual, always eager to please. "I won't keep you from your lunch a moment longer that is necessary but I wondered if you could fill in some gaps for me?"

"Yes, anything I can do to help Kate– you only have to ask."

Where is Jason Rayner

"You are fond of Mrs Rayner?"

"I like her very much and I think she likes me," he said his cheeks reddening. "As friends of course, nothing more."

"But you would like it to be more." It was a statement not a question. The young man nodded.

"At one time, yes, but I never told her of course, especially not after she got married."

"I understand."

"What did you think of her husband?"

"I didn't know him, never met him. But I know Kate was head over heels about him."

"She told you?"

He paused then said, "Er, not exactly," adding, "but I could tell. As soon as she met him, I knew I didn't stand a chance."

"Do you know where she met him?"

"In a café, wine bar, somewhere like that, I think. Not sure though, I don't think she ever did say, exactly."

"And you never saw them together."

"No. But I could always tell when he was meeting her after work. She was excited, couldn't wait to get away."

"I see, and she didn't let on that she was getting married before the event, I understand."

"Not to Tracy and that crowd. But she did mention it to me. Told me not to say anything."

"And you didn't." Richie could imagine him keeping her secret and had no doubt it was why she'd confided in him in the first place.

"No, I didn't. She said they were going to Las Vegas to get married in one of the wedding chapels on the strip." He was plucking at the end of a paper napkin resting on the table. "What's happened to her, Mr Stevens?"

"I don't know, Oliver. But I intend to find out and I promise, when I do, you will be one of the first people to know about it."

Catherine's story

Chapter 19

"Just to re-cap. You were staying with your aunt and still hadn't made contact with the police? Is that right?" he asks.

The recording machine hums softly in the silent room. I can hear his breathing. He sounds as if he has sinus problems. This is getting difficult now; I have to be careful not to trip up. I nod and carry on.

I needed a change of clothes, as I'd not anticipated staying with Rita for any length of time but her accident changed my plans. The John Lewis store was busy; it was Saturday morning and the weekend shoppers were out in force.

It felt good to be wandering around familiar territory, even though it had been ages since I'd done so. I began my shopping expedition by having a drink in the coffee shop on the first floor then joined the throng of customers in women's wear whilst searching for items in my size.

I was contemplating whether to buy an emerald green cotton sweater or a more wearable charcoal grey one when I saw him. I tried to follow but he disappeared into the throng of shoppers. Was I imagining it? What was he doing in Sheffield? What was he doing on the train? Thoughts of continuing shopping evaporating in a mist of confusion, the pleasure of the day had vanished. I put the emerald green sweater back on the rack and hurried towards

Where is Jason Rayner

the exit and out into the street, praying I wouldn't see him again and fearing that I would.

When I arrived home, Rita was waiting to see my purchases. "What is it, love? Nothing suit you, did it? Sit down; you're as white as next-door's washing. I'll put the kettle on." She stood up but I put a hand on her shoulder and eased her back into the chair.

"I think I might be coming down with a cold, Aunt. Would you mind if I spent the rest of the day in bed?"

"Of course not, I don't mind at all; off you go now. Just shout if you want anything. I'll bring you in a hot milky drink; you'll soon perk up. I can manage the kettle now, so don't you worry about me."

The panacea to all ills, I thought dejectedly. It would take a lot more than a hot drink to make me perk up. I doubted whether I would ever 'perk up' again. I couldn't tell Rita. How could I, she didn't know I'd married Jason Rayner in the first place so I couldn't tell her I was beginning to suspect I'd imagined it all. My marriage was dissolving in front of me. What if the rest of my life was going to be filled with images of my husband around every corner?

The following morning I was able to think about it all more clearly. For my peace of mind I needed to speak to him. I could only hope an occasion would arise whereby I'd see him again and follow him; perhaps the police were right and he'd left me for

Where is Jason Rayner

another woman. Would it make any difference if he explained his reason for leaving me?

I thought about contacting Richard Stevens but realised he'd probably take it into his head to drive up to Sheffield and I didn't want that to happen, not now. I didn't want to let them know where I was, not yet. Rita was my main concern.

But the thought of talking to him again was uppermost in my mind and I couldn't rest until I'd contacted him. I had a decision to make and I couldn't consider anyone else this time. I'd spent my life being managed by other people, now it was time I took control.

"You appear agitated, would you care to take a small break, stretch your legs?" he asks.

"Yes, perhaps, for a moment."

"Coffee?"

"Thanks, black, no sugar. I'll be fine in a minute." I stood up and walked towards the window. The trees in the park opposite were swaying in the breeze like a drunk on a Saturday night, their branches linked arms and as I watched, they seemed to wave in my direction.

"We are in no hurry. Take your time," he said. "It's important that you explore the reason why Jason Rayner appeared in the first place."

Chapter 20

The coffee has calmed my nerves and I place the cup on the table at my side. He waits for me to continue but I decide to let him wait, whilst I think of how to explain it all to his satisfaction. It matters. It's one of the conditions I have to fulfil as a result of being accused of wasting police time. My disappearance when I was sixteen didn't help matters. They couldn't let it all go unpunished and this is my penance. The police psychiatrist recommended this man to them. She said he is an expert in his field. She believes I need him to untangle my confused psyche.

He interrupts my thoughts. "You do realise that at the end of this session, I will make a report to the police?"

I nod and smile at the trees outside the window.

"But I don't want you to become concerned. It's routine. Patient confidentially still applies; the report will contain no detailed transcript of our sessions just a summary of your state of mind. So you must feel free to talk without any constrictions."

This is no penance. It's part of the plan; we anticipated this was going to happen, and knew it's the only way to stop the questions and put an end to the investigation. Today it will be over, this session is the culmination of weeks of therapy. I'm ready to continue.

Where is Jason Rayner

The next day, feeling a bit uncomfortable about the way I had refused to contact Sandy after she had been so kind to me, I walked towards Starbucks, opened the door, and found a seat with a good view of passing shoppers, I drank my coffee and decided that when I returned to Lockford, I'd visit Richard Stevens and explain why I felt the need of secrecy.

"Cathy?" A middle-aged woman wearing a shabby coat stood in front of me. "I thought it was you. How is Rita, I haven't seen her down at the centre for some time?"

I thought about saying she'd mistaken me for someone else but soon realised I couldn't get rid of her so easily.

"She's fine, " I replied, hoping it would be enough.

"I could call round, if you like? See if she'd like to join us for Bingo on Saturday night."

"That won't be necessary. I'm staying with her for a while and we have other plans for Saturday night."

The woman sniffed. "Haven't changed, have you? Tell Rita I asked, don't forget." She shuffled off towards the door and I watched her carrying a selection of plastic carrier bags in the direction of the bus stop.

I winced – people like Brenda Cox, with their endless questions, were one of the reasons I'd left this town in the first place. Why she would think my aunt would want to go to Bingo, of all things, was beyond me. Glancing at my watch, a thought occurred to me. It was Monday morning. I tipped up my mug, drank the dregs of my coffee and rushed

Where is Jason Rayner

out of the door, wishing a breath of fresh air would wash away my childhood.

It started to rain as I walked towards the school. Mid morning break time had ended and the yard was empty. By now the slight shower had turned into a torrent. I sheltered under a tree across the road from the school gates but my hair was already plastered to my head and had started to curl annoyingly around my forehead.

At midday, I heard the electronic buzzer, which long ago had superseded the clanging of the school bell, followed by the excited chatter of children's voices as they spilled into the playground or ambled through the gates to go home for lunch. A short while later, I saw him. It had stopped raining but he was wearing a navy mackintosh with the collar turned up. The wind was blowing through his hair and I felt an ache somewhere in the region of my ribs, I wouldn't think about my heart and how it had broken.

Rita didn't comment on the fact that I was wet through, other than to say, " Still raining then?"

"How are you?" I asked. I could hear the sound of her television coming from the front room.

"Getting there, it's just the pain."

"You must take the painkillers the doctor gave you. I know how you hate taking them but it's important."

"I will, I promise, you don't have to worry about me, Catherine."

I walked to the window and looked across the road. The windswept trees and rain soaked pavements stared back at me. Rita had too much to worry about at the moment. I couldn't tell her that I'd seen him and that I thought I was losing my mind. Anyway, I wouldn't know where to begin and I was used to hiding things, it was the best way.

"I'll put the kettle on," I said, going into the kitchen.

As I waited for the kettle to boil, I mechanically measured coffee into three cups and let my mind wander to what I was going to do next. I thought about ringing Richard Stevens but something held me back. Perhaps it would be better to confront him, ask him to explain why he'd left me. I shook my head to rid myself of such thoughts; to speak to him would prove I was mad.

I felt anger bubbling up inside me as the kettle boiled and the cut off switch clicked. I stared blankly at the three cups, tipped the contents of the third into the bin and poured water over Rita's and mine. It was the first time I'd let myself feel the loss of my uncle. Anger and sorrow mingled with frustration as I turned my thoughts back to the matter in hand. There was no way this was going to be easy; I was going to see him again and again.

He blows his nose and the sound seems loud, echoing around the dimly lit room. Not sinus problems, probably hay fever, I decide. Dennis Bridgeman used to sneeze his way through the summer. A picture of sitting in the classroom studying the text of *Romeo and Juliet*, waiting for a sign, slides unbidden into my mind and I shake my head. I must not be diverted. I must not think of him. It might show. My pulse begins to race so I take a

Where is Jason Rayner

deep breath, wait until he's finished snorting into his handkerchief, and continue.

The Investigation.

Chapter 21

"DI Flintlock on the phone for you," Sandy said, as Richie sat back and drank his third cup of tea that morning.

"Put him through please, Miss Smith."

The detective sounded as if he was standing outside, Richie could hear the steady hum of motorway traffic in the background. "There have been some developments I thought you might like to hear about, Mr Stevens. The body found near the estuary has still not been identified but our forensic team have agreed that the cause of death was non-accidental. It's now believed that the unidentified male was struck from behind which precipitated his fall into the river."

"I see," Richie said.

"Have you heard from Mrs Rayner again?" Flintlock's voice faded as his mobile's signal dipped. "Can you hear me?" he asked.

"I hear you. And the answer is still, no. She's not been in touch with this office since the last time we spoke and her mobile is unreachable on that number."

"Any ideas where she might have gone?"

"None, I'm afraid."

Putting down the phone, Richie stroked his chin. He hadn't lied but he hadn't been exactly truthful either. He didn't know where Kate Rayner was but something Oliver Watts told him had led him to believe that she had a relative up north somewhere

Where is Jason Rayner

and Richie was beginning to wonder if that was where she was. In addition to which Flintlock had said the caretaker of the block of flats where she lived had admitted their forensic team, in order to look for traces of her husband's DNA. It seemed that they'd taken a sample of hair from one of her jackets for elimination purposes and removed items of clothing from the flat for testing. However, it appeared there were no traces of any DNA samples other than those of Mrs Rayner in the entire flat. Either she was a fanatical cleaner or she lived alone and had done so for some time.

It was lunchtime and Sandy had popped out for sandwiches for them both. Richie walked into the outer office towards the water cooler and, as he filled a polystyrene cup with ice-cooled water, something on Sandy's desk caught his eye. She was an assiduous creator of doodles, especially when there was case in progress. He picked up her notepad and saw that she had been repeatedly writing the name Kate Newson. She'd begun by printing it in large capitals then slicing up the letters as if completing an anagram in a crossword puzzle and reforming them. Finally he noticed that she had left the Christian name untouched and focused on the surname. But the last name she had written was KATE NEWperSON.

One of the attributes he admired about his PA was her ability to think outside the box. He valued her opinions and suggestions, without which many of their cases would have remained unsolved.

"No sausage sarnies to-day – they've had a run on them – BLT do?" Sandy arrived and as usual brought with her a breath of fresh air.

Where is Jason Rayner

Richie was still holding her note pad. "Did you know you're a star, Miss Smith?"

"I have my moments. What is it this time?"

"Kate Newperson?"

"I thought it possible." She walked towards the small kitchen area, put the sandwiches on a couple of plates and made a cup of coffee for Richie and a camomile tea, which was her latest preference.

"More than possible. The woman has reinvented herself. The question is, who was she before?"

"I suppose we could start with the date she began working for Arbuthnot and Trent and then scour the past editions of the national newspapers for anything that might establish a link." Sandy bit into a tuna and cucumber sandwich.

"Good place to start but it will be an almost impossible task, I should think. Especially if there are no newspaper reports relating to her; why would there be?"

"Yes I know but as we've nothing else to go on, I don't mind making a start," Sandy replied with a grin. "Besides, if someone reinvents themselves it's usually because they are trying to get away from something in their past. I think it's a quite plausible hypothesis."

"What would I do without you?" Richie grinned. "And while you're doing that, I'll ask Oliver Watts to come over for an interview. This time I need to find out everything he knows about Kate Newson/Rayner, in minute detail."

It was nearly six o'clock and Richie was alone in the office as Sandy had been searching through archived newspaper reports most of the afternoon and he'd told her to go home at five. At six on the dot he heard footsteps climbing the stairs followed by Oliver Watts opening the office door.

"Come in, Oliver. Coffee?" Richie offered.

"Er, no thank you, Mr Stevens."

"Sit down, I'll try not to keep you longer than is necessary. I need to ask you some further questions regarding your friendship with the lady you first knew as Kate Newson."

"Have you found her?" the young man asked eagerly.

"I'm afraid not, neither the police nor I have any idea where she might be and it is imperative that we find her as soon as possible." Richie drummed his fingers on the desk. "The police have been unable to find a photograph of her so that it could be circulated in an attempt to find her. I wonder if perhaps you might have one in your possession?"

Oliver shook his head.

"No office party snapshots, for example?"

"I don't think so. You see Kate wasn't a party girl. She wasn't like the rest. She was different."

Richie smiled. "And that's why you liked her?"

He watched the young man's face change colour by degrees until it became fiery red. So it was more than just liking, Richie thought – he was mad about her.

"Yes, I'm not much for parties and the like, either. I thought at one time she liked me too but then she met Jason Rayner and I didn't get a look in."

"And you never met him?"

"No. As I said, I don't think any of us in the office, did."

Where is Jason Rayner

"A bit unusual, wouldn't you say?"

Oliver bit his lip. "Not if you knew Kate. She was a very private person. She wouldn't have liked to become the subject of office gossip."

Something in his expression gave Richie the distinct impression that this man would have wanted something from the friendship, if he couldn't have the relationship he so desired.

"You haven't been straight with me, have you, Ollie?"

Richie watched him running a finger around the inside of collar, his face permanently flushed. "I'm ssorry?" he stammered.

"The photograph. You took one on your mobile didn't you?"

He breathed a sigh of relief. "I, er - how did you know?"

"I didn't but you just told me."

Oliver hung his head. "She would have hated to know I had it. But I liked her so much. We met one lunchtime in the park and ate our sandwiches on the grass while we watched some children feeding the pigeons." He looked up and smiled. "She was so intent on watching them that I risked taking a snap then pretended I was looking at the weather forecast on the Internet. "But it wasn't a good one, it was only half her face really."

"Do you have it with you?"

The young man hesitated. "I don't want her to get into trouble," he said.

"Right, well for the moment, let's just say this stays between us. I'll use the photo to try to find her and only give it to the police if not to do so might put her in danger. What d'you say?"

Where is Jason Rayner

"Er, I suppose that would be OK. Shall I Bluetooth it to you?"

A year ago Richie wouldn't have had clue what he meant but Sandy had changed all that. He switched on the Bluetooth connection on his laptop, waited for Oliver to send the file then accepted it as Sandy had shown him.

The photograph was grainy and as Oliver said, it wasn't a good one. Nevertheless, in the morning he'd get Sandy to have a look at it. There was something she could do with the Photoshop programme, which was totally beyond him; maybe she could make the image clearer.

"Thank you, Mr Watts. I'll let you know if I trace your friend."

"Will you explain about the photograph?" he asked.

"Don't worry," Richie tapped the side of his nose. "Our little secret," he said.

Where is Jason Rayner

Chapter 22

The day following Richie's conversation with Oliver Watts, Sandy rang to say she was making progress and hoped to have something to show him later that afternoon. Richie opened the post and listened to the wind howling as it swept around Hastings Buildings. Summer in the UK - he shivered; it was as cold as winter, a season where memories of the family he'd lost would resurface. It was November when Philip Hatton, sodden by drink, had ploughed his car into Lucy's and although time had eased the pain, there were days, especially when the anniversary of the death of his family approached, the memory became almost intolerable.

The sound of his telephone ringing cut into his thoughts. It was DI Flintlock.

"Mr Stevens, I thought you might like to know that in view of her disappearance, we are now looking for your client in connection with the murder of a male victim answering the description of her husband Jason Rayner. You no doubt understand that because we are still no further forward in our investigations as to the identity of the murdered man, it is imperative she contact us immediately. If she does get in touch with you, please inform her of our conversation."

Flintlock spoke formally and Richie replied in the same manner. "Certainly Inspector."

Putting the phone down, he opened his laptop and accessed the file where the photo of Kate Rayner

Where is Jason Rayner

was stored. If only Sandy could improve the quality of the image they might have something to work with. But he knew he was clutching at straws – the woman had disappeared without a trace.

There was nothing more he could do until Sandy returned later that afternoon so switching on the answering machine and texting Sandy to say he'd see her later, he left the office and walked across the road to the offices of Arbuthnot and Trent.

The girl called Tracy was standing in reception. She recognised him.

"Heard from Kate yet?" she asked, whilst nursing a mug of coffee.

"Have you a spare moment, Tracy?" Richie approached her. "I'd like a word, confidentially, of course." He looked over his shoulder conspiratorially. It did the trick. Tracy was a woman who loved intrigue and he knew she'd be unable to keep a secret for longer than one minute.

"Yes, it's my coffee break and anyway, it's as dead as a doorknob in here." Richie wanted to laugh…doorknob? "We could use this interview room, if you like?"

"Fine, " he replied, following her long legs encased in shiny tights, or could it be stockings? The room, which was little more than a cupboard with a small desk and two chairs facing each other, smelled of perfumed polish, the desktop shining as if newly cleaned.

"Right, what's new?" she asked, sitting opposite him and sliding her pencil slim skirt up her thighs as she crossed her legs.

"I know you were the only one in the office in whom Kate might have confided." Flattery was always a good starting point with the Tracys of this world, he thought. "And I'd like to take you back to the moment Kate Newson first started to mention Jason Rayner. You don't mind if I take notes?" He could see that rather than minding, Tracy was impressed.

She thought for a moment, tapped her red-painted fingernails on the desk then said, "She'd been out buying doughnuts, I think, and came back all flustered. I asked her if she was OK and she did the thing she usually does when she doesn't want to talk."

Richie looked up from his notebook. "What thing?"

"She puts her head down, twists the end of her hair around her fingers and hurries away." Tracy was in full flow. "But I wasn't having any of it. I said, you've met someone haven't you? I could tell – she was all soft and squishy. She used to be like that with Mason Trent until she found out what he was like. He's a real…."

Desperate to get Tracy back on track, Richie said, "But you didn't actually see Jason Rayner?"

"Er, no."

"You hesitate? Why, has something occurred to you?"

"No, well, the flowers, I mean, I suppose she could have sent them to herself but I was with her when she first saw them. She was genuinely surprised. She picked up the card, read it, twirled her hair again then clammed up, said they were from a friend. I made some comment about it being a BOYfriend but she insisted they were just from a friend."

Where is Jason Rayner

"But you didn't believe her?"

"Not a bit of it. And I was right – a couple of days later she broke a date – well it wasn't really a date – with Ollie. And, well, it was obvious. She couldn't wait to leave the office to meet him, started taking trouble with her clothes and hair, you know."

"How do you mean?"

"Like, usually she dressed in a dark suit for the office but if she was meeting Jason she brought a change of clothes with her."

"That's not unusual, surely?"

"No but these were the sort of clothes you couldn't imagine her wearing – bright, in your face clothes, sexy. Not at all like her."

Richie closed his notebook. "I see, thank you Tracy, you've been a great help."

"Have they found him? There was something on the news about the police wanting to find Kate."

Richie stood up. "No, Mr Rayner is, as yet, still missing but I hope to find his wife soon."

As he walked back to his office Richie felt the note of optimism he'd expressed was fading. Where on earth should he start? 'Up north' covered a large area and, although Oliver Watts was sure his client had mentioned relatives living in the north of England, it wasn't much to go on.

He was flicking through the file Sandy had compiled on Kate Rayner when he heard the sound of footsteps taking the stairs two at a time. It was impossible to mistake Sandy's arrival. She burst into the office like a ray of sunshine on a dull day and once again he marvelled at her ability to change her persona at will. Today she was the competent researcher dressed in a smart navy trouser-suit and crisp white blouse, her long fair hair was tied up in knot on the top of her head from which tendrils escaped to frame her face.

It was obvious she was excited, even though she tried to hide it. He watched as she placed her laptop case on the desk and took her time sliding back the zip and removing the impossibly thin computer.

"Well? " he asked.

"Very."

"Miss Smith!"

"OK, yes, I think I've found something. I was able to transfer the details to a memory stick so that you can see for yourself." She accessed a file on the laptop as Richie read the newspaper report over her shoulder.

Running his fingers through his hair he said,"This puts a whole new light on the case. I seem to remember this story but it was a while ago and I'd never have associated our client with little Cathy Barton."

"So now we know where to start?"

"Excellent work, Miss Smith; as you say, now we know exactly where to begin."

Where is Jason Rayner

Jack's Story
via his laptop

Chapter 23

If I were to be asked, I'd say I liked my work. It was a joy to get up every morning to know that during the day I'd be responsible for opening up young minds to the pleasures of English Literature. It made the four years I'd spent at Bristol University worth the effort and heartache. The downside was leaving Emma and only corresponding via email and text for most of each year. Then during my second year, the emails stopped, the text messages dwindled, followed by the phone call I'd dreaded.

She'd come straight to the point – she'd met someone else. It was as simple as that and nothing I could say had made any difference. She said she was sorry but long distance love affairs never worked.

After she dumped me, I'd gone out with my mates, got drunk, got laid, let my studies slip until I woke up one morning with a stranger in my bed and the realisation that I was letting my life slide down the tubes without raising a hand to stop it. From then on it was work all the way until, at the end of my third year, I'd achieved a creditable upper second-class honours degree in English. Teaching had always been my aim, so after a further year completing my teachers' training course, I finally left Bristol with the qualifications necessary to pursue a career in my chosen profession.

Where is Jason Rayner

I'd no intention of going anywhere near Sheffield where I was likely to see Emma and her husband but fate had taken my hand and led me there. My widowed mother was a terminal patient in the Northern General Hospital for the foreseeable future and there was nothing I could do about it, other than to apply for a job where I'd be near enough to visit her during the time she had left.

Applications and interviews for schools in the area began in earnest until the day arrived when I opened the letter advising me that I'd been successful in my submission to join the staff of Westbank school in Hallum. Westbank was a relatively newly refurbished establishment, having once been Hallum Comprehensive School and I was pleased at the prospect of starting work there after the summer holidays.

I seem to remember the weather during August was unusually hot especially in the centre of town. I visited mother on most days and could see a rapid decline in her health. It saddened me to see her looking out of the window from her hospital bed at the blue sky and endless sunshine and not be able to enjoy it.

On one such day, mother looked at me, took my hand in hers and said, "I want you to enjoy your life, Jack, don't keep coming here every day. Have a holiday before you start work."

"I'm fine, mother, don't worry."

"You are not fine. Do as I say! Take that trip to Rome. Relax, before you have to deal with the terrors of the sixth form or whatever they're called these days." Her attempt at asserting her authority made us both smile.

Where is Jason Rayner

"OK, OK, I give in. I'll see if I can get a last minute deal."

"Good boy." She sighed and closed her eyes.

Rome was unbearably hot. The heat seemed to rise up from the cobbles and the air was so thick you could cut it. I loved every sweltering minute of it. My hotel was small, clean and near enough to the centre of the city for me to walk in each morning and lose an hour or two sightseeing. I visited the Coliseum and imagined the Gladiator fights and the Christians being fed to the lions; I could almost hear the roar of the long dead crowd in my ears as I slipped back in time, sucking up the atmosphere under a blisteringly hot sky. I wandered through streets where around every corner there was a building, relic or artefact requiring further investigation. Totally enthralled at the spectacle and being able to travel back in time in my imagination, I felt history seeping out from every ruin along the route and was able to put my mother's health to the back of my mind, which I knew had been her intention. When the heat became too intolerable, I made for a bar and a cool drink, whilst soaking up the sounds of Italy, the language, and its people - Sheffield briefly forgotten.

The day before my holiday ended, the temperatures rose still further and by mid morning I sought the relative cool of the Pantheon. Sightseers milling around the circular structure congregated at the altar or stood with hands on hips, necks bent backwards as they inspected the oculus through which sunlight sliced like a laser.

Where is Jason Rayner

I wouldn't have called myself a spiritual person and wasn't given to flights of fancy but as I joined a small group of tourists standing under the oculus bathed in the midday heat, I felt at peace. Closing my eyes, I breathed deeply, experiencing the comfort of countless worshippers sweeping over me and felt at one with the world. It was an event that I would re-live in order to cope with a future, which at the time was waiting to unfold, and the last occasion when my life would be totally free from complications.

The flight home was on time and I arrived at Manchester airport in time to catch the connecting train to Sheffield. It was raining. A fine drizzle clung like cobwebs to my clothes and the scent of autumn was in the air as I opened the front door of the semi detached house I'd shared with mother before I went to university. It was almost midnight, the house smelled as if it had been shut up for more than just two weeks. In my bedroom, I opened the window, stripped off, and flung my clothes on a chair then, exhausted, slid into bed and was asleep before the town hall clock struck the hour.

The next day, as I walked into the Northern General Hospital, I was looking forward to telling mother about Rome, anticipating the pleasure on her face as I recounted the splendours of the Sistine chapel and the majestic buildings, some of which had stood since biblical times. I was smiling as I walked towards the side room to find her.

Two nurses were switching off the monitor at the side of her bed as I opened the door. My mother's face was waxen and I didn't need a stethoscope to diagnose her condition.

"When?" I asked.

Sister Morris left the bed and placed a hand on my arm. "In the last hour, she didn't suffer at the end."

"Did she ask for me?" I felt helpless and at a loss to know what to do next.

The younger nurse looked up from the bed, opened the bedside locker and handed me an envelope. "She asked me to give you this. She wrote it a few days ago, before her decline."

I felt a lump in my throat as I looked at the thin spidery writing of my name on the envelope. "What happens now?" I asked, slipping mother's last letter into my pocket.

Sister Morris said, "Your mother's things will be waiting to be collected from the bereavement office on the ground floor, together with the death certificate. If I were you, I'd stop off at the canteen first, have a cup of coffee, give them time to get it all together for you, and give yourself some time for it to sink in."

In the lift, I pressed the button for the ground floor and let the tears flow, thankful that I was alone. I'd known this day would soon come but it hadn't made it any easier to cope with. Removing my glasses to wipe my eyes, I waited for the lift door to open then followed the directions to the canteen unaware that in doing so my life would change forever.

Chapter 24

The coffee was hot and glutinous. I sat down at a table in the corner of the canteen and looked though the window into the car park. Visitors' carrying bunches of flowers, children's balloons or carrier bags containing the inevitable bunch of grapes, left cars and headed for the hospital entrance. During mother's illness, the staff on Beryl ward had encouraged me to visit at any time and not to wait for visiting times so I'd missed the crush in the lift and the general stampede towards the wards.

I looked at my watch. It was visiting time. I sat in a daze unable to believe that when I'd finished my coffee, all I'd have left of mother would be her 'things' and death certificate. My father had died before I was old enough to remember him so this was my first experience of losing someone I'd been close to. I didn't know how I should feel – I was numb.

"Anyone's seat?" She was young and pretty.

"No." Words of one syllable were all I could manage.

She didn't say anything more as she drank her coffee and munched on an apple. Then, as I was about to leave, I saw she was crying.

"Are you OK?" I asked.

She nodded as a tear dropped off the end of her nose on to the table. She sniffed.

I pulled out a handkerchief from the pocket of my jeans. "Here, it's clean," I said.

She took it and wiped her face, "I'm sorry."

"No need, if you'd seen me five minutes ago, I was fighting to keep them at bay myself?"

She looked at my handkerchief. "I'm afraid I've made a mess of this."

"It's only a handkerchief. Do you want to talk about it?" I asked.

She bent her head and twisted a strand of hair around her fingers.

"Not really. You?"

"My mother just died."

She nodded, didn't comment; there were no 'poor yous' or 'I'm sorrys'.

"What will you do now?" she asked.

"I have to pick up a few things from the office then I'll go home." The thought was not appealing but the rest of the day had to be got through somehow.

"I must go too."

Before I could rationalise my actions, I said, " I don't suppose you'd fancy a quick bite and a drink in the pub before you go home?"

She looked at her watch, hesitated then tucking my handkerchief into a satchel-type bag at her feet, said, "I do actually."

She'd come on the bus. She told me she lived in Beaufort Avenue. So I drove to a pub I knew nearby and said I'd drop her off at her place later. In the middle of the afternoon the pub was relatively free of clientele. At the bar, a man with a lived-in face sat reading the racing post. A pair of young lovers, sitting in a corner steadily drinking their way through a bottle of red wine, looked up as we walked in and sat down.

"What will you have to drink?" I asked.

"Lager shandy – half – please."

"The menu appears to be on the board, I see. Won't be a sec, just getting the drinks."

I was standing at the bar when I saw her making for the toilets. When she returned I saw that she had repaired her makeup and I felt my stomach flip. She looked lovely. Recognising the signs, I swallowed. Not the time, or the place, I thought.

"It's my aunt. She's in the hospital. She and my uncle are the nearest people I have to parents," she said, twisting her fingers together.

"Rotten," I replied, lifting my pint to my lips. "How is she?"

"She's had a routine operation and it's gone well." She sniffed. "I suppose being in hospital reminded me of the time my parents died and you caught me at an off moment."

She lifted her eyes from her hands. "Mostly, I'm OK. But today I just lost it."

"Don't we all at some time or other." I reached across the table and took her hand in mine. " Anytime you want to talk, just give me a ring. I'll write my number on this beer mat for you."

She smiled. "That's awfully kind but you don't have to, really."

"My pleasure."

I suppose it was mainly because I was at a low point and she was going through a similar experience, otherwise why would I keep thinking about her? She was pretty but far too young for me to be interested

Where is Jason Rayner

in her in any way other than a compassionate one. But as the days passed and I didn't hear from her I found that I was longing to see her again.

After we'd left the pub on the day mother died, I'd driven the short distance to her home. It was a large detached house, which had seen better days, situated in a tree-lined avenue conveniently near to the centre of the city. She'd thanked me for the lift and stood at the gate. In the rear view mirror, I saw her watching until I drove away before turning and walking in through the gate.

It wasn't until I'd reached home and closed the garage doors behind me that I realised I didn't even know her name

The days passed and I was busy with tasks I'd have preferred not to complete. Clearing out mother's bedroom and sending her clothes to the charity shops was the worst part of it. I could smell her scent wafting up from the folds of her clothes in the chest of drawers, see her face the last time she had worn the flowered dress with the lace collar hanging in the wardrobe and hear her laughter when she'd tried on the fur hat I'd bought her last Christmas, which had been far too big for her.

Swallowing the lump in my throat, I'd dusted and vacuumed until every material trace of mother had drifted away on a burst of feverish activity. But the memories remained along with the photographs showing happier times. Afterwards, the house seemed emptier than I'd ever known. Although there had been times when I'd relished the idea of freedom, to get a place of my own, unencumbered by caring for her, now that she'd gone I felt lost.

Where is Jason Rayner

However, I had a new job and I supposed life would go on as usual in spite of mother's death.

There were three days left before I was due to start work. The autumn term at Westbank began on Monday. During the week since I'd seen the girl, I'd prepared my lessons for the start of term and so the weekend stretched before me like an empty page waiting for me to write on.

Saturday night was mine to enjoy, without worrying about how mother was coping, so I rang my good friend Brad.

"Hi, it's me. Yes, thanks, yeah, I'm OK. Fancy a night on the town?"

"Sorry mate, heavy date. Remember that girl, I met in Starskeys, Liz?....." And Brad was off on one. I held the phone at arms length until he finished.

"No problem. I'll be in touch."

"Erm, hang on a bit. What if I ask Liz if she's got a friend? We could go to that new club – 'Benny and the Jets'. Liz and I were thinking about going. What d'you say?"

I hesitated, then thought, what the heck, it couldn't be worse than rolling around in an empty house with no one but a ghost for company.

We arranged to meet at LaCie's, a wine bar near the club. I left the taxi and strolled to the bar wondering who Liz had brought along for me. Inevitably it would be a let down, no doubt one of her friends who looked like the back end of a bus and couldn't get a date on a Saturday night. I gritted my teeth at the thought.

Where is Jason Rayner

The bar was crowded. I scanned their faces until I saw Brad's raised arm. Liz and he were sitting at a table near the bar; a girl with long dark hair sat with her back to me – she certainly looked OK from the back, I thought cynically.

"Hi, Jack, over here," Brad shouted above the din. "Come and meet Cathy."

Chapter 25

"Hello again," she said.

I was stunned. "Good heavens, what a coincidence."

Liz looked at Cathy and then at me. "You two know each other?"

"Not really, we met in the hospital," I explained, "the day Mother died."

The air in the bar seemed thick, I could hardly breathe.

"That's great then," Brad said. "What'll it be, pint or stick with the red wine?"

The rest of the evening passed in a haze. I was aware of her, smiling at me, making no demands, dancing when I asked her to and sitting quietly at my side when I felt all talked out. Liz and Brad called it a night at half one but we stayed at Benny's until the grey light of dawn filled the streets outside.

We ate breakfast at the all-night café just around the corner. It was as if we wanted the night to never end and I couldn't believe my luck.

"What are you thinking about?" she asked.

"Me? Oh nothing much. Just how much I've enjoyed this evening."

"Morning."

"Yeah, that too," I said taking her hand across the table. "Can I call you?"

"I'd like that."

She scribbled a mobile number on a paper napkin and handed it to me. I didn't see her home. There were things she needed to do, she said, as the sun rose in the sky and church bells rang out over the city.

When Monday arrived, I felt apprehensive. It was a new school, new staff and new pupils. Butterflies did a dance in my stomach as I drove into a parking space behind the science block then entered the building.

"New boy?" A tall thin guy with a beard and curly brown hair held out his hand. "Mike Tomlinson, Head of Physics."

"Jack Robinson."

"You've met Friar Tuck, I presume?"

I grinned, Barry Didsbury, the head, with his paunch and circular bald patch fitted the description exactly.

"Beginning of term briefing, in the hall, and then we're let loose on the rabble. I wish you luck."

"Do I need it?" I asked.

"Depends. Show them who's boss from the off, old son. That's my advice."

We reached the hall and joined the rest of the staff gathered for the start of term pep talk before the pupils arrived. Didsbury introduced the new members of staff of which there were three, myself, Vanessa Rawlings and Robert Williams.

Afterwards, Vanessa caught up with me in the corridor as I made my way to the staff room. She was slim, approximately five three with blonde hair that was tied back into a ponytail and looked as if she should be in year ten, not teaching them.

"Hi, I'm scared witless, first day and all that," she said, falling into step alongside me.

Where is Jason Rayner

"Don't let them see it, pretend you've been teaching for years and know exactly how to keep them in control. Blagging it usually works. What's your subject?"

"Geography but I'm to fill in for P.E. as well apparently; yours?"

"English."

She stopped outside room 8. "This is my lot." She took a deep breath.

"Looks like I'm next-door. Pop in if you have any trouble but remember don't let them know how you feel – it's half the battle."

She smiled." Thanks, Jack, see you later."

My first class were year nine kids and after the usual half-hearted attempts at flexing their muscles, they soon fell into line and began to ask sensible questions regarding the text. I focused on work and gradually my grief at losing mother took second place to the living, breathing, rabble.

During the lunch hour, Vanessa and Robert joined me in the canteen to discuss how each of us was managing on our first day. Robert seemed preoccupied and grunted into his pasta that one child was much like another, regardless of their environment, an opinion with which Vanessa strongly disagreed. I was ambivalent and managed to work my way through a plate of spaghetti bolognaise adding to the conversation only when not to would have been awkward. Having lived with mother's rules for a lifetime, I suppose I was a firm believer in the old adage 'manners maketh man'.

The afternoon session began with the year eleven pupils, who were studying for their exams. I quickly read out their names, noted three absences and began

Where is Jason Rayner

the lesson. Most of them were well behaved with one notable – Dennis Bridgeman. Dennis was bored and when he was bored, he was a nuisance. I'd met a few like Bridgeman before and they all conformed to the same blueprint. First they started to annoy another pupil, either by talking or flicking pieces of paper in their direction then they turned their attention to whoever was teaching them. Usually they were troubled children who'd had enough to cope with in life already.

I ignored the first flexing of Bridgeman's muscle then said, "Right everyone, listen up. I'm not bothering to read from texts at the moment. You all know that we are to begin with Romeo and Juliet." There was a loud groan from the boys. "So instead, I'm going to cast the characters. As I don't know any of your capabilities I'm going to run down the register choosing each of the main players randomly." When it came to picking someone for the part of Romeo, I said, "Dennis Bridgeman – Romeo."

One of the girls gasped, a couple giggled and a lone male voice whispered, "That's a laugh!" But I noticed the imperceptible lift of Dennis Bridgeman's shoulders and knew I'd made the right choice.

It was a different scenario with the last two lessons of the day, which involved a double period with the year twelve who were studying the text of the Duchess of Malfi. They seemed to know the importance of adapting themselves to the work and I envisaged no problems in that direction.

In the corridor, as the last buzzer of the day sounded, I met Vanessa leaving her classroom.

Where is Jason Rayner

"How did it go?" I asked, falling into step beside her.

"Could have been worse, I suppose. But there are one or two that need watching."

"Aren't there always?" I said. "Anyway fancy a quick drink in the pub on the corner, after we've cleared away the debris of the day in the staffroom?"

"I do, see you later."

Mike Tomlinson was standing at the bar when we arrived. He raised his hand to us indicating a table near the window where a couple of members of staff were sitting.

"Join us?" he asked.

Afraid that this was going to be a long night, I hesitated.

"Don't look so worried. It's just a couple before we head off home, not entrance into the Hellfire Club," he said.

Afterwards, I gave Vanessa a lift back to her car." Worst day over," I said. The word 'worst' had seemed innocent enough at the time.

Where is Jason Rayner

Chapter 26

The following day set a pattern for the week. The relationship between the three of us new recruits strengthened and when Friday came I felt as though I'd settled into my new position without any problems. In the staff room there were the usual grievances amongst the staff but nothing of any consequence.

"Not coming to the pub for a quick one tonight?" Robert and Vanessa asked as I opened my car door and slid into the driver's seat.

"Have to give it a miss."

"Date?" Robert winked.

"Hope so, if she hasn't decided to stand me up," I replied with a grin.

It had been over a week since I'd seen Cathy and three days since I'd spoken to her on the phone. She'd had a heavy cold but was sure she'd be able to meet me in the wine bar at the corner of the High Street and Castle Square at eight on Friday night.

At first I wasn't sure if it was her–she looked younger. I supposed it was after seeing teenagers all week or maybe it was that she was wearing less make-up than when I'd first met her with Brad and Liz.

I bought the drinks and we sat at a table away from the bar, where a crowd of university students were celebrating someone's birthday.

"How's the cold?" I asked.

"Better, thanks."

"Fancy a film and a meal after? Or if you'd rather do something else?"

She smiled. " No, that's fine. There's a new Meryl Streep film on at the Plaza, I'd like to see it, if possible, I mean, if that's OK, or do you fancy something else?"

We were at the stage of dancing around each other's feelings, as neither of us knew each other well enough.

"Great, Meryl Streep it is then. If we finish up here we should be in time for the eight fifty showing.

I didn't really enjoy the film, it was a fluffy romance but she loved it and so I lied. Afterwards, we stopped off at an Indian restaurant in a back street, and over a curry, I attempted to find out more about her. At first conversation was stilted but as the wine flowed so did the words. She told me she hoped to work in advertising, if a suitable job opportunity arose. I was content to let her talk and then I told her about my time spent in Bristol Uni., leaving out the bit about Emma. Later, as I kissed her goodnight in the car outside her house, I realised I hadn't mentioned that I'd started work at Westbank. I hadn't got around to it; understandable in view of the fact that the kiss led to me driving back to my place and asking her in for a nightcap and things had got a little out of hand.

After I'd eventually driven her home in the early hours, I parked in the garage and sat for a while putting off the moment when I'd enter my empty house. I'd enjoyed the evening. Cathy was good

Where is Jason Rayner

company and she'd entered my life at a time when I was vulnerable, I suppose. It's no excuse, I know, but that was the reason for how we'd ended up in bed so soon. She seemed to understand and had gone along with it with enthusiasm. But did I want to see her again? Self-analysis has never been my strong point; I found my thoughts spiralling until I wasn't sure of anything any more.

Opening the car door, I sighed, and entered the house through the door at the back of the garage leading into the hall. The sound of the grandfather clock at the bottom of the stairs echoed in the silence.

Monday morning was wet and dismal. As I showered, rain battered the bathroom window in a never-ending onslaught. However, even the darkest sky couldn't depress my mood. I was actually looking forward to the day. Shakespeare and year eleven – even Dennis Bridgeman couldn't destroy my optimism. I whistled as I backed my car out of the garage and drove in the direction of Westbank School. Nearing the building, I saw the usual untidy line of schoolchildren, some hurrying to avoid the showers, others walking without raincoats, obviously impervious to the rain. It was a rite of passage, they believed that anything was better than looking uncool, into which category raincoats and umbrellas definitely fell.

Vanessa tapped the roof of my car as I switched off the engine and picked up my books.

"Nice weather for ducks," she said, as we rushed towards the entrance, dodging the puddles.

Where is Jason Rayner

Wolf whistles and comments followed us as Vanessa said, "When will they ever grow up?"

"Soon enough, I expect." I stood aside to let her enter the building.

"At least someone has manners," she said smiling up at me.

The morning passed without incident, until it was time for the double period with year eleven. Romeo and Juliet clutched under one arm and a pile of exercise books under another I pushed the door open to room 2B with my back, eased through the doorway and lowered the books on to my desk. I could hear the hum of background conversation gradually increasing in volume.

"Right, that's enough now, settle down and open your copies of Romeo and Juliet to page number 42, everyone."

Amid the inevitable rustle of books being opened and backpacks clattering to the floor, I selecting the passage they would be studying that afternoon then glanced around the class.

When my eyes met Cathy's, Romeo and Juliet slid from my fingers.

Where is Jason Rayner

Chapter 27

She looked unconcerned. Her eyes met mine for a moment then she picked up her book and flicked through the pages until she found the relevant section.

I felt my cheeks burning and ran my finger around the inside of my collar, which had begun to feel tight. She was a pupil? Uncomfortable images slipped into my mind, each one more embarrassing than the last. How old was she? She was in year eleven, so at least she could be over sixteen – what if she wasn't?

"Read the next scene and when you've all finished we'll discuss it," I said, ignoring the chorus of disapproval that had started with Dennis Bridgeman who, like the others, wanted it to be acted out, as before. I knew I was being unfair, so muttered something about getting on with it or finish it in the Sinbin after school. But I was aware of her sitting in front of me in her school uniform and my hands began to shake. Opening my laptop, I accessed the year eleven register page, typed in the password and found her date of birth. What was I going to do if she turned nasty, gossiped to her friends, spread the word we'd slept together? I looked at the screen. It was my worst nightmare – she was fifteen.

When the buzzer sounded for the end of the lesson and thankfully the end of school, I waited until I was alone in the classroom and the chatter of voices drifted down the corridor. Cathy hadn't looked at me as she passed my desk. She'd held her head high and followed the rest of her classmates just as if nothing had happened between us. Was that a good sign? I hadn't a clue.

Outside, I walked to my car in a daze.

"Are you OK, Jack?" Vanessa caught up with me. "You walked right past me. You did say you'd give me a lift – my car's having a service and MOT, remember?"

Would she be able to tell, I wondered? " Sorry, in a dream, of course, here, let me open the door."

Vanessa slid into the passenger seat. "Are you sure, you're OK?" she asked as I closed the door behind me.

"Not really, I've just found out the girl I've been seeing recently is a year eleven pupil and she's fifteen." The words left my lips by their own volition. It was too late to take them back.

"Oh, I see."

She didn't look as if she did, I thought, anyway, how could she? "I had no idea," I started to explain, easing out of the car park and trying to avoid the usual throng of stragglers making for the bus stop.

"I didn't think for one moment you did. Look, let's stop at the Wheatsheaf for a bite to eat and you can tell me all about it. My car won't be ready until six then perhaps you could drop me off at the garage, afterwards."

I agreed with a sigh of relief. At least she wasn't shocked, at least I could talk to someone about it – the mere thought of it was already beginning to scare me to death   I could see the newspaper headlines –

Where is Jason Rayner

Teacher's career ruined by sex with pupil - jail sentence for paedophile teacher.

The Wheatsheaf was quiet; it was an odd time to eat, after the lunchtime rush and before the evening 'Earlybird' menu attracted parents with young children. We sat at a table overlooking the car park, away from the large seating area near the bar.

After we'd eaten, Vanessa said, "You don't have to tell me about it, if you'd prefer not to, you know."

"No, no, I want to, it will be a relief. It's just - I don't know where to begin."

She smiled and patted my hand. "At the beginning is a good place, I always find."

Somehow I managed to tell her, how we'd met, about mother, everything up until the moment when we made love, had sex, made out, whatever, I couldn't find the words to describe what it had actually been.

"I don't need it warts and all, Jack, don't look so worried – it happens."

Suddenly I understood – "you?"

"That's why I applied to this school – far enough away from my old one. They all look older than they are, some more so than others, anyone can make a mistake. It's how we deal with it that matters."

I felt stupid, almost like crying. "Where did it happen?" I asked.

"A comprehensive on the outskirts of Brighton."

"It must have been hard for you, leaving your friends, family?"

"Friends, yes, family no – my father was a member of the school governors, he couldn't wait to see the back of me,"

Where is Jason Rayner

"Surely not."

"You don't know my father."

I sighed. "You have no idea how your revelation makes me feel. To know you understand - it means the world. I've been feeling like a pervert all day. How about picking up your car tomorrow and you joining me at mine for a good old drowning of our sorrows? I've a spare bedroom; you can stay the night or get a taxi back to yours, whatever you decide."

She didn't hesitate. "Do you know, Jack, I think I will. It's been too long to keep it all in and now you and I have something in common other than lessons. Besides, you'll be the first friend I've made since I've been living here."

Where is Jason Rayner

Chapter 28

Vanessa stayed the night in the spare bedroom. I awoke to the chill of an autumnal morning with a slight hangover, yawned, slipped on my dressing gown and padded over the beige carpet to the window. The sun was just coming up, fingering the trees in the avenue with strands of gold. Vanessa had rung the garage from the Wheatsheaf yesterday and it appeared there'd been some problem with obtaining a new clutch and it wouldn't be ready until later today. At least it was Saturday – no school. It felt good to have someone in the house again, I thought, as I went downstairs, picked up the morning post from the mat in the hallway then walked into the kitchen to make some toast and coffee for us.

I was humming to myself, the post still unopened on top of the unit, when I heard Vanessa coming downstairs.

"Great smell of coffee, just what I could do with."

"No hangover then?"

"No, bit thirsty – you?"

"I've taken a couple of pills, the headache's going, I've been worse. We did sink a few, if I remember."

"We did indeed, and I think it did us both good. You look much better today, in spite of the dressing gown."

I smiled. She was wearing my rugby shirt, which came down to her knees. I thought she looked cute. "Take a seat, the toast will be ready soon."

"You'd make someone a lovely wife."

"Why don't you stay until the garage has finished with your car? We could crash out, relax, it is Saturday after all." I hesitated, perhaps I was a bit too eager for company. "Or not, if you're busy."

"No, it's not that."

"What then?"

"I thought maybe you'd want to see Catherine to sort things out with her. It could be very awkward on Monday, if not."

I put the toast and two mugs of coffee down on the table. "Oh God, I hoped I'd dreamt it all. I really don't want to face her. What on earth am I going to say?"

"Take it from me, it won't just go away, Jack."

I took a deep breath as reality sunk in. "I know."

"Look, you could use me as an excuse."

"How?"

"You could say that you were sorry, you didn't know she was so young etc., and that you have a girlfriend. It might stop her thinking that it could go on."

"You wouldn't mind?"

"Well, technically, you wouldn't be lying. I am a girl and I think I am your friend?"

Picking up the mug, I began to feel as if things might turn out OK after all. "I suppose, I should ring her, ask her to meet me?"

"I think that might be best. Better not tell her over the phone. Although it won't be easy, either way."

Where is Jason Rayner

"You can say that again. I'm dreading it."

Vanessa leaned across the table and patted my hand. "Best get it over with."

By the time, I'd found her number, and plucked up enough courage to ring her, it was half past ten. I could hear Vanessa in the shower; she was singing.

I heard the ringtone followed by her voice. "Cathy? It's me, Jack. I think we should meet, don't you?"

"I knew you'd phone. Where?"

"The Black Swan café on the Water Street, at eleven?"

"Fine."

I'd chosen the Black Swan because it was in a side street, well away from the cafés frequented by teenagers on Saturday mornings.

She was outside waiting for me when I arrived. I opened the door, led her to a seat in a corner, paid for our drinks and carried them back to the table.

"I had such a shock," I began.

She was smiling. "Me too."

"I had no idea you were so young."

"It doesn't matter. I'll be sixteen the month after next."

"Oh but it does, Cathy. You must see that. I could be arrested, lose my job…"

She reached over and touched my arm.

"Don't stress – I won't say anything. We can still meet, we'll have to be careful, that's all." Her fingers stroked my upper arm, her touch as light as the feathers of a young bird.

"It's impossible. I can't see you anymore." I removed my arm from her reach.

Where is Jason Rayner

She didn't answer but when I could see she was struggling not to cry, I felt as if I'd hurt a child. "Please, don't cry, Cathy. If there's anything I could do to make this better for you, I would, but my hands are tied."

"What if I was sixteen already?" She sniffed and I gave her my handkerchief.

"It wouldn't make any difference. I'm your teacher," I replied.

"So you don't love me?"

This was harder than I thought possible.

"Another place, another time, things might be different. But you must understand, I can't let this go any further between us. I could be arrested, sent to prison."

Without another word, she stood up and walked away from me, her shoulders drooping, her hands in her pockets. She looked what she was, a very young person struggling to cope with adulthood. Well that was that, I thought. But it occurred to me I hadn't mentioned the bit about having a girlfriend.

I finished my coffee, picked up my car from the car park and drove down the High Street. She was sitting on a bench outside Marks and Spencer. A vision of how she had comforted me when mother had passed away, slid into my mind. I stopped the car.

Looking around for anyone who might recognise us and seeing no one, I said, "Get in." Waiting until she closed the passenger door, I accelerated down the street and turned left into Winterbourne Road, which led to the road skirting the moors on the edge of town. Then parking up in a secluded area with a

Where is Jason Rayner

view of the bleak Derbyshire moors in front of us, I turned towards her.

Where is Jason Rayner

Chapter 29

My mobile was ringing as I drew up at the traffic lights. It was Vanessa. I let it go to answerphone then turned on the loudspeaker to listen.

"The garage rang and offered to drop off my car at your place. I'm at home now. Obviously you've had a harrowing day. Can't imagine what's been going on, you've been gone so long. Anyway, give me a ring when you have a spare moment."

Beads of sweat trickled down my forehead. I wiped them away, wishing I could do the same to the past few hours. By the time I reached my place, I was bathed in the stuff. I opened the front door, leaned against it and closed my eyes. If only I hadn't stopped my car, if only I'd left her looking as if the bottom had dropped out of her world, instead of trying to make it better.

I took the stairs two at a time and in the bathroom, ran the shower, stripped off and stood beneath the spray, letting the water wash away the events of the past few hours. I was a fool. I closed my eyes and wished I could turn back the clock to the start of the day. But wishing didn't make it better, the bitter taste of my actions lingered like bile on my tongue.

Sitting at the kitchen table as dusk turned into night, nursing a glass with a large measure of brandy, still untouched, I heard the message signal on my mobile ping twice in succession. I stretched out my hand and opened the first message. It was from Vanessa.

Hi. Any news? How did it go? X

If only she knew, I thought, opening up the second message. It was, as I'd feared, from Cathy.

Hi. Thanx so it's OK now?

I shivered and lifted the glass to my lips. The brandy hit the back of my throat and I spluttered. I couldn't answer either message with honesty. Switching off my phone, I tipped back my glass, drank the contents then refilled it. Oblivion was my only solace.

Sunday passed in a haze of indecision. I lost count of the number of times I picked up my phone to ring Vanessa then put it down again. There were no further text messages from her, but as the afternoon wore on, I found six messages from Cathy, one saying how much she was looking forward to seeing me for a double period of English on Monday morning, three saying how happy she was that we'd cleared up the little misunderstanding and two asking me to ring her.

It was nearly eight o'clock when I rang Vanessa.

"At last!" she sounded a bit peeved.

"Sorry, sorry, I've been putting off this call."

"Why, what happened or can I guess?" I hadn't been mistaken; the tone of her voice said it all.

"I feel such an idiot."

"Again?"

"I know. I have no excuse. I'm really in the shit now."

Where is Jason Rayner

I heard a loud sigh from the other end. "You're telling me. What do you intend doing now? Do you realise how serious this is becoming, Jack?"

"That's the question I've been avoiding all day. The answer is I haven't a clue. And I'm dreading tomorrow. She's been sending me texts all day. How can I face her and Romeo and Juliet?" I felt like laughing hysterically at the thought.

"A bit ironic, wouldn't you say? Look, I don't want to state the obvious but this has to stop now. You've already landed yourself in a big heap of trouble. If you want my help, you'll have to stick to what we agree - no deviations – no sympathy kisses, or worse."

"Anything, I can't believe you're still willing to help." I knew the relief, I felt at having Vanessa's continuing support would be a temporary, unless I sorted this out. There was no way out of this, other than to face up to what I'd done head on. But with Vanessa on my side, it did make a difference.

"Right then, I'm coming over. I'll spend the night – in your spare bed, I hasten to add and we'll turn up at school tomorrow, together. We'll discuss it all in detail later."

My hands were shaking as I replaced the phone. In the bathroom, the face that looked back at me from the mirror was grey, dark shadows, rimmed my eyes, a glimpse of my future, unless I could sort this out. I turned away from the mirror, removed clean linen from the airing cupboard and made up the bed in the spare room.

The following day, sitting in my car in the school car park, we waited, until we saw Cathy. She was

Where is Jason Rayner

walking in through the gates alone, her school skirt skimming her knees, her bag bouncing against her hip, hair tied back in a tight ponytail, skin, devoid of makeup. She seemed so young compared to the group of girls walking in front of her, each with a skirt length leaving little to the imagination, eyes still ringed with the remnants of weekend eye-liners, a ton of lip-gloss shining in the crisp morning air.

"Right, here goes," Vanessa opened the passenger door and closed it with a slap. "Hurry up, darling," she called to me in a voice she usually used to stem the buzz of conversation in the classroom.

I saw Cathy turn her head in our direction. My heart pounded, I was sure my face was glowing traffic-light red. As we'd discussed the previous evening, I walked towards Vanessa, kissed her cheek and, slipping my arm around her shoulders, accompanied her to the entrance. When we passed a group of gawping girls and Cathy, I looked straight ahead without even a glance in her direction and entered the building.

Inside, I removed my arm and whispered, "I didn't think it was possible to feel even worse than I did yesterday."

"You're doing OK. It's the only way, Jack. Ignore it, it never happened remember. And if she insists it did – her word against yours – be firm, remember what we said."

My shoulders stiffened, I held my head high, as I walked into the staffroom with Vanessa. She was right - my word against Cathy's.

Where is Jason Rayner

Chapter 30

Somehow I got through the day. Whenever possible, I avoided her. During the double period English lesson with year eleven, which I'd been dreading, Dennis Bridgeman read the part of Romeo and Sally Walker read Juliet; this took up most of the first lesson, after which a forum debate took place as to the merits of the play and the acting skills of Dennis and Sally. Cathy contributed nothing to the debate, she kept her eyes glued to her book and, during the second period essay session, wrote silently, twisting a strand of her hair around her finger with her free hand. I thought she seemed to hang back as the buzzer indicating the end of the lesson sounded, but my, 'hurry up everyone, Miss Sanders is waiting for the room,' spurred her into movement and she was swept along on a tide of short skirts and hairspray with the rest of the girls.

I didn't see Vanessa until we were leaving the building at the end of the afternoon session. She just raised her hand to me as she walked towards her car, then drove away, confirmation if I needed it that she had been avoiding me all day.

Driving out of the school gates, I searched in my rear-view mirror for any sign of Cathy, and finding none turned in the direction of home. I half expected her to be waiting for me outside my house

Where is Jason Rayner

or to have left a succession of messages on my home phone or mobile but discovering that there were none, I breathed a sigh of relief that the day had passed without mishap.

By the end of week, I was beginning to think I'd got off lightly. I'd seen Cathy during lessons but, as on Monday, she'd been silent, only the condemnation in her eyes speaking of my ill treatment of her. Vanessa asked me briefly if I was OK but afterwards she too became quiet and withdrawn in my company. It didn't help matters to know I deserved every slight, every cold shoulder.

Saturday morning dawned with a stiff wind blowing down the drive and whistling around the house. Opening the bedroom window to let some fresh air into the room, I saw a figure standing outside on the pavement. I blinked, sure it was Cathy but then an older woman emerged from a car parked at the curb and joined the young girl and I realised it wasn't her after all.

After lunch, my mobile rang. It was Robert.

"Mike and I are making a night of it, meeting in the Old Dungeon at six, downing a few or maybe more, then finishing up at Starskeys. What d'you say, fancy joining us?"

I hesitated before replying. I'd been to neither venue with Cathy so thought it was probably safe to agree. Although why I should be so concerned about hiding from her didn't make any sense. Obviously she wasn't bothered.

"Great, see you at six," I replied.

Afterwards, I tried ringing Vanessa to see if she fancied meeting us in the Dungeon, but her phone went to voicemail and her house phone remained unanswered.

The usual Saturday crowd were gathered in the Dungeon, which comprised of schoolteachers, students and young women who wanted to be linked with the profession either by association or implication. Robert and Mike Tomlinson were chatting to two dark-haired girls at the bar. They looked so cosy that I regretted my decision to arrive late. I glanced around, somehow hoping to see Vanessa but she was nowhere to be seen.

I admit to being half cut when I saw Brad at the bar. "Thanks a bunch," I said. " What were you trying to do? Get me arrested?"

"And hello to you too, Jack. If I knew what you were on about it would be a start."

"Cathy?"

He looked confused then realisation dawned. "Yeah, Cathy. How did you get on by the way?"

"You didn't know, did you?"

"Know what?"

"That she was fifteen."

"Jeezus – you're not kidding me?"

"And she's one of my pupils."

He sniggered and it was all I could do not to punch him in the face. "You think it's funny?" My voice was rising.

"Hold your horses, Jack. I had no idea, honestly. Liz has a friend called Jen who was telling her this sad tale about a neighbour of hers, pretty little thing, she said, who lives with elderly relatives in a large old house and doesn't have any friends. And Liz being Liz said she'd do what she could to help, ask me if I had any mates who fancied a night out etc. That's the whole story, the rest you know."

I could see he was telling the truth so I bought him a pint and told him of my predicament. I couldn't see there was any harm in telling Brad, we'd been friends since schooldays. Of course, I didn't count on the fact that he was bound to tell Liz. And pebbles in a stream create ripples, the extent of which could drown a man.

Where is Jason Rayner

Chapter 31

When Brad rang and told me he was sorry but Liz had mentioned it to Jen and it he wasn't sure who else, I was horrified. I had to put a stop to the gossip, straight away.

"Tell Liz, she's got the wrong end of the stick. Cathy has a crush on her teacher – nothing more, especially as he's got a girlfriend and has had for some time. We'd broken up the night I came out with you on that blind date, tell her, make sure she understands."

"But, I thought – at the Dungeon, you said…"

"Drunk mate, not sure what I said. I know I was mad at you for not telling me my date was underage and to complicate matters she is in my English class and has been making moon eyes at me ever since. I was just letting off steam. Tell Liz it's a storm in a teacup and if she has any sense, she'll forget it."

"Right." Brad didn't sound convinced but I soon got him talking about how the City were doing and he finished by saying we must go out for a drink one evening soon.

Nevertheless, it was obvious to me that I'd have to do something drastic to stop Liz and her mates spreading rumours. I rang Vanessa.

'Hi, it's me. Could we meet up? There's something I need to discuss with you."

Where is Jason Rayner

Reluctantly she agreed to meet me the next day after school for a drink at the Wheatsheaf.

It was fortunate that I didn't have year eleven that day and so didn't see Cathy, that was, until I was making for my car. Vanessa was parked alongside me and she called out, "See you in five then, Jack," as she drove past me. Cathy was standing a metre or so away. She held my gaze for a moment then rushed off, out through the school gates and into the road. I waited until I could see her cross the road at the zebra crossing and join a group of children waiting at the bus stop and then started my car and drove in the opposite direction, taking a circuitous route to the Wheatsheaf.

Vanessa was waiting at the bar when I arrived. I joined her, bought our drinks then steered her in the direction of a secluded table overlooking a brick wall.

"Nice view," she commented. " I suppose this is your idea of a private chat?"

She was still mad at me.

"I don't know how many times I can say I'm sorry. I do understand if you want nothing more to do with me."

"You're your own worst enemy, Jack."

"Yeah, I know, I know."

"Well go on then. What is so urgent this time?"

"I'm in desperate need of your help. I don't know how to handle this thing with Cathy. Especially as I'm in more trouble after blurting out too much to Brad." I tried to explain how I'd made him believe it was just a schoolgirl crush.

Where is Jason Rayner

"You have to hope he believes you or it may have repercussions. It seems perfectly clear to me. I told you I was willing for you to tell her you have a girlfriend. But you have to keep up the facade or I'm not sure if that offer still holds."

I sighed. "I thought you'd say that. I don't blame you. I don't like me so why should you?"

"OK, forget the hair shirt and tell me why you wanted to see me."

I took a sip from my pint. "I think I should explain first. You see, I did tell her that I couldn't see her but she left before I could mention the 'girlfriend' thing. Then as I drove past her sitting on a bench, she looked so lost and I remembered how supportive she'd been when Mother passed away and, well, I felt a rat so I stopped to give her a lift."

"So you said before. Don't tell me – and that's when things got a little out of hand? I'm right?"

"Of course, you're right. How it happened is a mystery to me. I just don't seem safe in her company."

"It's sex, Jack." She looked at me over the top of her glass.

"I suppose so. She's young, attractive and I have no will power where she's concerned."

"I don't have to tell you how dangerous this relationship is. You'd be a fool not to realise it."

I ran my fingers through my hair in frustration. "It's not a relationship – it's not anything and you're right again – it's just sex. I'll have to control it but I do need help."

She smiled then and I sensed a weakening of her resolve to hate me.

"You will?"

Where is Jason Rayner

Vanessa nodded. "This is absolutely the last time though, I mean it."

"Yes, of course, I understand. What do you suggest we do? I'm at my wits end."

She thought for a moment and the silence between us lengthened. Then she said, "I suggest we up the girlfriend/boyfriend thing to such an extent that the staff room gossips have a field day. It won't take long for the kids to latch on and we'll take it from there."

"You'd be willing to be the subject of gossip and tittle tattle for me?" I was astounded. "After the way I've acted?"

She reached across the table and patted my hand. "As long as you remember to keep your side of the bargain; you have to realise that I'm not willing to go through with this unless you stop this thing with Cathy immediately - no secret meetings no lingering looks – no contact of any kind, other than in class – right?"

"Right," I agreed.

"I told you. I remember what it was like and I wouldn't wish my worst enemy to go through such an experience. Besides, I sort of like you, Jack. At least I like the sensible side of you, not the one who is led by his willie."

I spluttered and our laughter filled the space between our table and the bar where to my dismay I saw Cathy standing with Liz.

I grabbed Vanessa's hand and kissed her fingers. Realising what was happening she raised my hand to her lips in a similar gesture.

Where is Jason Rayner

"No time like the present," she said and, as we stood up, I put my arm around her waist and we walked past the bar and out into the car park.

"There, that wasn't too bad, was it?" Vanessa asked, kissing my cheek. As I smiled and thanked her, I felt as if I'd just run over Bambi.

Where is Jason Rayner

Chapter 32

During the following weeks, Vanessa and I worked on our strategy. News of our relationship spread like wildfire. Whenever we were together, wolf whistles followed our progress across the school grounds and in the staff room we were subjected to the usual comments.

Robert and Mike were intrigued.

"When did this happen?"

"You two are a pair of dark horses."

"When's the engagement party then?"

They kept it up for a while until they got fed up, but the bit about the engagement party set me thinking. It was still difficult in class and although Cathy had said nothing, since she'd seen us in the Wheatsheaf, I felt like a rat when I saw her sitting there desperately trying to appear as if nothing had happened between us. It wasn't an exaggeration to say I felt every shaft of her pain like arrows piercing my skin as I guided year eleven towards their English exams.

I suppose it was bound to happen. We spent so much time together. At first it was a joke between us. We were acting a part, lovers on the surface but friends in reality. It was at the end of a particularly harrowing week when I'd had to suffer year eleven every day. Dennis Bridgeman had resorted to type and was making it difficult during the study periods as I attempted to focus their minds on preparing for the exams. Denis had a short attention span and spent most of his time annoying the other pupils. On the Friday morning he turned his attention to Cathy who, to be fair, ignored him most of the time but it was during a double period at the end of the day that I saw he'd got under her skin. I noticed her head drooping, her eyes filling with tears.

"Bridgeman! I've had enough your nonsense today. Go and wait outside the staffroom for me. I'll see you after this lesson finishes."

He sloped off and I knew he'd be nowhere near the staffroom at the appointed time but making his way home on the 92 bus. However, I had to get rid of him somehow before he caused more trouble.

I was relieved when the end of day buzzer sounded and the usual mad rush for the door occurred. Picking up my books and laptop case, as the last pupil left the room, I heard a soft voice saying, "Thank you, sir." I looked up and she held my gaze.

"Don't mention it, Cathy. I hope you have a nice weekend; try to forget all about Bridgeman."

She nodded and followed the rest into the corridor as I bent to pick up a copy of book that had slipped from my grasp.

Afterwards, Vanessa joined me in the entrance hall and we walked to our cars.

"Bad day?" she asked, slipping her arm through mine.

"Bad week."

"Fancy making a night of it? Robert and Mike are going to the Dungeon and asked if we wanted to tag along."

Where is Jason Rayner

I hesitated. "Do you mind if we don't. I'm not saying I wouldn't like to make a night of it but what if we just go for a meal and a drink somewhere quiet, just the two of us?"

"Like an old married couple?" She grinned and reached up to kiss my cheek, the inevitable catcalls following us as we reached our cars.

"What if we dine locally? The Piping Pie is usually good and there's a nice view of the river then we could finish up at mine. Stay the night if you like?"

She thought for a moment. "Why not? Sounds good to me. I'll see you at yours at seven."

"Seven it is," I replied, opening my car door.

The restaurant was, as I'd described it to Vanessa, discreet, with no likelihood of bumping into pupils – not their scene - and the food was excellent. We'd walked from my place, along the river path. The air was warm and the scent of roses from the gardens along the way drifted into our nostrils. A small cruiser passed us, a young woman in a striped bikini lounging on the deck. Vanessa smiled, her hand in mine and said, "Must be nice to have money. I've had to work for everything I've got and what have I got to show for it? A ten year old car that keeps breaking down and a grotty flat in a run down area."

It was the first time, I heard her speak about her past, except for the bit about having gone through similar circumstances as myself, and I suddenly realised that I knew nothing about the person who had been willing to help me out of such a difficult situation. I leaned forward and kissed the top of her head.

Where is Jason Rayner

"What was that for? There's no one about."

"Just a thank you for all your help."

During the meal I began to relax and afterwards, at home, we opened a bottle of wine, curled up on the couch and I listened whilst Vanessa talked about her life as a child growing up in a run down inner city area.

"London can be a lonely place when you're a kid, unless you have money, connections or a supportive family," she said.

I reached out, took her hand in mine and stroked it. "You've survived, that's what's important."

Her rueful expression, as she replied, spoke volumes. "Don't get me wrong, I didn't have it as bad as some and my parents weren't as inadequate as many but they didn't really want another child. My brother and sister were grown up and had left home by the time I started school and resentment at having to deal with an unwanted pregnancy seeped out of every pore.

Three months after Mum died prematurely of ovarian cancer, Dad won the lottery, ironic really when there'd never been enough money to splash out on a holiday when Mum was alive. The first thing he did was book a fortnight in the south of France for us both then moved to Brighton with me in tow like unwanted baggage. He mixed with a different crowd, became a school governor and was sort of proud when I qualified and ended up teaching at the same school. Until, of course, I became involved with a pupil. It wasn't anything like you've experienced though. He saw us kissing and it was enough for him to warn me off and insist I get a job as far away from Brighton as I could."

Where is Jason Rayner

"Let's drown our sorrows, forget about what's gone on before and start afresh tomorrow. This time, I won't get sucked into feeling sorry for Cathy and how I've treated her. It began in all innocence and I don't want to think about the rest."

Vanessa held out her empty glass for a refill. "I agree. Tomorrow is another day."

When I awoke the next morning, my head was thumping like a jackhammer. I stretched and my hand touched hers. Oh God, I thought, I don't remember how last night ended. I was wasted.

Vanessa groaned. "Jack? I..."

"You don't remember either?"

"Er, no, not exactly. I think we overdid the wine. I feel like death."

"You and me both."

She began to giggle. "At least we are both in the same boat. I suppose we had a good time?"

"Certain of it, " I said leaning over her and kissing her mouth.

"Shower and two painkillers for me, I think," Vanessa said, sliding out of bed then realising she was naked, started to reach for the sheet but soon abandoned the idea. "What the heck," she said, allowing me an uninterrupted view of her naked rear, as she walked into the bathroom.

Our relationship changed from that day on. Vanessa and I played out our parts in school. The gossip in the staffroom altered its focus from us to the deputy head's new baby, whom, it seemed, was distinctly darker in colour than its father. The exams came and went and the long school holiday break began. Cathy still tugged at my heartstrings but I learned to ignore the feeling with Vanessa's help.

The weather in July and August was hot and sunny and Vanessa moved into my place during the first week of August, as she was selling her flat. It was meant to be a temporary measure until she found something more suitable. During the second week of August the exam results came through and I watched the pupils anxiously searching the school notice boards for news.

Cathy had excellent results and it was with a sense of relief I knew my 'little indiscretion', as I now thought of it, hadn't hindered her work.

"Well done, Catherine," I said. "You'll stay on for A Levels and go on to Uni?"

She looked up at me. "No, sir. I'm leaving school."

"Surely not." I was genuinely concerned that she'd be wasting her talent.

"I've enrolled at a college of further education and intend to do a crash course in business studies. I'm leaving Sheffield and moving down south."

She walked away and left me standing with my mouth open. I wanted to say, don't go, stay with me, we'll work something out, but thankfully the words didn't come.

"You OK?" Vanessa slid her arm through mine. "I saw you talking to Cathy."

I sighed. "Yeah, I'm fine." I looked at my watch. "Should be finished in ten minutes. How d'you feel about going into town and checking out the travel agents? I think we could both do with a holiday."

The Investigation

Chapter 33

Richie Stevens read the newspaper report on his laptop. Cathy Barton had disappeared from her home in Sheffield where she had been living with her elderly aunt and uncle, since the death of her parents. Her uncle had just died; she was sixteen and had only recently finished her school examinations. A nationwide search had begun on the day after she'd received her exam results. Her aunt said she'd had excellent results, she couldn't understand why she'd have just taken off like that, it didn't make any sense, except that she'd been very upset by her uncle's recent death, maybe that was it.

It was some time before the police interviewed her English teacher, Jack Robinson, who informed them that the last time he'd spoken to his pupil, she'd said she was going to study at a sixth form college in the south of England in September. He hadn't seen her since.

Sandy was looking over his shoulder.

"You agree?" she asked.

"Most definitely, Miss Smith. As usual I'm sure you're right. The photograph is an old one, I grant you, but there are enough identifying features to link them to our client. I'd say you've hit the nail on the head, our mysterious Kate Newson is Cathy Barton."

"Her aunt was distraught. There were rumours in the newspapers that she may have been murdered, but then came the letter." Sandy was thoughtful.

Where is Jason Rayner

"Turn to the next page and there's a transcript of the letter she sent to her aunt."

Richie dutifully did as requested.

Dear Aunt, I'm sorry to see that my departure has caused you so much concern. Please don't worry any more. I'm fine. I can't explain, but I needed to get away in a hurry. As you know I have the money my parents left me; I've been planning this for some time, you see. You'd be proud of me; I've been so resourceful. I'll be in touch to let you know how I'm getting on. It might not be for a while, not until all the fuss has died down. I'm sixteen now and well able to take care of myself. Love to you, as ever. Catherine.

Richie ran his fingers through his hair. "So," he said, "we know Cathy, Kate or whatever she wishes to call herself, is resourceful."

"According to her aunt she had good exam results," Sandy commented, "and I see the police were still looking for her when she'd phoned her aunt a few days later and confirmed that she was studying in a college of further education in Bristol. But there was no mention anywhere of her changing her name to Kate Newson. What was she running away from, I wonder?"

"And where is she now?" Richie stood up and walked to the window. The offices of Arbuthnot and Trent were clearly visible through the morning drizzle sliding down the windowpane.

Sandy sat at her desk and rhythmically tapped the back of her left hand with the fingers of her right, a sure sign that she was concentrating. Richie turned away from the window and smiled. She was young, talented and eager; if he'd created a perfect partner

Where is Jason Rayner

he couldn't have been more successful. Partner in the working sense, of course; he was forty five and losing his family in such tragic circumstances had robbed him of ever wishing to look for anyone to share his life with again and certainly not anyone as young as Sandy Smith. At work, he was in a good place – his Private Investigation business, while not exactly thriving, was providing a living for him and Sandy – he enjoyed the work, which wasn't so dissimilar from working as a detective in the Metropolitan Police Force, so he had no complaints.

"Do you think we should tell the Devon police about our suspicions?" Sandy asked.

"Mmm? Not yet. At this point, we are assuming that Kate Newson and Cathy Barton are one in the same. I don't think there's much to be gained by informing them, until we have something more substantial to show them."

Sandy stopped drumming her fingers. "Sheffield?"

"Sheffield. We could travel up first thing tomorrow and come back on the last train. I need to think and driving is too distracting."

"I could drive, save us the train fare?" Sandy offered.

"No worries, Miss Smith, I think our finances will run to a couple of return fares to Sheffield but thanks for the offer."

The following day, Richie and Sandy sat opposite each other, she with her laptop plugged into the train's Internet connection, he working on the Telegraph crossword puzzle. They spoke little during the journey, which suited them both, until after they'd eaten their cardboard tasting sandwiches from the buffet car.

"Are we agreed that we should start by visiting the Aunt first and then checking on her old school and any friends who knew her?" Sandy asked, opening the notebook on her phone and compiling an itinerary.

"You have all the addresses on your phone?"

"Does a dog like chasing rabbits?" She grinned. "Did I just say that? Corny or what?"

"Definitely corny."

"I've been thinking."

"Did I doubt it?"

She raised her eyebrows at him. "What if we scare her off? If she's living with her aunt, she might do another runner."

"It's a possibility. That's why I want you to do what you do best."

"And that is?"

"Re-invent yourself. I've seen you do it time and time again, probably unconsciously but you've become an expert at it. When we arrive at Sheffield Railway Station we'll take a cab into the city centre. I'll grab a coffee somewhere and leave you to buy the necessary accoutrements. I suggest you make out you're an old friend from her schooldays who thought you'd caught sight of Cathy in town and would like to catch up – that sort of thing. Of course, we'll have to make sure she isn't in the house first, or as you said, she might take off."

"And while I do, you'll be at the school?" Sandy asked.

"Hopefully I'll be able to speak to one of her teachers, at least."

Where is Jason Rayner

Later, sitting in a café wedged in between a large department store and a travel agents, Richie waited to see Sandy's transformation. Half an hour later, he saw a non-descript dark-haired young woman wearing glasses waiting in the queue to be served. He turned back to his crossword puzzle and waited for Sandy to join him.

Where is Jason Rayner

Chapter 34

Fortunately for Richie, the inner city bus stopped right outside Westbank School. He stood on the pavement and, looking at the building, tried to imagine Kate Rayner in school uniform, rushing through the gates. It was lunchtime and the school grounds were awash with children, a tide of navy and white uniforms ebbing and flowing. A young woman with blonde hair drawn back into a ponytail, wearing shorts and a white tee-shirt adorned with the school's logo, was patrolling the grounds for signs of trouble. He approached her.

"Excuse me, Miss. I wonder if you could help me. I'm from Blurb Magazine and I'm writing a follow up piece about a young girl who disappeared from here a while ago – Cathy Barton."

The young woman's mouth twisted into a tight line and her face lost its colour.

"I've nothing to say. Now if you don't mind, I'm busy."

Richie was nonplussed. It wasn't a reaction he'd been anticipating. Watching the young woman walking towards a group of children messing about near a dustbin, he wondered what was the connection between Cathy Barton and this woman, for he was in no doubt that there was one.

Barry Didsbury, the headmaster, reminded him of Friar Tuck. He stood up as Richie entered his study.

Where is Jason Rayner

"Mr Stevens. Please, take a seat. You said on the phone this is to do with Catherine Barton, who was once a pupil at the school."

Richie abandoned his former unsuccessful pretence of being a magazine reporter. "First, let me apologise for not fully explaining the reason for my visit. I don't really know why I didn't come clean on the phone." He looked downcast, "In my line of business, I've found people less than willing to talk to a Private Investigator."

Didsbury frowned. "Really? I would have thought talking to a reporter would have had the same effect."

Richie laughed ruefully. "Perhaps you're right. Anyway, thanks for not throwing me out."

"I don't know what I can tell you, other than what you already know. Catherine Barton was a bright kid – it was quite a shock when she left straight after her exam results and didn't enter the A level course. And then, when she disappeared, it was an even bigger shock. She was such a quiet, well-mannered girl. I wasn't aware of her having any problems at home."

"I understand there was some talk at the time that she'd been murdered?"

"Er, yes, it spread around school like a forest fire. We were all interviewed by the police, of course, a very uncomfortable feeling, I don't mind telling you."

"Was there anyone she was particularly close to, friends, members of staff?"

Didsbury, shook his head and thought for a moment. "She didn't have any close friends, as far I remember, a bit of a loner I would say. However,

Where is Jason Rayner

Jack Robinson, who taught her English, seemed to get through to her. I believed at one time, she had a slight crush on Jack but after he and Vanessa got engaged, she seemed to get the message. It's an occupational hazard, I'm afraid, young girls fancying their teachers."

Feeling that Barry Didsbury would be quite safe in that department, Richie asked, "Could I speak to Mr Robinson, do you think?"

"He doesn't work here any more, I'm afraid. He and Vanessa split up and he went to work somewhere in Manchester, I think. Vanessa still works here of course."

Richie looked up expectantly.

"But I wouldn't suggest you talk to her. Still a bit touchy on the subject of Jack."

"Oh, I see. She wouldn't be the young woman wearing shorts on patrol in the school grounds?"

"Ah, so I see you've already met her."

Richie stood up. "I have indeed but thank-you for your time, headmaster. If there's anything that springs to mind, please give me a ring." He handed Barry Didsbury his card.

By the time Richie reached the school grounds, there was no sign of Vanessa Robinson or the children. He wondered how Sandy was getting on and whether she'd had more success with the Aunt. The bus arrived, soon after he reached the bus stop, and he joined a group of afternoon shoppers making their way into the centre of town whilst taking advantage of the city's free bus system.

He was sitting on a bench in the park wondering if Sandy had been more successful than him. The

Where is Jason Rayner

earlier drizzle had made way for glorious sunshine and he inhaled the after-rain smell of newly washed vegetation rising from the well-tended border plants. Closing his eyes, he waited for Sandy to join him. He'd fallen asleep, the sun was warm on his face and he was dreaming of his days in the Met. DCI Freeman, his old friend, was asking him how he was doing on the Slater Road killings. 'Wake up - no time to sleep' – Norman's voice had suddenly changed – he sounded almost feminine. He felt a hand on his shoulder and grunted awake to see the black outline of someone blocking the sun.

"OK for some," Sandy said. "The boss sleeps in the sunshine, whilst the assistant works. Budge up a bit."

Richie swallowed, and forced DCI Freeman back into the dream. "Miss Smith?"

"The same. Any luck at the school?"

"Not really. I'll explain over a cuppa, shall I?"

Sandy looked around. "It's nice here. Why don't I fetch us a take away coffee. You slip back to your dream and I'll be back in a bit."

Waiting for Sandy to return, Richie wondered how they could find Jack Robinson. It was a long shot but he might be more involved with Cathy Barton than Barry Didsbury had led him to believe.

When Sandy returned, he outlined his visit to the school and his feeling that Vanessa Robinson was hiding something. When he'd finished, he asked Sandy how she'd managed with Rita Ferris.

"As we know her husband died before Cathy left home and Rita, lives alone in a large house on Beaufort Avenue. It's a big old place for one person and needs maintenance but I had the feeling some

Where is Jason Rayner

superficial work had been recently carried out, trees trimmed, borders cut back, front door re-painted. Rita's all about though and invited me in when I said I was a friend of her Cathy's." Sandy sighed. "I must admit I did feel rotten about lying to her."

"Our business can be a messy one at times, as we know only too well."

"We certainly do. Apparently she had a phone call from her niece a few weeks ago and she did visit but only for a short while and she hasn't seen her since."

"Did you ask her about Cathy's disappearance, after her exams?"

"I did. But she looked a bit confused and said, Cathy liked to do things on her own, she had her inheritance and was used to looking after herself. Oh, and by the way, I think I know why our client talks the way she does. Rita told me that her sister, Cathy's mother, didn't have her until she was well into her forties. She was childless and thought she was on the menopause, when she suddenly became pregnant. It would seem she'd been surrounded by much older people, when she was young. Rita has a very old fashioned way of speaking too and I suspect her sister was the same. It's like stepping back in time in the house. You'd have to see it to believe it."

"When and how did Bill Ferris die exactly?"

Sandy hesitated, and drank the remains of her coffee before replying, "It's odd. I'm sure I had the impression from our client that Bill Ferris had died recently. But it's not so; he died just before Cathy left home, when she was sixteen. Rita said he'd been struggling with his health, bronchitis and a dodgy knee, nothing too serious. Apparently, he was unsteady on his feet, fell down stairs and died as a result of the fall."

"I see but an odd thing to lie about surely?"

"That's just it. The more we look into Cathy Barton's personality the more difficult it is to get a clear picture of her. It's as if all our first impressions keep shifting perspective."

Richie leaned towards her. "I knew your first class psychology degree would come in useful some time."

Sandy raised her eyebrows. "I'm not sure how to take that remark."

"Take it in the manner it was meant, Miss Smith. I really don't know what I would do without you."

Her laughter competed with the tinkling of the waterfall spilling into the lake in front of them as they walked back to the park entrance.

"How do you feel about staying on here for a day or two? Give your nephew Harry a ring. See if he'd like to man the office for a bit. You did say he was down from Uni?"

"He's finished, yes, just waiting for the right job to come along. I'm sure he'll be glad to make a bit of extra money. He's planning to go to Peru in August."

"Great, he knows the drill and that Bernard has the spare office key."

Sandy nodded. "Dan has taken Jane and the kids to Spain. Harry, being so much older than Chloe and Adam, decided not to go so he's staying with Dad at the moment, helping to look after Bruce who is getting a bit of a handful in his old age. "

"Surveillance dog, Bruce?"

Where is Jason Rayner

"Bit too old for that now, but yes, the dog we've used as a cover many times before." Sandy grinned and followed Richie towards the taxi.

Where is Jason Rayner

Jack's story
via his laptop

Chapter 35

At the beginning of term, Vanessa and I continued to act as if we were lovers; only this time there was no fabrication. We spent most nights at her place and when she sold her flat she moved in with me. We still got the occasional jibe aimed in our direction but most of the pupils soon lost interest.

It was during the fourth week of term that the police arrived at school to interview everyone about the disappearance of Catherine Barton. Vanessa joined me for lunch in the canteen.

"What's going on? Have you any idea, Jack? Rumours are rife, I even overhead some of the kids saying she's been murdered."

My heart began to pound in my chest. Murdered? The word sent an icy shiver down my spine. It was bad enough that I wouldn't be seeing her again; the rest was unthinkable.

"She told me she was going to study at an FE college but she didn't say where exactly," I said, following her to a seat overlooking the netball pitch. "I explained to the police and they said they were putting out an appeal for her to get in touch with them, on the six o'clock news."

"I expect she will, once she knows they're looking for her. All this seems to have been brought about by her aunt not having heard from her and assuming the worst, I suppose."

"Yes, I'm sure you're right."

Where is Jason Rayner

Vanessa looked up at me. "Are you sure you're OK? You've gone very pale."

"I'm fine, bit of a shock seeing the police, you know how it is." My excuse sounded hollow even to my ears.

The next day being Saturday, Vanessa and I stayed in bed until half ten, got up and then went into the Meadowhall Shopping Mall. She wanted to buy a dress for a wedding to which we'd both been invited. We were walking towards John Lewis when I saw Brad and Liz. I smiled, waved, and was left holding my hand in the air like a fool, my grin fixed like a frozen rictus.

"Did you see that?"

"They probably didn't see us."

"They're not blind. Besides, when have Brad and Liz ever been seen in a bookshop? A diversionary tactic, if ever I saw one." I was mad. Why were they avoiding me? Could it be to do with Cathy's disappearance?

Following Vanessa through the doors of the department store, I wondered how many people knew about Cathy and me and how dangerous that could be in this present situation. Surely they couldn't think I had anything to do with her taking off? Questions spun around in my brain and for none of them did I have any satisfactory explanations.

"What d'you think of this?" Vanessa asked, holding up a blue dress.

"Great," I replied, neither knowing nor caring one way or the other. But Vanessa was no fool.

Where is Jason Rayner

"Go and have a coffee and I'll join you once I find something," she said pointing me in the direction of the coffee shop.

Coincidences occur when you least expect them, I always find. I was flicking through the morning paper when I became aware of a hand placed on my shoulder. Looking up, I saw a young woman with short spiky hair, wearing denims and a pop-band tee shirt. She looked like a student.

"It's Mr Robinson, isn't it?" Oh God, not a pupil wanting some advice, I thought. It was Saturday, for goodness sake. But I didn't recognise her as one of ours. "I wasn't sure if it was you, at first. You were a friend of Cathy Barton's?" she said.

I felt my stomach flip. She was waiting for an answer; so she wasn't an ex pupil.

"I taught Catherine, yes." I replied cautiously.

"No, I meant you were more than just her teacher." Was there malice behind the words, which were said in an even tone?

"I liked her, she was a good student, a clever girl." My hands, holding the paper began to shake so I placed it on the table.

"My name is Jennifer Teague, I live next door to Rita Ferris, Cathy Barton's aunt. It was me who suggested to Liz that Cathy could do with some male company. But I had no idea she thought Cathy was old enough to be involved with someone of your age."

She spoke as if I was Methuselah.

"Ah yes," a non-committal response was best, I decided.

"I gather you became more than friends with her."

Where is Jason Rayner

"Rumours, nothing more, you know what young girls are like, crushes on their teachers are an occupational hazard. No. Once I realised the situation, I made it clear to Catherine that there had been a mistake."

"I see. Do the police know?"

Now, I knew. There was no mistaking where this was leading. But before I could act with righteous indignation at the suggestion, Vanessa joined us.

"I've just heard the news. Apparently Cathy Barton's been in touch with her aunt. It's all been a storm in a teacup – she's been living in Bristol all the time." I could hear the relief in her voice and wondered whether Jennifer Teague was aware of it too. "Oh, hello, I'm sorry, am I interrupting something?"

Before I could reply, the young woman shook her head, mumbled a negative reply and walked away. It would seem as one door opened another one closed. Cathy was safe but I couldn't say the same for me as Jennifer Teague obviously had other ideas. I could only hope it was the last I'd see of her but my gut feeling was that our paths were destined to cross again.

Where is Jason Rayner

Chapter 36

You would have thought I'd be relieved that the police had stopped looking for Catherine Barton, but I couldn't settle. What was she doing? How was she managing on her own? Was I to blame for her living away from her family, away from me?

"What's wrong? Something *is* bothering you, you've been waking up at five o'clock every morning this week."

"Sorry. I'm disturbing you. I'll sleep in mother's room for a bit, until I recover my normal sleep pattern."

Vanessa sighed, stretched out her arm and patted my shoulder. "You don't have to do that, Jack. I'm just worried about you. Does it have anything to do with this Cathy business? You should forget her now – it's all in the past – let her get on with her life and us with ours."

She was right, of course.

"Will you marry me?" I asked. I wasn't really sure I'd said the words but once they were out, I thought, why not? She was right, I should move on and this was the perfect way to do it.

"Is that the reason, you haven't been able to sleep? You were worried I'd refuse?" She laughed with relief.

I looked suitably shamefaced.

"Come here, silly. Of course I'll marry you – the sooner the better, I should think."

Where is Jason Rayner

We were married at the end of the month, during the half term holiday. It was a quiet civil ceremony in the registry office, Robert and Mike were our witnesses and we spent the rest of the week in a hotel in Derby, walking the moors by day and making love by night.

When we returned to the school on the following Monday morning, we were greeted by congratulatory wishes and gifts in the staff room, the news having been spread by Robert and Mike and the grapevine going into overdrive. I felt relieved to be focusing on our future and not looking back at my past for once.

The weeks flew by until we broke up for the Christmas holiday. I spent a frantic Christmas Eve searching the shops for a gift for my new wife and eventually, having found a shop selling gym equipment, managed to buy one of those boxed vouchers entitling her to full membership of the prestigious Harry Lloyd complex. Vanessa had been dropping hints for weeks.

Realising it wasn't exactly a romantic gift, I saw a small shop selling lingerie and walked inside. I didn't feel at all uncomfortable examining the merchandise, as most of the customers were men who were obviously in the same predicament, frantically searching for last minute gifts for their wives and partners.

I was paying for a set, which I thought looked particularly sexy, when I saw her.

"Gift wrapped, sir?" the shop assistant asked, and when I didn't reply added, "Sir?

Where is Jason Rayner

Dragging my eyes away from the front of the shop, I replied. "Er, no thanks, just pop it in a carrier, I'm in a hurry."

The girl sniffed, rammed the underwear unceremoniously into a bag, her chance to show her artistic talents having been thwarted, and handed me the card reader.

Outside, I searched the street for sight of her. I hadn't been mistaken, I was certain I'd seen Cathy looking in at the window and even more certain that she had seen me. I was frantic, my pulse racing, I had to find her. Then I stopped – why?

"So, you got married then?" I didn't turn around. I was rooted to the spot. "Congratulations."

"Cathy," I began, as I spun around to face Jennifer Teague.

"Just good friends, eh?" She leaned towards me. "Pull the other one, Mr Robinson."

The Salvation Army Band struck up a chorus of Hark the Herald Angels Sing and a sudden influx of Christmas shoppers slid between us. But before she disappeared altogether, I saw my accuser was no longer alone and this time there was no doubt in my mind who had taken her arm and was leading her away.

Chapter 37

Christmas morning arrived, along with a light dusting of snow. Vanessa went for a run in the park. I'd learnt from experience not to try to dissuade her so started to prepare lunch. Somewhere in the back of my mind was a niggle that wouldn't let me rest and its name was Jennifer Teague. What did she want from me? Blackmail was an ugly word but the only one springing to mind as I peeled the potatoes and inhaled the appetising smell of turkey cooking.

The day progressed with lunch, during which we both drank too much wine, followed by lovemaking in front of a roaring fire, falling asleep to the sounds of an old Frank Sinatra download on my IPad and spending the evening in front of the TV screen.

It was during the third week after Christmas that the snow began to fall in earnest. I'd had trouble digging the car out of the drive and had eventually given up.

"We'll get the bus, if they're running," I said, as we both abandoned any thoughts of getting to Westbank by car.

"You'd think old Didsbury would have closed the place, the weather being as it is." Vanessa stamped her feet on the frozen pavement.

"He couldn't make a decision to save himself, the old fool. Good, at least the 74's running. Here it comes."

It was a surprise to both of us to see how many staff and pupils had turned up. The kids were

Where is Jason Rayner

making the most of the snow by pelting each other with snowballs in spite of the freezing temperatures. Most of the car park and grounds in front of the entrance had been cleared of snow; health and safety issues obviously having been dealt with, I thought, wishing that Didsbury had been more lax in that department and abandoned all hope of opening up the place. I shivered and followed Vanessa inside.

The day was unremarkable, except for one thing. At two thirty-five I received a text that would alter the course of my life. The snow had been falling all morning and by lunchtime even Barry Didsbury was considering how he was going start his car. After dithering for a further hour, he eventually made the decision to close the school.

Vanessa and I managed to get on a bus but had to stand all the way home. My phone received a message as the bus took a corner into Layton Avenue but I didn't bother to check the text; it was too inconvenient to remove my mobile from my pocket because one hand was clutching the overhead strap and the other steadying Vanessa, as the bus skidded on a patch of ice.

"There's more of this to come, I'm sure," Vanessa said, hanging on to my arm as we left the bus and walked towards our house. "At least we'll have a lie in tomorrow."

"I thought Didsbury was never going to make up his mind. I had visions of being snowed in over night."

"Perish the thought." She grinned at her choice of words.

The air inside the house was warm, the central heating operating on the thermostatic control. We peeled off our outer clothes in the hallway and I put my mobile on the hall table. It was only later, when we were going to bed and I went to turn off my phone for the night, that I saw the message icon lit. Remembering the message alert on the bus, I clicked on the symbol and read.

I KNOW ALL ABOUT YOU AND CATHY. I WON'T LET IT REST. MEET ME AT THE BANDSTAND IN THE PARK AT TWO ON SATURDAY. JT

There was no mistaking the implied threat in the text.

"You OK, love? You look as if you've seen a ghost." Vanessa, dressed in a pair of unflattering fleece pyjamas, came and sat beside me on the bed as I switched off my mobile and placed it on the bedside table.

"What? No. I… Just wondering how long this weather is going to last. I hate the snow," I lied.

She sighed, slid under the covers and as I joined her, I shivered but it was not because of the falling temperatures.

Where is Jason Rayner

Chapter 38

The snow had stopped and been replaced by brown slush, which covered the pavements. Thankfully, it had also melted from the roads due to an increase in traffic, as commuters made their way to work. Vanessa was in the gym making the most of her Christmas present when I drove towards the park for my meeting with Jennifer Teague. I had no idea how I was going to handle the situation, whether to deny it vehemently or to ask her what her intentions were. In the event, I decided let her do the talking.

She was sitting on a seat under the roof of the bandstand. She was wearing a navy puffer jacket, green knitted beanie hat, and gloves. She looked younger than she was and a vision of Cathy, the second time I met her, hit me like a punch in the face.

"You came. I wondered if you'd have the guts."

"What's this all about?" I asked, whilst using the voice I kept for the Dennis Bridgemans of this world.

"As if you didn't know," she sneered. " Cathy Barton was a child when you abused her and I intend to make you pay for it. The law comes down heavily on paedophiles, Mr Robinson."

So now I knew. She had no intention of going to the police, well, not before she'd seen how much she could squeeze out of me first.

"That's ridiculous. If you'd spoken to Cathy, she'd have told you so."

Where is Jason Rayner

"Cathy was just a child, fifteen is, as you well know, under the age of consent in this country."

"I had no idea she was fifteen," I was explaining. I knew I shouldn't do that – never apologise – never explain.

"Ignorance is no excuse – the law is plain."

When I'd first seen Jennifer Teague in the Mall, I thought she looked like a student. It occurred to me that she might be studying the law - she seemed so knowledgeable on the subject. Perhaps I was her guinea pig, a project. I was clutching at straws when the facts were plain to see. She was nothing more than a blackmailer.

"How much?" I asked, dreading the answer.

Her laughter was more a bark of incredulity. "You think I want money?"

I admit to being surprised. "What *do* you want, then?" I asked.

"I want you to make it right by Cathy. She's suffered enough."

I remembered that it was indirectly because of her that I'd met the girl in the first place. She was a friend of Liz's and had asked her to find someone to take Cathy out on a date.

"What are you - Catherine Barton's guardian angel?"

"You could say that." She was full of surprises. I don't know what I expected her reaction to be – perhaps get mad – perhaps make up some excuse.

"As I said, I lived next door to Cathy when she was growing up. First she lost her parents, then there was her uncle – a real pig of a man and now you."

Where is Jason Rayner

She stood up and stamped her feet to restore the circulation. I waited. There was nothing more I could think of to say to her.

"Anyway. I expect you to do the right thing by her. You dumped her and carried on your relationship with another teacher, right under her nose. She was distraught. No wonder she ran away."

"She told me she was going to college."

"She would – she did – but the fact remains, she'd have stayed, if you'd been more understanding of her feelings. She was a young girl for goodness sake."

I didn't think it possible to feel any worse than I already did about Cathy but I was wrong. "I'll sort it out," I said, "but I don't know how to get in touch with her."

"Problem solved." She removed a piece of paper from her jacket pocket and handed it to me."

"Bristol?" Had she chosen Bristol because I'd told her it was where I went to University? It was possible, I thought.

"You'll soon find it."

She started to walk away but then turned slightly and over her shoulder said, "I'll know if you don't go."

It sounded like a threat and I had no doubt she meant it. I looked again at the address on the piece of paper, memorised it, and threw it in a litterbin near the bandstand.

When I returned home, Vanessa was in the shower. I could hear her singing. We were happy and it would have been so easy to forget about my meeting with Jennifer Teague but something was

Where is Jason Rayner

telling me it would be a big mistake to even think about it.

Where is Jason Rayner

Chapter 39

Deciding to let things slide for a bit, I did nothing about trying to find the address I'd memorised by accessing Google Earth on my computer, believing if I just ignored it, it would go away. But a week after my meeting with Jennifer Teague in the park, I received another text, this time asking for an update on the Cathy situation as she called it.

I was sitting in my car in the car park of the gym complex waiting for Vanessa. It was a Saturday morning and the air was crisp and clear. Sunbeams danced on the dashboard as I screwed up my eyes and replied to the text message.

IN HAND WILL GO DOWN IN HALF TERM. CAN'T DO ANYTHING BEFORE WITHOUT AROUSING SUSPICION.

It would have to do, she could like it or lump it, I thought, sliding my phone into my pocket as Vanessa appeared, hot and sweaty from her workout. I thought she looked great and if it wasn't for Jennifer Teague I could relax and enjoy my life. I suppose, at this point, I should have told Vanessa about it. But I didn't and I was to come to regret the decision.

As the school term limped along to half term, I tried to think of a reasonable excuse for staying away for the night. However, fate intervened.

"Jack?" Vanessa put down her mobile. I recognised the tone of her voice.

Where is Jason Rayner

"OK, what d'you want? A lift into town, new dress, picking up for a girls' night out?"

She grinned. "You know me so well. None of those, BUT.."

Here it comes, I thought, slipping an arm around her waist and pulling her towards me.

"Nicola's hen night. It's not a drink with the girls in town as I'd imagined. She's booked a night at a health spa for us in half term. I'll be away for two days and a night."

"How *am* I going to cope?" I asked, kissing the top of her head, whilst unable to believe my luck.

"You don't mind?"

"Not at all, my sweet. Actually, I was thinking of popping down to Bristol to see Ben Jennings. He's an old friend from college days who, by coincidence, contacted me only last week. He's planning a get together with some of our old college pals and wondered if I'd like to join them."

"Really? That's great." She was walking away when she said, "And what a coincidence."

That night, after Vanessa was in bed, I opened up my laptop, accessed Google Earth and zoomed in on the address, which was by now imprinted in my memory. The flat was near the centre of the town. I estimated the time it would take to drive down and then went to bed but my dreams were of a young girl, with dark hair and a smile that tugged at my heartstrings.

As the half term holiday drew nearer, I began to feel nervous about my meeting with Cathy. I believed that her guardian angel would have informed her of my proposed visit but still I wondered what her reaction to me would be.

The day I'd been alternatively dreading and longing for eventually arrived. As I kissed her goodbye, Vanessa said, "Have a good time." Then she frowned. "What is it?"

"Why?"

"You seem a bit preoccupied." She picked up her overnight bag and headed for her car. "Missing me already, are you?"

"OK, I admit it, " I replied and blew her a kiss as she backed out of the drive.

Adding Cathy's address to my Sat Nav, and making a mental note to delete it later, I drove into the road and headed for the motorway. It was Monday morning and the start of the school holiday. I passed caravans making their way to the coast and a stream of holiday traffic, which cut my speed considerably for most of the way. Stopping off at a service station sometime later, I suddenly began to feel relaxed at the prospect of seeing her again. I imagined our conversation during which I would tell her of Jennifer Teague's indirect threats in the hope that she would have a word with her and put a stop to it.

It took me nearly four and a half hours to reach the outskirts of Bristol. Traffic leading to the centre of the city was nose to tail, so I eventually reached the flat at ten to one. It wasn't in the best of areas; refuse littered the street and graffiti defaced every possible surface. Guilt at the way I'd treated her washed over me like an unstoppable tide as I parked the car and walked the short distance to her flat.

Where is Jason Rayner

The paint on the front door was cracked, the wood rotten in places. I pressed the buzzer to flat 14b and waited. No answer. I tried again as a Rastafarian wearing a striped knitted hat opened the front door. He eyed me suspiciously for a moment then moved away.

"Excuse me," I called after him. He turned, hesitated, then said, "Yeah?"

"I wonder if you could help me. I'm looking for Catherine Barton, she lives in 14b."

"No man, you got it wrong - 14b is empty. There was a young girl living there but she was called Kate Newson - nice young kid - left a couple of weeks ago - no idea where she went."

"Long black hair, blue eyes?"

He frowned. "Blue eyes, yeah, black hair but not long." He indicated a point just below his chin. He stopped and looked at me more closely. "Not a cop are you? I can usually smell them."

"No, just a friend."

"Well looks like your friend's flown the nest, man."

"Right, well thanks."

"'Aint no problem. If you find her, tell her Baz said hi," and with that he walked away and I was left with a sinking feeling in the pit of my stomach.

Sitting in my car, I searched my mobile for Jennifer Teague's number. I'd added it to my address book under the name B Didsbury 2, to avoid any awkward questions Vanessa might ask. I was about to disconnect the call when she answered. It sounded as if she was walking along a pavement, I could hear the steady hum of traffic.

Where is Jason Rayner

"I'm outside her flat now and she's gone," I explained.

"Gone?"

"Yes, it appears she left here a week or two ago and one of the residents, living on the floor below, said he doesn't know where she's gone. Do you have any idea where I can find her? Oh, and she's calling herself Kate Newson for some reason."

"Not a clue. I don't understand it. Kate Newson, you say?"

"Yes."

"I wonder why…"

Not wishing to continue the conversation, I interrupted her, "Well, you can't say I haven't tried. There's no point in me hanging about here. If she does contact you, just tell her I'm sorry."

"Yeah, well, sorry doesn't do it for me."

I was starting to get angry. "Look, do what you like. I've tried, that's all I can do," I replied cutting the call.

I didn't fancy leaving the car in such a run down area so drove into the centre of Bristol, parked in the Cabot Circus car park and went to find a restaurant for lunch. The hum of conversation around me as I ate, rather than giving me solace made me feel lonelier than I'd ever thought possible. Realising I'd spent the journey down anticipating seeing Cathy again brought me to the conclusion that the reason for my depressed mood was staring me in the face. Her disappearance from the flat meant that I was never likely to see her again and I couldn't bear the thought. However, I had no idea then how my future would be inextricably woven with that of Cathy Barton's.

The Investigation.

Chapter 40

"So, I'll talk to Vanessa Robinson, while you go to see Cathy Barton's next-door neighbours?" Sandy said over breakfast in the dining room of the small hotel.

Richie nodded. "Maybe she'll open up to you. She was a bit suspicious of me."

"And you said, she was fit, athletic looking?"

"Very."

An hour later, Sandy joined Richie in the foyer of the hotel. She was dressed in a pair of jogger bottoms, running top, and trainers. Richie smiled. "Resourceful as ever I see, Miss Smith."

"I try to be, Mr Stevens. See you later. I'll text you."

He nodded, accepting her remark about texting him later without the usual fear of stepping into the unknown. Much to his children's dismay, he'd shied away from technology but Sandy Smith had educated him in more ways than one. He'd had to find his way around a computer for work but Smart phones, Xboxes and their offshoots left him drowning in a sea of confusion. Sandy would have none of it; she'd shrugged off his indifference but somehow managed to steer him towards technological advances without him kicking and screaming. It had been an insidiously deceptive assault and one for which, he had to admit, he was grateful.

The houses on Beaufort Avenue were detached and, with one notable exception, well kept. The house where Cathy Barton had lived with her aunt and uncle was in need of general maintenance; the windows needed replacing, the roof too, but Richie could see the garden had been tidied up and the front door repainted. He rang the bell of the house next-door and waited. He'd seen a man, presumably the husband, leaving in an Audi hatchback a moment or two ago and hoped there was someone in.

A middle-aged woman answered the door. She was in her late forties with mousy curly hair.

"Yes?" she held the door partially open and spoke to him through the gap.

"Hello, I'm so sorry to bother you. My name is the Reverend William Henry. I'm looking for a young lady named Kate Newson. Does she live here?"

"No, you've got the wrong address," she replied opening the door a fraction wider.

"Oh dear." Richie attempted to look suitably downcast. "It's quite important that I speak to her and I was given this address. This is number 32 Beaufort Avenue?"

The door was opened to its full extent. "I think you've made a mistake, number 32 is next door but there's no one living there called Kate Newson, I'm afraid."

"No one, oh dear me." Richie fumbled into his pocket and removed the photograph that Oliver Watts had given him. "This is the young lady, I'm searching for. I don't suppose you know her by any chance."

A shaft of sunlight fell across her face as she looked at the photograph. She blinked. "Kate Newson, you said?

"That's correct."

"This photograph looks a bit like Cathy Barton, although I can't be sure, and she does live at number 32. Well that's not quite right. She used to live there. She's living somewhere down south at the moment or so I understand." The woman looked tired, dark shadows ringed her eyes.

Richie frowned. "This is so unfortunate. My parish is in Lockford, which is on the south coast," he hesitated.

"Lockford, you say? Now I come to think of it, I believe my daughter Jennifer once told that was where her friend was living." She sighed and blew her nose.

"I wonder, if I could trouble you still further – a glass of water?"

She looked at him and he could see her coming to a decision, the dog collar, no doubt helping him to gain her confidence. "I've just put the kettle on, you could come in and tell me why you want to get in touch with Cathy, if you like."

"Very kind, very kind indeed," Richie muttered, wondering how long he had before the husband arrived back home.

Later that afternoon, when Sandy and he were sitting in a café overlooking a park making short work of the afternoon tea menu, Richie said, "Right then, time to compare notes I think, Miss Smith."

Where is Jason Rayner

Sandy began, "I managed to catch up with Vanessa in the gym complex. She was in the coffee shop and I admit to feeling a bit like a stalker when I asked if I could share her table, as the place wasn't exactly full. Anyway, I made some excuse about wanting a view of the pool and she didn't appear to think it an odd request."

"Good."

"To cut a long story short….."

"Always a good idea, Miss Smith."

"She is very tetchy on the subject of Jack Robinson. I had a feeling it might be because he left her for another woman a while back, so after chatting about the advantages of using the facilities in the gym, I made up some story about my boyfriend dumping me and in order to forget him I'd thought of getting in some healthy exercise."

"Good thinking."

"And after a bit, she mentioned that most men were rats, her husband included."

"Husband, not ex-husband?"

"Husband. He left a letter for her on the kitchen table one morning and just disappeared."

"And she hasn't heard anything from him since?"

Sandy shook her head and Richie complimented her on managing to find out so much in such a short time.

"Hang on, I haven't finished," Sandy said, taking a sip of her coffee. "Once she started talking about him, she couldn't stop. It was like a dam bursting; I think it had been bottled up inside for ages and talking to a complete stranger about it seemed to work for her."

Richie sat back in his chair and listened.

Where is Jason Rayner

"She said, Jack Robinson and she started work together on the same day but just before the school term began, her husband had met a young woman and the relationship developed into one of intimacy almost immediately. However, he was unaware that the girl was only fifteen and was further shocked to discover that she was one of his pupils."

"Cathy Barton?"

"Or Kate Newson?" Sandy continued. "Vanessa helped him cope with the situation and even went to the extent of suggesting he use her as a 'sham' girlfriend to get the girl off his back."

"And the rest is history? They ended up married and his affair with an underage girl was hushed up?"

"That's one of the reasons why she's so mad. He's made a fool of her."

"Hell hath no fury." Richie said. " So he's gone off with Cathy Barton?"

"She's not sure. She thought so at first but then decided he couldn't risk it. If it was discovered he could still be convicted. She doesn't think he'd take the chance, in view of the fact that he was so relieved to know he'd got away before."

"Bit odd she told you and not the police. If she was that vindictive you would have thought she'd be running to the police with wings on her heels."

"I found that odd too. Maybe she still loves him?"

"Love and hate, two sides of the same coin if you ask me. But I must say, excellent work, Miss Smith."

"So?" Sandy asked. "How did you get on with the next-door neighbour? Did the Reverend William Henry inspire confidences?"

Where is Jason Rayner

"Of a sort. Mrs Teague is a nice down to earth woman who told me Cathy Barton grew up in the next-door property with her aunt and uncle, until he died. At first she was reticent but I gradually gained her confidence, I think."

"And?"

"Yes, well, it was when she mentioned the uncle that my suspicions were aroused and I asked her how old Cathy was when she came to live with them."

Sandy sat forward in her seat.

"She was nine. But I gathered that her daughter Jennifer had no time for Bill Ferris and she let something slip. She didn't say so, well, not in so many words, but I believe she thinks Cathy was abused by the uncle."

"Really?"

"I have a very uncomfortable feeling that this is only the tip of the iceberg. We need to find our client, Miss Smith and the sooner the better."

Following Sandy out of the café into the afternoon sunshine, Richie frowned; something was bothering him about Mrs Teague – where had he heard the name before? For the life of him he couldn't quite remember.

Where is Jason Rayner

Chapter 41

Waking up the following day, Richie rang Sandy's room.

"I've been thinking," he began.

She groaned.

"Sorry to disturb your beauty sleep. But how do you feel about booking in for another few days? Like we said yesterday, we've got to find her soon, before this thing gets out of hand and the Devon police step up their nationwide search for Kate Rayner. It won't take them long to discover Cathy Barton and she are one in the same and I'd like to avoid them complicating matters before we've finished here."

"I'll ring Harry, as soon as I'm awake," she replied cutting the connection.

It was gone ten when Sandy met him in the foyer ready to continue their investigation.

"So you'll see Rita, and I'll give Norm a ring and see what he can tell me about the original missing persons' inquiry concerning Cathy Barton."

"We'll meet for lunch at Paulo's on the High Street?" Sandy suggested.

"Why there, dare I ask?"

Sandy shrugged, tossed her fair hair over her shoulder and replied, "Vanessa recommended it."

"Oh, I see. You're not just a pretty face, Miss Smith."

Where is Jason Rayner

They parted company outside the hotel and Richie headed for the park, clutching his mobile phone and notebook. The sun was warm on the back of his neck. He walked through the park gates as two women, jogging along the path, passed him gasping for breath, their overweight, out-of-condition, bodies protesting in the crisp morning air. Finding a bench under the bandstand with a good view of his surroundings and where he would be aware if he were being overheard, he rang DCI Norman Freeman of the London Metropolitan Police Force.

"Richie, my old son, good to hear from you. I've done as you asked and I think you'll be interested in the result."

Richie listened, raised his eyebrows and finished by asking about Cheryl and the family and promising to visit them in the not too distant future. Afterwards, he closed his eyes and started to think about his next course of action. A picture of Cathy Barton was beginning to emerge and it was one which was at odds with the Kate Newson he had met in Lockford.

Later, sitting in the small bar of an Italian restaurant, Richie yawned. "It was pure coincidence Norm said." He took a sip of his beer and continued, "There wasn't much on file about the disappearance of Catherine Barton, probably because she turned up unharmed and the case was swiftly closed down. But as luck would have it, one of Cheryl's friends is a WPC who was working on the South Yorkshire Force at the time, so Norm gave her a ring on our behalf."

Where is Jason Rayner

"Certainly helps if you have friends in high places," Sandy said.

"My years of working at the Met have paid off at last then?"

'So it would seem," replied Sandy with a grin. "Come on then, spill your guts."

Richie spluttered at her choice of words and put down his pint. "Apparently there was talk amongst some members of the staff at Westbank that one of the teachers had been 'friendly' with Cathy Barton but his engagement to one of his colleagues scotched the rumours before they'd had time to spread."

"Jack Robinson?"

"The same. Vanessa was telling the truth not simply venting her anger by trying to blacken his name. I suggest we talk to him and soon. But where to start looking might be a problem. No one we've talked to seems to have heard from him for quite some time."

"DCI Freeman might help?" Sandy looked up expectantly.

"Possibly but only if he's committed a crime. I can't see the Met putting out a missing persons' bulletin on a hunch. But I'll have a word with him, off the record, see if he can ask around."

"What's the plan for tomorrow?" Sandy asked.

"I think we should concentrate on speaking to the aunt again, as you were unable to get her to answer the door today. You were sure she was inside?"

"Positive, I saw her hiding behind the curtains in an upstairs room as I walked away."

"Right, Rita Ferris it is, although I have a strong feeling the house, with the neglected front and god-

Where is Jason Rayner

knows-what at the back, might hold more questions than answers."

Chapter 42

The house looked even more neglected in the crisp morning light. Richie opened a wrought iron gate as they followed the cracked path which skirted the drive and led them to the front door.

"The next door neighbour told you Rita Ferris lives here on her own? It's a massive place to maintain," Sandy observed, gingerly picking her way over the broken crazy-paving stones.

"Mm, I wouldn't fancy it – expensive too. I wonder what sort of life Cathy Barton had here after her parents died?"

"Maybe we're about to find out."

Richie had reached the front door; he rang the bell and waited. At an upstairs window he saw a curtain twitch. She was in then, good. He bent forward and opened the letterbox.

"Mrs Ferris. My name is Richard Stevens. I'm here on behalf of your niece Catherine." Not strictly true but near enough, he thought.

After a while, they heard the sound of footsteps crossing the hall and the clunk of a lock being slid back. The door opened a fraction.

"Yes?" The voice was reedy, the tone querulous.

"We're sorry to bother you. It's about Catherine. I'm a Private Investigator working on her behalf and this is my PA Miss Smith."

Sandy stepped forward.

Where is Jason Rayner

"I was with Cathy when her husband disappeared. Do you think we could come in and have a chat, Mrs Ferris."

"Husband? My Cathy?"

"That's what we'd like to talk to you about," Sandy replied, taking a step nearer the door. "It won't take long."

"Well, you'd better come in then. But I don't know anything about a husband."

Richie raised an eyebrow as Sandy passed him and walked inside.

"In here," Rita Ferris said, indicating a door on her left. They followed her into a room overlooking the front garden. The overgrown bushes had been trimmed but were sprouting again and a tree, badly in need of a tree surgeon, obscured the light from one of the windows. A faded carpet and worn furniture competed with a new sofa, upholstered in bright red leather, all of which ruined the once elegant proportions of what could still be a pleasant room.

Rita Ferris sat down on a chair with an upright back; her coloured hair was beginning to fade and an inch of grey roots showed through like a white line in the middle of the road. But she was wearing a pale blue cashmere cardigan, which suited her and on her feet were a pair of obviously new slippers in a darker shade of blue. She winced as she sat down.

"My aunty had the op," Sandy said, "she's fine, it gave her a new lease of life.

"Hip was it – like mine – or knee?"

"Hip."

Where is Jason Rayner

"Now, what's all this nonsense about my Catherine having a husband?" She gave a snort, of derision.

Richie wondered whether to step in but decided to leave it to Sandy, who seemed to have created a rapport with the woman.

Sandy delved into her oversized canvas shoulder bag and removed a wafer thin tablet notebook. "You don't mind if I write some of this down, Mrs Ferris?"

Rita shook her head.

"We're trying to find out as much as we can about our client in order to give her the best possible help. You see it appears that, some time ago, she married a man called Jason Rayner who has since disappeared. Catherine employed us to try and discover what happened to him."

"I had no idea, she didn't let on. P'raps, it's just as well her uncle has passed on. He wouldn't have liked the idea of her being married and not telling us."

"How old was Catherine when you and your husband came to live here, after her parents died?"

"Nine, and pretty as a picture. My brother and his wife died within weeks of each other, Norma from cancer and Jim six weeks later – a stroke - delayed shock they said but I knew he died from a broken heart. Poor Cathy, it was awful what happened when Jim died, too terrible to think about." She looked out of the window and sighed. "They only had little Catherine, Norma couldn't have any more besides she was too old. But before she died, she made me promise to look after her daughter, if anything happened to Jim."

Where is Jason Rayner

"That must have been difficult for you both," Sandy suggested.

"Not really. I thought Bill might have kicked off about it though. We weren't young and very much stuck in our ways, you know how it is." She peered at Sandy then said, "No you wouldn't –you're too young."

Richie frowned; he'd been under the impression that Kate Newson's parents had died in a traffic accident. So was *he* confused or was it another lie?

"Anyway, it worked out OK in the end. Bill loved our little girl, couldn't do enough for her."

"What about Catherine? It must have been hard living with older relatives."

To Richie's surprise the old lady laughed. "Not so, my dear. My sister was born before me. Catherine always had an old head on young shoulders – Jim and Norma were both much older than her friends' parents. She was used to it; used to living with older people."

So there was the explanation for her odd mannerisms staring him in the face, Richie thought. He could imagine the young child living in this house, with her elderly parents and thought the image of her he was building up was become clearer.

"And you said, your husband and she were close?" Sandy asked.

Richie bit his lip; she was good, you had to hand it to her.

"Yes, no, not exactly close. Bill followed her around like a puppy. I was amazed at how well he'd taken to having a child in the house, especially as we hadn't been blessed with any of our own but Catherine didn't want to be fussed. In the evenings,

Where is Jason Rayner

she would sit as close to me as she could, and if Bill offered to read her as story before bed she always said, 'No, let Aunty Rita do it.' He tried to shrug it off but I could tell he was hurt."

Sandy leaned forward. "How did Catherine get on in school?"

"She did very well, she's a clever girl."

"So why did she leave after her exam results?"

"That's always been a mystery to me. It was a terrible time." Her voice broke. "My Bill died, then Catherine went missing. It was like the Queen once said - an Anus horribilus – although at the time Bill thought it very funny - when it happened to the Queen, I mean; he kept repeating it." She stopped as Sandy looked on uncomprehendingly. "He used to call it a horrible bum." She put her hand over her mouth and giggled.

The whole atmosphere in the room seemed to lighten as Sandy burst out laughing and Rita tittered behind her hand. Richie waited to see how Sandy was going to retain the equilibrium and she didn't disappoint him.

"How awful for you – to effectively lose the two people closest to you at the same time."

Rita Ferris removed a paper tissue from the sleeve of her blue cardigan and blew her nose.

"It must have been a relief when Catherine turned up safe and well though?" Sandy added.

"Yes, you can't imagine it. As soon as I heard her voice on the phone, I felt as if a weight had been removed from my chest."

"Did she visit you much, during the years following her supposed disappearance?" Sandy tapped away on her digital notebook.

Where is Jason Rayner

"Not as much as I would have liked. She was busy; first there was her college course then her job with that firm of solicitors in Lockford. But she always came up for Christmas." She hesitated. "Except for last Christmas. She had flu - she said - didn't want to give it to me."

"So you never met Jason Rayner?"

"Who?"

"Her husband, Jason Rayner."

"I'm sure you've got your wires crossed, dear. Don't you think she'd have told me if she got married?"

Outside in the fresh air once more, Sandy inhaled. "What was that smell?"

"Camphor. Moth balls, I expect."

"So what now?" Sandy asked.

Richie looked at his watch. "I noticed a bus stop further down the road. It's nearly lunchtime. I suggest we visit Vanessa Robinson and see if she'd like to join us."

Where is Jason Rayner

Chapter 43

It was fortunate that, as Richie and Sandy arrived at Westbank School, Vanessa Robinson was striding out of the gates to walk the short distance to the Wheatsheaf pub for lunch. It was also fortunate that she was alone.

"Mrs Robinson?" Richie held up his business card. "I spoke to you briefly at your school and I think you've spoken to my PA previously. I'd like to ask you some questions about your husband, if you have the time."

She sighed loudly. "Mr Stevens, I no longer have any interest in discussing Jack Robinson and his affairs are entirely his alone. I haven't forgotten your little ruse of trying to pose as a reporter either, or you," she said pointedly to Sandy.

"I can't apologise enough, it was shameful and I do understand your reluctance to talk to us but it is important. Would a free lunch change your mind?" Richie asked.

She was about to turn on her heel and walk away but Sandy intervened. "We're not trying to rake up old memories, which you'd prefer to forget, it's just we need to discover whether our client is telling us the truth and, unless we can trust our source, we are in a mess." She sighed. "It would only take a few minutes and then we'll leave you to finish your lunch in peace."

Vanessa made a few disgruntled responses but reluctantly agreed and led the way into the pub.

Where is Jason Rayner

Richie winked at Sandy who ignored him and began a conversation with Vanessa about the best workout necessary to obtain a flat stomach.

After ordering lunch for them all at the bar, Richie joined the two women at a table overlooking the car park.

"Right, to get straight to the point. Where do you believe your husband is living as we need to contact him urgently?" Richie asked.

"He said he was moving to Manchester to be with an old girlfriend whom he'd met by chance a few months ago."

"And you believed him?"

"I don't know what to believe any more, where my husband is concerned. I've given up trying to untangle his lies. If he's with her then he's a bigger fool than I thought he was."

"Cathy Barton?"

"Yes, or whatever she's calling herself these days."

"She says her husband has disappeared and that his name is Jason Rayner."

"In that case, he's probably done the same to her as he did to me. He likes young girls, Mr Stevens. But although the initials are the same, I can't see him being so inventive and knowing Jack, he'd want to get as far away from temptation as possible, in her case."

Richie frowned. "So he's done this before, with another young girl."

To be fair, she had the grace to shake her head. "Just with her, but a leopard never changes his spots and if he's done it once there's nothing to stop him doing it again, is there?"

"And have you seen him since?" Sandy asked.

"Not since the day he left."

"So what made you suspect he might be with Cathy Barton?" Sandy persisted.

"At the time I thought he couldn't help himself but now I'm not so sure. He wouldn't take the chance. It would be too big a risk. It's just, I used to think she had some sort of hold over him."

"Could she have been blackmailing him?" Richie asked. "Threatening to expose him for having underage sex with her, do you think?"

"Possibly, and I did think he started to act strangely after receiving some text messages but to be truthful, I think it was just that he couldn't help himself where she was concerned. Even after I did everything I could to stop him from ruining his career and his life." She was getting annoyed. "I don't care one way or another, they're welcome to each other."

Richie stood up as the meal arrived. "Miss Smith and I will eat ours at the bar," he instructed the waitress then turning to Vanessa Robinson said, "Thank you, Mrs Robinson, we won't bother you further and we'll be in touch should we have any news of your husband."

"Please don't bother, Mr Stevens. I have no wish to know how he's living his life and will be initiating divorce proceedings as soon as I'm legally able to do so without his agreement."

Leaving the Wheatsheaf sometime later, Richie said, "Well, what d'you make of that?"

Where is Jason Rayner

"It fills in a few gaps and I think it gives us a little more understanding of Jack Robinson's nature. However, whether it gets us any closer to finding him is another matter."

As the bus arrived to take them back to their hotel, they saw Vanessa Robinson walking back to school. She moved with grace, her back ramrod straight, her head held high. "I have the distinct impression she would have backed him through thick and thin as long as he'd kept away from Cathy Barton," Richie said.

"But how far would she go to make sure that happened, is the question?" Sandy replied.

A cool breeze had sprung up by the time they reached their hotel.

"Time to pack up and go home. I don't think we're gaining anything by staying here," Richie said.

Jack's story
via his laptop

Chapter 44

I left Bristol and went back to Sheffield, hoping that Jennifer Teague would leave me in peace now and I could get on with my life with Vanessa without having to look over my shoulder to see if the police were going to arrest me.

The daily routine continued, Vanessa and I went to work, came home, made love and at weekends met our friends. Three months after I'd gone down to Bristol, I was shopping in the city centre, looking for something to buy Vanessa for her upcoming birthday, when I saw her. At first I thought I was imagining it and that the girl was someone who just happened to look like her.

She was sitting in a café with an older woman, presumably her aunt. If she'd been on her own, I would have approached her, spoken to her, asked her how she was getting along. But as it was, I just watched the way her newly cut hair shone as she tipped her head slightly to drink her coffee. I stood mesmerised. If anything she was more appealing than I remembered her and more enticing.

I shouldn't approach her; I knew it would be a mistake. I should pretend that I hadn't seen her, convince myself that it was someone else. But my feet weren't listening and before I knew what was happening I was standing at her side looking down at her.

Where is Jason Rayner

"Hello Cathy," I heard the words, but wasn't aware that I'd spoken them.

"Hello, Mr Robinson. Aunt, this was one of my teachers at Westbank," she said to the woman sitting opposite her.

The woman squinted up at me, and under her scrutiny, sense suddenly returned.

"Good to see you again. You had everyone worried when the police started looking for you," I said, the words sounding like an accusation.

"A mistake. It was just a mistake," she said, refusing to look at me.

"Well, it's nice to see you. Are you back for good?"

This time her aunt spoke. "She's only visiting. She's got a good job for herself in Lockford. Hadn't heard of the place until a week or two ago, when Catherine wrote to me. She won't be coming back up here that's for sure."

I felt a chill settle somewhere in the pit of my stomach at the thought but managed to reply, "I see. Enjoy your visit. Goodbye then."

My legs felt like lead as I walked away, refusing to look back, and wondering if she had turned her head in my direction. In the jewellers, opposite the café, I bought Vanessa's birthday present, a small gold locket on a fine-link chain. Afterwards, having paid for my purchase and waited whilst it was gift wrapped in black and gold paper, I left the shop and looked across to where Cathy had been sitting with her aunt. A young woman with a baby in a buggy had taken their place. She had disappeared; it was as if I had imagined the whole encounter.

Where is Jason Rayner

It was later, when I reached home, I remembered the name of the place, Lockford. It shouldn't be too difficult to find, I thought, locking the car and entering the house by the back door.

Vanessa was at the gym so I had the place to myself. I hid her present underneath some junk in my bedside drawer, made a cup of coffee and liberally laced it with sugar to stop my hands from shaking. I couldn't trust myself. That was the top and bottom of it. I was hopeless where Cathy Barton was concerned. If only she'd stayed away, if only I hadn't seen her again, if only I could wipe her image from my mind. But as the glutinous liquid slid down my throat and warmed my body, I could see her face in front of me as plainly as my own staring back at me from the bathroom mirror every morning. I closed my eyes and prayed that I could fight the impulse to rush down to Lockford as soon as I could.

Later, after Vanessa returned and we'd eaten dinner, she said, "You're quiet, Jack. Do you fancy hitting the town tonight?"

I resisted the urge to tell her that I'd seen Cathy that afternoon. "I'm fine. Forget about living it up tonight. I suggest we have an early night. You have to be ready for tomorrow."

She smiled. "What have you got planned?"

"Birthday surprise, nothing to get too excited about, but it's not every day you're twenty eight."

"Funny, lovely, man." She leant across and kissed my cheek. Vanessa was great and I sometimes forgot how lucky I was.

Where is Jason Rayner

The following day, I woke her with breakfast in bed, her locket in its shiny wrapping sitting alongside a glass of champagne and orange juice. "Oh, darling, it's lovely, " she said, "help me put it on."

I fastened the chain around her neck then sat back to enjoy the view. We made love after breakfast and I tried to ignore the vision of Cathy's face sliding between us. At lunchtime, we dressed and walked the short distance to our local where Robert, Mike and Vanessa's friend Imogen and her husband were waiting to help celebrate my wife's birthday. After lunch, we walked through the pub garden to the river, a tributary of the River Don, and boarded the cruiser, which I'd hired for the occasion. The rest of the day was spent enjoying ourselves with all thoughts of Cathy Barton placed firmly to the back of my mind.

Later, as I turned the key in the lock of our front door, Vanessa rested her head against my shoulder. "Thank you for the best birthday ever, Jack."

I should have been contented with my lot. A loving, beautiful wife, a job I enjoyed and a comfortable home. Most people would be satisfied. But if turning back the clock to the day I first met Cathy Barton and changing things were possible – would I? I shuddered at the answer, which I was afraid to contemplate.

Chapter 45

The weather changed, a week after Vanessa's birthday; summer arrived with a vengeance. The heat ratcheted up a few degrees higher every day and by Friday afternoon, every window in the school was thrown open, there being no such thing as air conditioning in the place, as Sheffield was unused to being considered warm enough during the summer months to require such an extravagance.

"I'm off to the gym for a work out and a swim, care to join me?" Vanessa asked on the way home.

I shook my head. "No ta, I'm going to stretch out on the back lawn with a cool beer."

I wasn't lying. It had been my plan and I had every intention of sticking to it. But the phone rang as I was opening the fridge.

"Hello, is that Jack Robinson?" I didn't recognise the voice but I believed it might be Jennifer Teague. "If you want to make it right with Cathy, she's staying at her aunt's place; it's number 32, Beaufort Avenue, but then you'd know that, wouldn't you, Mr Robinson?"

My suspicion being confirmed, I began to answer but she cut the connection. So, I could ignore it, take my beer into the garden and forget that Cathy was only a short drive away, which is what I should have done but I put the beer back in the fridge, picked up my car keys from the hall table and drove towards Beaufort Avenue.

Where is Jason Rayner

What was I going to say to her? How could I make it right and satisfy Jennifer Teague at the same time? My pulse began to race as I drove into the Avenue and parked outside the house, which was still badly in need of repair. Picking my way along a cracked pathway, I stood outside the front door and hesitated. Why was I here? What would Vanessa say? Questions tumbled around me like confetti blowing in the wind.

I pressed the bell and waited, part of me hoping she would answer and not her aunt. The footsteps crossing the hall were slow and measured, the woman looked as if I'd woken her from sleep. There was a smell coming from the hallway. It was unpleasant.

"Hello?"

"Mrs Ferris, I'm Jack Robinson, I taught Cathy English at Westbank; we met in the Mall."

"My Catherine?"

"Yes, I wonder, could I speak with her, please?"

She shook her head. "You're too late. She's up and gone again."

I felt as if a sledgehammer had hit me. "Gone?"

"Back to her flat in Lockford. I hoped she'd stay a bit longer this time but she said she had to get back to work or she'd have the sack."

"I see. So she's working; where exactly?"

"Arbuthnot and Trent, solicitors in Lockford High Street." She took a step back and peered at me. "Why do you want to know so much about my Cathy?"

I thought on my feet. "A friend of hers was asking about her and I said I'd look her up. Someone told me she was staying with you."

"Well, she isn't. So if you'll excuse me."

She shut the door abruptly and left me staring at the chipped paintwork wondering if I had the guts to go through with a plan that had begun to form in my mind.

My car was where I'd left it but Jennifer Teague was leaning against the driver's door waiting for me.

"I tried. She's gone. Now leave me alone," I said.

"No such luck," she replied spitting a ball of chewing gum into the gutter and standing aside to let me open the car door.

I drove away, and in the rear view mirror, I saw her waiting until I turned out of the Avenue and joined the main road. I still wasn't sure exactly what she wanted of me. She hadn't demanded money, or threatened to tell Vanessa. But the danger, of her being able to topple my carefully controlled life like a delicately constructed pile of playing cards, still remained.

It was at the end of the summer term when Vanessa received the letter. It was from her father's solicitor. Her father had died without contacting her but as she was his next of kin she'd inherited his estate, which included the family home. So she made an appointment to visit the solicitor, a family friend with offices in Brighton, the following Saturday.

"I wonder whether we should go by train, or drive down?" I asked.

"You don't have to come. It will be a real bore. I'll catch the train. You could take me to the station and pick me up though."

Where is Jason Rayner

"I don't mind; if you want me to come, I'll come, it's up to you."

"Better if you don't. You've got enough to do keeping the garden in order – everything is growing like wildfire, after the rain."

So it was decided. Vanessa left on the Friday evening. She'd booked into a B&B planning to stay overnight on Friday, Saturday and Sunday and to be home later on Monday afternoon. She said it should give her enough time to check out the house and make arrangements to put it on the market.

I was all set to get busy on the garden when I saw Jennifer Teague cycling up our drive. Anger at her persistence rose up in me like lava, hot and immediate; I was furious. I opened the front door.

"What d'you think you're doing? This smacks of stalking – coming to my home – badgering me about Cathy Barton. I've had enough of it. You can do as you like."

I started to shut the door in her face when she asked, "Have you quite finished? I'm here because I've been asked to come and speak to you. Rita Ferris has found something belonging to Cathy and I think you'll want to know exactly what it is. Look, can I come in? It's starting to rain."

Reluctantly, I stood aside and ushered her into the kitchen. She sat at the table but I refused to prolong her visit by offering her a drink.

"And?" I asked impatiently.

"She was cleaning Cathy's room and apparently she came across a diary hidden behind a bookcase."

"Hidden?"

Where is Jason Rayner

"Well. Rita thinks it was hidden. I suppose it could have slipped behind some books; anyway she read it. She told me she knew she shouldn't have done it but she wanted to relive some of the happy times before Bill died, when Cathy was still in school, before she disappeared."

I shivered and stretched up to close the window. I had a strong feeling I knew what was coming next.

"Cathy wrote it all down, Mr Robinson."

"I see." I sat down as my world collapsed around me.

"What does her aunt intend doing about it?"

"So far she's only told me and I said it was probably nothing, just a crush on her teacher."

I frowned. "Perhaps I should rephrase my question then. What do you intend doing about it?"

"I need money, Mr Robinson. My parents aren't wealthy and student loans are so expensive."

So now we have it, I thought. It is blackmail after all.

"Rita Ferris is an elderly lady. I think I can convince her not to go to the police."

I thought about calling her bluff but I had no fight left in me. "I'm a teacher, I'm not rich," I began.

"But you're not poor, are you? This house, two cars, your wife working."

"How much?"

"Five grand for starters. I'm not greedy. Then we'll see shall we?"

I sighed. "A cheque?"

Her smile was slow and measured. "I don't think so, do you? You can get the cash first thing in the morning."

"It's Saturday tomorrow."

Where is Jason Rayner

"I'm sure you'll find a way, credit card withdrawal, cashpoint. Under the bandstand at half ten; I'll be waiting for you, Mr Robinson"

I nodded, stood up and closed the front door firmly behind her. I had some serious thinking to do.

The investigation

Chapter 46

The office smelled of liquorice. Richie opened the window and smiled. Sandy's nephew Harry had inherited his aunt's flair for efficiency – not a paperclip out of place, post neatly arranged in his in-tray and all computer files up to date. If he had a failing, it was his love of liquorice allsorts, thought Richie, standing at the window and inhaling the fresh morning air.

He'd told Sandy to take the day off, to have a lie in after their visit to Sheffield but he had no doubt she'd turn up soon, as bright and shiny as a new penny. He yawned, stretched, filled the kettle, and was in the middle of making a cup of coffee when he heard the outer door clang shut and footsteps as light as air skipping up the stairs. He smiled; he was never wrong where she was concerned.

"Couldn't sleep?" he asked, as Sandy, the efficient PA once more, sat down at her desk.

"He's still addicted then."

"Who?"

"Harry," she replied, removing a half eaten bag of liquorice from her desk drawer and dropping it into the waste bin.

"Black, no sugar," Richie said, placing a mug, with the words HE THINKS HE'S THE BOSS written in large letters across it, on her desk.

"Thanks. What now?"

"First, I think I'll ring Norm. See if he's heard anything new."

Where is Jason Rayner

But before Richie could pick up the phone, it rang. It was DI Flintlock.

"We've called off the search for Kate Rayner. The body in the river has been identified. It was an alcoholic who'd been living rough – one of his fellow drinkers got into an argument with him and the rest is the usual sordid tale."

"I see, so there's still no sign of my client?" Richie asked.

"Nothing." He hesitated before continuing. "But although she's not involved in this case, I would be interested to know when she does get in touch with you, as there is still the problem of her wasting police time by not getting in touch with us and of course there is still the missing husband to consider."

"That's if there is a missing husband," Richie said. "I can't find anyone who's ever seen him. Either way, I'll be in touch, if she turns up."

Replacing the phone, Richie ran his fingers through his hair.

Sandy looked at him over the rim of her coffee mug. "You didn't mention about us suspecting that Kate Rayner was once Cathy Barton."

"No."

"Why?"

"I'm not sure but considering they no longer believe she murdered her spouse and dumped him in the river, I don't think it's relevant. She's started a new life; I think she should be allowed to call herself anything she wants.

"OK. I'll update the file but first I must tell you about my chat with Vanessa before we left. I wanted to leave it until we were back in the office because I needed to think about it first."

"Give me a moment to ring Norm and then come into to my parlour, Miss Smith."

"Said the spider to the fly," she replied.

He was smiling as he turned his back to her and walked into his room with a view of the High Street. He was told DCI Norman Freeman was off on the sick with flu. He didn't ask to speak to anyone else, although there were one or two detectives working at the Met who still remembered him. They would remember how he'd punched Phillip Heaton's face to pulp and how he would have lost his job if it hadn't been for DCI Freeman. They would have remembered that Heaton deserved what he'd got and that everyone's sympathy had been with the man who had lost his family at the hands of a fool. It was the usual tale of someone who'd been driving under the influence, whilst being banned. They would also have remembered how Richie had been unable to continue working in London and had moved to the south coast to get away from his memories. But they wouldn't have known that his memories travelled with him no matter where he went.

As he replaced the phone, he heard Sandy crossing the floor in the outer office and waited until she was sitting opposite him.

"Fire away, Miss Smith," he said stretching his legs and tipping his head back to rest on his joined hands.

"OK. We know Vanessa Robinson is very bitter about what happened between Cathy Barton and her husband." Sandy tucked a stray lock of hair behind her hair and continued, "It's understandable; she'd stood by him when he was in danger of losing his job and worse, because of his involvement with the young girl. So it must have been a terrific blow to discover he'd left her for another woman."

"And?" urged Richie, this was old news as far as he was concerned.

"She said, he left a note, that he'd met someone he knew from his days at University and they'd fallen in love, he was sorry, etc.etc."

"Yes?"

"Well, that's just it. I've been thinking about that invisible note and I wonder, do we believe it or was it fabricated in order to lay a false trail? What do we know about Vanessa Robinson? She's a spurned wife. How angry she must have been. What did she do about it?"

"Go on."

"What if it really was a smoke screen – suggesting he left to be with Cathy Barton?"

Richie sat upright. She was only voicing his suspicions but somehow it made the supposition all the more plausible.

"So, let's assume that to be the case. Where is he now? You can't be suggesting that she's done away with him and hidden the body?"

Sandy was silent.

"So, for the moment, let's forget about Vanessa Robinson being a murderer, which is a bit far fetched, you have to admit; if he was with Cathy Barton as is a strong possibility then where was he when Jason Rayner was on the scene? And where is he now?"

Sandy shrugged.

Where is Jason Rayner

"Yes well. I know you're going to say it's rubbish but Jack Robinson – Jason Rayner?"

"You'll have to stop doing crossword puzzles, Miss Smith – it's causing confusion." He chuckled. "It's a bit too obvious but taking into account our client's transformation from Catherine Barton to Kate Newson, you could be right. Also he couldn't risk being discovered as Jack Robinson, Cathy Barton's teacher, who would have been arrested and added to the sex offenders' register or worse. Nevertheless the question still remains – where is he? Or should I ask where are they?"

Where is Jason Rayner

Chapter 47

Tracy sat opposite Richie and inched her skirt higher then crossed her legs.

"Fancy seeing you again," she said, accepting the glass of wine Richie offered her, whilst unaware that he'd been watching her movements from his office window and noticed that every Friday evening, after work, she entered the wine bar alone.

"Not really surprising, as I work across the street," Richie replied. "Actually, I'm glad we bumped into each other as I was hoping to talk to you about Kate Newson or should I say Rayner."

Tracy bit her red-painted bottom lip. "Bit of a dark horse our Kate. Has she contacted you? She's been off for ages."

"Not lately. But having you on the inside so to speak is a definite advantage." He'd found the Tracys of this world were always up for a bit of flattery, where intellect was concerned, and she was no exception. She straightened her skirt and tried her best to look intelligent and she would have been convincing had it not been for her inability to keep her eyes focused on anything other than her appearance. Continually checking her image in the mirror above the bar, she said, " I always thought she was odd. Actually, I can tell you something, which might be useful."

Richie leaned forward.

"She rang Larry Arbuthnot only last week. Said she was looking after a sick relative and would be

Where is Jason Rayner

away for a bit longer. She was sorry but hoped he would understand and promised to be back before the end of the month."

Two weeks to go, thought Richie.

"Really? Thank you, Tracy, that's splendid, a great help. I'll keep in touch and you know where I am if you think of anything more concerning your colleague. Another glass of red is it?"

Leaving the wine bar and walking back to the car park in Hastings Buildings, Richie began to think a picture was beginning to emerge. It was indistinct, parts of it were missing, but the outline was starting to take shape. He believed Cathy Barton was running away from her past when she began living in Lockford and Jack Robinson was only a small part of it. Then there was the question of her mannerisms – old fashioned – oddly spoken – older than her years. What had happened in her youth to make her different from her contemporaries?

When Richie arrived at his flat, he had a quick chat with the old boy who was effectively a night watchman but who spent most of the night sleeping behind his desk. The river level was lower than he'd seen it for a while and the heat of an early summer wrapped around him like comfortable memory.

Inside, he opened all the windows to remove the stale air, took a cool beer from the fridge and switched on the TV. The theme tune to a hospital drama accompanied by the rolling cast list filled the screen followed by the introductory music to the nine o'clock news. Richie put his feet up on the old sofa that he refused to replace in spite of its faded and grubby material and raised the can to his lips. His reluctance to part with the sofa was due to the fact that it was all that remained of the suburban house he'd shared with his family and if he closed his eyes he could still see his wife bending over a knitting pattern and Tess reading a trashy paperback.

Lost in thought, he missed the headlines but caught up with the story, as a reporter was interviewing Vanessa Robinson.

"I have no idea where he is and I'd be grateful if you'd take your camera out of my face and let me pass," she said.

Richie sat up. The report was focusing on a murder, some time ago, of a young woman called Jennifer Teague, who had been found strangled in some woods at the back of Beaufort Avenue. But it was the name of the young girl that unlocked his memory.

"Of course, what a fool I've been," he said to himself, the reason why the name Teague was familiar to him suddenly becoming clear.

Richie was thinking about his visit to Jennifer's mother and the proximity to his client's family home as his mobile began to ring. It was Sandy.

"I've seen it," he said, before she could speak.

"The plot thickens," Sandy replied, and he could hear music in the background and the sound of conversation.

"It does indeed, get back to your life, Miss Smith and I'll see you on Monday morning."

Where did Jennifer Teague fit in to all this, thought Richie, as the night closed in and the lights of Lockford shone in the distance? Maybe Sandy would be able to paint a picture of her in his mind. He needed something to concentrate on, to stop from going around in circles. Cathy Barton, Jennifer

Where is Jason Rayner

Teague and the Robinsons were intertwined and he had to find the link that connected them. It wasn't a great leap of imagination to believe that someone who could be charged with paedophilia was open to blackmail, but who was doing it - Jennifer Teague, Cathy Barton or Vanessa Robinson?

The answer to this question could be the lynchpin to the whole case. But knowing where to start was the thing. After a good night's sleep, which mercifully had been devoid of dreams, he decided, a good place to start was always at the beginning.

Where is Jason Rayner

Jack's story
via his laptop

Chapter 48

I had no intention of succumbing to blackmail but what could I do about it? There had to be another way. I looked at my watch as my mobile bleeped. It was Vanessa texting to say that she'd arrived in Brighton, was shattered, and would ring me tomorrow. I texted back to say that the landline was playing up, as road works had disrupted the cable line, so to ring my mobile. Driving to the nearest cashpoint, I removed the maximum amount possible using my card then drove to the supermarket where I bought a loaf of bread, some biscuits and a bottle of water, paying with my card and choosing the cashback option. It was a start, together with the cash I kept in the house for emergencies, which was considerable as I'd long ago slipped into mother's habit of filling a cake tin with cash and putting it on the top shelf in the kitchen and stacking a couple of thousand under a loose floorboard in her bedroom.

Vanessa said she would be back on Monday evening. I decided, in order to cover my tracks, I'd write a note telling her I was leaving her and moving in with a previous girlfriend of mine who lived in Manchester. The city was large enough to make my actual destination vague in order to deter her from trying to find me. Although I guessed she'd be so mad she would do no such thing.

I slept little that night and was up before five. I was thinking on my feet, an idea formulating as I packed a case, placed the note on the hall table, and left the house I had shared with my mother and later my wife without a backward glance.

I was waiting for Jennifer Teague under the bandstand. It was half past ten.

"Here," I handed her an envelope. "You understand that this is an end to it. There'll be no more, whatever threats you decide to make."

She opened the flap of the envelope, looked inside then, satisfied, said, "I'll be seeing you Mr Robinson," before walking away from me.

The roads were fairly quiet as afternoon approached. The journey was unremarkable until I reached Manchester and booked into a B&B in the centre of the city. The next day, I withdrew more money from the cashpoint machine, spent Sunday wandering around the city before returning to the B&B and waiting for Monday morning when the banks would be open again.

I went to bed early that night to think about my immediate future. In order to establish the veracity of my story, I'd have to spend a week or two in Manchester and withdraw enough money to set up a new identity in Lockford. In the unlikely event of someone trying to trace my whereabouts, it could be established by the use of my credit card that I'd at least spent some time in the city. I was sure Vanessa would ring and it would give me time to think up a suitable story to keep her from having any hope I'd return.

It was Tuesday; Market Street was a hive of activity when I arrived outside the branch of my bank. I'd phoned the day before to make an

Where is Jason Rayner

appointment to see the manager. It was after I'd spoken to Vanessa who had rung my mobile, spat out a stream of invective regarding my actions and finally told me she never wanted to lay eyes on my cheating face again. Neither of us had mentioned my house, so I presumed she had every intention of staying put and under the circumstances there was no way I was going to insist on going to solicitors to claim my half. I decided it was a casualty of the events instigated by Jennifer Teague, who I considered was mainly to blame.

The bank manager smiled as I entered his office, "Sit down, Mr Robinson. I understand you wish to close both your accounts with our Sheffield branch and withdraw the funds in cash and banker's draft?"

"That's right."

"It's a bit unusual but I've had a word with Mr Blakely, the manager of your branch and he gave me a full and accurate description of you." He smiled and I began to relax." He said he's well acquainted with you as you teach his son? "

"I do." I breathed a sigh of relief. I'd expected all sorts of checks and questions; I silently thanked heaven for Reece Blakely's dad.

"Under the circumstances, I can't see any problem. You said you wished the banker's draft to be made payable to John Rice, is that correct?"

"It is." Acutely aware that I was reduced to replying as sparingly as possible, I tried to force my features into a smile. "I'm moving into the area shortly and will be transferring funds from the sale of my property in Sheffield to your bank and initiated new accounts, here in Manchester as soon

Where is Jason Rayner

as possible. Mr Rice is an advisor who is dealing with the transaction."

This explanation seemed to satisfy him, for after completing a few standard security questions, he made arrangements to comply with my request, shook my hand and accompanied me into the banking hall.

Leaving the bank and walking towards my car, I felt ready to start my new life unencumbered by the likes of Jennifer Teague and Rita Ferris. I was John Rice. I'd thought it all out; I had to think of a name bearing the same initials as my former self for a variety of reasons, one being my car. I had the registration plates Vanessa had bought me for my birthday – A1 JR and as it was a new model, I was determined to keep it to avoid the necessity of having to tax and insure another vehicle in my new name. I was thinking ahead, but in reality had little concept of how to proceed successfully.

The following weeks were filled with planning how to continue with my new life. It took some time to think out how I was going to succeed without the police looking for me in connection with Cathy Barton, if her guardian angel suddenly decided to tell them of my involvement with an underage girl.

After Vanessa's initial tirade, she rang once more to discuss some mail, which had arrived and said if I gave her my address she would forward it. However, I asked her to open it, as I wasn't expecting any urgent mail. Then I told her to put the rest in the bin. She cooled down a bit, when I apologised yet again and thanked her for standing by me. I'd expected another stream of invective but she just sighed and said, I was my own worst enemy and she wanted to

Where is Jason Rayner

forget about it all, by which I inferred she was not going to drag it up again by going to the police.

I'd been gone from Sheffield for nearly a month when I rang an estate agent in Lockford and arranged to rent a flat in the area. Afterwards, I packed my meagre belongings into the boot of my car and equipped with enough money to see me through until I was more settled, drove out of Manchester, heading south.

Following my Sat Nav's instructions towards Lockford, I stopped at service stations along the way and gradually slipped into the skin of my new persona. John had been easy (JFK had used either name), Rice I'd arrived at after eating my first meal as a new man in Manchester; it had been curry and rice. Although not world shatteringly inventive it was inconspicuous enough not to be instantly recognisable, which was all to the good.

I arrived in Lockford when dusk was beginning to colour the sky with a pale orange glow as the sun set. The temperature gauge on my car read 24 degrees. It looked as if tomorrow was going to be another sunny day.

My flat wasn't in the best area but I had no intention of wasting money. I knocked on the landlord's door; he lived in a house in the next street, which was a distinct improvement on the shabby houses he was renting on Cornwall Road. I introduced myself as John Rice and paid the bond he required in cash. He hardly looked at me, grunted a few instructions and handed over the key.

Cornwall Road had seen better days. It consisted mostly of student accommodation and houses with

Where is Jason Rayner

For Sale or To Let signs standing in small front gardens like sentries. There were three flats in the house where I was to live. The ground floor flat was unoccupied, and a student with long greasy hair tied back in a ponytail mumbled a greeting as he passed me on his way to the attic. My flat on the second floor smelled of curry overlaid with disinfectant, the aroma filling my nostrils as soon as I opened the door. There was a small desk under the window, a table and chairs against one wall and a sofa and armchair in front of a small TV. The room was divided into a lounge and small kitchen area, with a fridge, cooker and washing machine. The bedroom contained a single bed, chest of drawers and a table and there was a communal bathroom and toilet on the landing outside my front door. It was adequate, and that was the best way I could describe my new accommodation.

   I slept fitfully that night dreaming of Cathy and how she'd looked when I'd last seen her, interspersed, with Vanessa and I celebrating our wedding. They were confused, disturbing dreams and when I awoke I felt I deserved to be plagued by such nightmares. Breakfast consisted of toast and coffee both of which I'd bought before I'd left Manchester. My cupboards were bare so a visit to the supermarket in a side street across the road from my flat was in order. And afterwards, I decided to drive into town to complete the second part of my transformation.

Where is Jason Rayner

Chapter 49

It was half past ten when I walked past the barbershop on the High Street, which was of the trendy variety catering for both men and women, but in a side street I saw the striped pole above a small shop and discovered a barber who had been cutting hair since the relief of Mafeking.

"Short back and sides, is it, sir?" he asked, whipping a white cotton cape around me like a Matador enticing a bull.

I nodded, "As short as you like," I replied, watching him selecting the right setting on his razor followed by my hair falling like a shower of dead leaves around me.

Later, in Specs-Express, I removed my glasses and chose some coloured contact lenses. I would have to wait a day or two for delivery the assistant told me but I could use a trial box, which were untinted, until then. I caught sight of my face in the mirror as I left the shop and thought, good, even my own mother would have trouble recognising me.

It was a short distance to a café on the High Street which was opposite the offices of Arbuthnot and Trent. From my table near the window, I had a good view of the front door. It was mid-day. I saw a tall blonde woman wearing a grey suit and white blouse leaving the office and walking across the road and into the café. She stopped at the counter, gave her order, waited for her take-away baguette and coffee, left, stopped to look in the window of a dress

Where is Jason Rayner

shop opposite then walked back to her office. I waited, my eyes fixed on the office door but the only person to emerge was a man wearing a pinstriped suit whose black hair flopped forward across his forehead.

When Vanessa rang, I ignored the call. I did feel a pang of guilt where she was concerned but what could I do? My transformation was just beginning. It would take some time before it was completed to my satisfaction after which I could approach Cathy but I had all the time in the world and I was in no hurry.

I stayed in my flat until I was sure everything was in place and there was to be no nationwide hunt for a missing person called Jack Robinson. After our initial conversation in Manchester, it was obvious, by her reaction, that Vanessa had read my apology, got mad, raged against me, and full of hate, ripped the note to shreds. Then when she rang a second time, I felt safe in the knowledge she'd get on with her life and forget I ever existed. At least I wasn't leaving her destitute. She had the house her father had left her and was living in my place, mortgage free. Under the circumstances it would be impossible for me to claim my share of the property so she would be OK, but what about me?

The previous day I'd bought a small safe and screwed it into the back of one of the kitchen cupboards behind the cleaning materials, then inserted a false chipboard backing, so if the landlord decided to pay an unscheduled visit whilst I was out, there would be nothing unusual for him to see. Also, although there was no immediate problem with money, I had to find some paid work as soon as possible. Luckily it was summer and Lockford was

Where is Jason Rayner

surrounded by countryside. I was fit and healthy and there were always cash-in-hand jobs on farms, fruit picking, washing-up in restaurants, casual labour; it would only be for a while, I kept telling myself.

However, I decided to take matters in hand in the long term. What were my skills, apart from manual labour? I was a teacher – I had a degree in English. In Lockford Library, I used one of their computers to print off a flyer – English Tutor – contact number. 07973705471 then attached the flyer to a notice board in the library with the help of a chatty junior librarian.

"My sister's looking for someone to coach her son, Mr Rice. I'll give her your number, shall I?" she asked.

In the corner shop near my flat, I paid a nominal charge and they attached my flyer to a board in their window; I advertised in the local paper and waited for the phone to ring. Credit cards were a problem but finance was the least of my problems, if Rita Ferris and Jennifer Teague had their way, making money would be the last thing I'd be worrying about.

As the weeks passed, I realised Lockford's education system must have been woefully inadequate; it was surprising how many pupils required my help. With the assistance of the library photocopier and a certain amount of creativity, I adapted my degree certificate to my new situation, framed a copy and hung it on the wall above my desk in the flat. I explained to my pupils' parents that I'd prefer to be paid in cash and by the hour - no one questioned it and before long I found I was busier than I'd thought possible. The summer

Where is Jason Rayner

holidays, with autumn term approaching, was the best time for their little darlings to get a march on their peers, or so it seemed. The rent of my flat was secure and with my weekends during the fruit-picking season catered for, I began to think that I could pull off my transformation without any initial problems.

During the following days I became a stalker. I sat in Starbucks and watched her arrive for work. I saw her having lunch with a gawky lad who also worked at Arbuthnot and Trent and sat in my car opposite the bus stop and watched her catching her bus then followed it until she arrived at her flat. At no time did I approach her and she was unaware on my existence.

I was in no hurry, as long as I could see her every day, it satisfied my initial need. I couldn't hurry things. I had to make sure she wouldn't run scared when I talked to her. It was obvious Vanessa had accepted my story and I'd kept my mobile in the early days when we'd had a few initial text messages of the kind where she ranted and I apologised. Later, I'd ditched my phone and bought a pay as you go with a new number and Sim card. I was John Rice and Jack Robinson had ceased to exist, since any trace of him would end in Manchester.

Complacency is a dangerous emotion, it leaves you vulnerable and my carefully laid plans could have disintegrated before my eyes on a September day when a cool wind was blowing down Lockford High Street.

I was approaching the café where I planned to sit and continue my vigil in the hope of catching sight of her. Some day soon I hoped to approach her, gauge her reaction to me and later explain how we should proceed but I had to be sure it was the right time. However, events did not turn out quite as I'd planned; she was crossing the road in front of me carrying a tray of doughnuts.

Catherine's story.

Chapter 50

The light outside the window is fading into evening, although it's only the middle of the afternoon. I hate these grey, damp, days when the sun forgets to shine and the faces of the passers-by merge into their surroundings. Inside the room the spotlight shines and he is still lost behind it. It's not a spotlight in the accepted sense. Radicals are not interrogating me but I prefer to think of it as such, otherwise I might become complacent. I must keep alert, as I need to have all my wits about me if this is to succeed. He waits and both of us know this is the point in my story from which there is no turning back. What constitutes truth and are we all capable of making lies sound like reality? The question hovers in the room as I take a deep breath and continue.

Although I was seeing him around every corner, I knew it was just my mind playing tricks. After a while, I decided to ring Richard Stevens. Someone called Harry Smith answered my call, he sounded very young. He told me that Mr Stevens and his PA were out of the office on business and wouldn't be back for a while. He asked if I'd like to leave a message so I said no, but I would call again in a day or two. I contemplated ringing the police in Devon but then decided to travel back to my flat in Lockford and put Jason Rayner completely out of my mind.

Where is Jason Rayner

Rita was upset; she'd hoped I'd be staying for good. I promised to keep in touch, kissed her and left by the mid morning train. Throughout the journey, I kept thinking about how I was going to deal with the problem of Jason Rayner. It was not an exaggeration to say he'd ruined my life. As the train drew into Lockford General, I had a good idea where to begin.

When Monday arrived, I opened the front door of Arbuthnot and Trent, walked into the washroom and hung my coat on my hook. I ignored Oliver's open mouth stare and Tracie's gasp by pretending that the past few weeks had never existed.

"OK, don't think you are getting out of this washroom until you've told me all." Tracy let the door clatter shut behind her. "You do realise there's been a police hunt for you."

"Slight exaggeration, wouldn't you say?" I ran a comb through my hair and spoke to Tracy's reflection.

"Explain!" she demanded and I could see that silence on my part would not satisfy her.

"I've spoken to DI Flintlock of the North Devon police force – there was a misunderstanding – I had no idea they were looking for me. I've been staying with an elderly relative who hasn't a TV."

"What about the body?"

"Body?"

"Come on Kate, it doesn't cut any ice with me – the body in the river."

"Oh that," I replied offhandedly. "Just an old tramp, it wasn't anyone special. They managed to identify him without any help from me."

Tracy looked downcast. She'd expected something juicy and I'd been a disappointment to her. She left me standing in front of the mirror with a feeling that this wouldn't be the last time I would have to explain it again that morning.

Mason Trent was no exception; you would have thought I was Rose West fresh from a killing spree the way he salivated waiting for some of the more salient points of my story to come his way. I must admit to playing him along for a while until dropping him from a great height. And when I did, I could see he was furious.

"Let's get on with some work then, shall we? We've wasted enough time this morning already," he said and then proceeded to give me a list of Herculean tasks to be completed that day.

After work, I went back to my flat, closed my eyes and rested against the door. I could still smell him, see him and taste him in my life. How long would it take to rid me of his presence? I'm not proud of what I did next but it was necessary. I went into the kitchen, made a cup of tea and removed my mobile phone from my handbag.

That night I tossed and turned in bed and when I finally did fall asleep, dreamt that the body in the river was his. I awoke at six, my heart racing - would the text prompt him to get in touch - what would I say - what would I do? My head full of unanswerable questions, I headed for the shower, dressed and walked to an all-night supermarket nearby to buy a carton of orange juice.

It was still only seven o'clock, far too early for work. So I decided to walk into the centre of Lockford. I'd tried ringing Jason Rayner on countless occasions but my messages remained unanswered. I had to face up to it - he'd disappeared

Where is Jason Rayner

for good. Luckily the Sweet Pea café opened early so I decided to have breakfast sitting at a table with a view of the offices of Arbuthnot and Trent. The walk took me twenty minutes and in the café I lingered over scrambled eggs on toast and a large cappuccino. I had a good view of the street and watched the pavement and road cleaners packing away their equipment and early morning cyclists and office workers, keen to get an early start, beginning to arrive for work.

A little way down the street was Richard Stevens's office and around a quarter past eight, I saw a young man with red spiky hair cycling by. He stopped outside Hastings Buildings and went inside. I was sure he was the person I'd spoken to on the phone, earlier. I waited until just gone half past eight then rang the number.

"Good morning, Richard Stevens Private Investigator, Harry Smith – how may I help you?"

"It's Mrs Rayner. I rang a few days ago. I gather Mr Stevens is still away. So I wonder if I could leave a message for him. Please thank him for his services and tell him I have come to the conclusion that my husband has disappeared for good, and no longer require his services. Please ask him to send me a bill, when he returns."

I rang off, feeling unaccountably satisfied.

The room has suddenly grown cold. I shiver.

"We are nearly there, Mrs Rayner. Stick with it," the therapist says; I want to laugh out loud. He has no idea. "You do realise now that there is no such person as Jason Rayner?"

Where is Jason Rayner

I do not answer right away and know that everything we have discussed over the past weeks hangs upon my answer. Today has been a culmination of my 'treatment'. It was a condition I had to fulfil or be charged with wasting police time on two occasions. Psycho-babble, counsellors, therapists, where were they when I needed them, when a lonely child had to cope with what happened to her parents, when Bill tucked me up at night? If I'd learned one thing in life, it was to keep important matters to myself and to give the rest of them the answers they wanted to hear.

"Of course. Jason Rayner was a figment of my imagination, as you suggested, and I understand I was at a point in my life when I needed a lover, someone who would make up for losing my parents and my uncle, as you explained." I answer. "I can see it all clearly and know why I acted as I did. I'm just sorry I wasted everyone's time and effort."

Satisfied with my reply, he stands up and closes the blinds. Outside, night has approached without me noticing it. He emerges from behind the desk-lamp and switches on the overhead light then steps forward to shake my hand. His eyes wrinkle at the corners as he smiles. "I'm glad to say that your treatment has been successfully concluded and I'm sending a copy of my report to the authorities. "Goodbye Miss Newson and good luck for the future."

I start to say, it's Barton, and then realise what a mistake that would be. How easy it would be to trip up, even now.

"Thank you for listening," I reply, and wonder if he has any idea how much this means to me. He has

Where is Jason Rayner

confirmed that Jason Rayner didn't exist, which was always our intention from the start.

The Investigation

Chapter 51

Rita Ferris bothered him. Whilst in the middle of an investigation, Richie liked to have a clear impression of the people involved. Although there were still many questions without answers where Cathy Barton was concerned, he believed he was beginning to understand what made her tick; Vanessa Robinson was an open and shut case, there was no mystery there, but Rita Ferris gave the impression of a frail elderly lady who wouldn't say boo to a goose. However, there was something about her that didn't ring true. It might be worth taking another look at Cathy Barton's early life, which might provide the answers to some of the questions that were keeping him awake at night.

To his surprise Sandy was already sitting at her desk when he arrived at eight the next morning. " I thought I was the only one who couldn't sleep, seems I was wrong," he said.

"I woke up at four with an idea that wouldn't let me sleep, so I got up, dressed and came to work."

"You've been here since five?" asked Richie incredulously.

"No, of course not, six," said Sandy.

"And the idea?"

"W..ell." She tapped the back of one hand with the fingers of the other, a gesture Richie had come to recognise with a degree of respect as it usually preceded something worthwhile. "For the moment, let's assume that Jack Robinson and Jason Rayner are the same person. So, he's created a new identity and is living under an assumed name and after a month or two he marries Kate Newson. Both parties having effectively put the past and anything to do with it far behind them, they can presumably carry on with their lives as a married couple without any problem."

"I'm with you so far."

Sandy sighed. "Why then has Jason Rayner disappeared? And why is it that we can't find anyone who has ever seen him? In addition to which I think it's odd that Cathy Barton suddenly reappears and is willing to accept the fact that her husband has run off with another woman."

"And?" Richie asked, resting against the corner of her desk.

"It's possible, Jason Rayner is a figment of our client's imagination but if it's as I suggested that Rayner is Robinson then we could be looking at a murder investigation."

"You think? So what has she done with the body? The Devon police have assured us that the body in the river has been identified. It's not him and if your supposition is correct, why did she bring Rayner's disappearance to their notice in the first place? It doesn't make much sense."

"Yes, that's what's been keeping me awake. Do we visit her again, in work?" Sandy asked.

"I don't think so. Technically she is not our client. We should move on."

Sandy raised her eyebrows. "You're not serious?"

"We won't be paid."

"Codswallop!"

Where is Jason Rayner

Richie laughed. " OK, you know me too well. But seriously, we can't spend too much time on it."

"So where do we go from here?"

"Start at the beginning."

"Sheffield?"

"Looks like it. It's fortunate that Harry is still around. But there are one or two things I have to do before we retrace our steps." He stood up. " Update the files, Miss Smith and I'll let you know our proposed itinerary in a day or two."

It was later that same evening, whilst Richie was watching the news, that he heard an update to a previous item about a body of a young girl being found in woods at the back of the house where she lived with her parents. It happened some months ago and the police were still looking for the murderer. Now, it appeared, they were asking for anyone, who had seen a man entering a lane at the side of the property on the day in question, to call the number appearing on the screen. Richie looked at the CCTV footage but it was so indistinct he doubted any identification could be made from the image alone. However, it appeared, there was some suggestion that Jack Robinson, who couldn't be contacted, had been involved with the girl. Police were asking, if anyone knew of his whereabouts, would they please contact South Yorkshire Police.

The laws governing coincidence were insubstantial and elusive and he had learned the hard way that it would be a mistake to ignore them when they occurred. Jennifer Teague, the murdered girl had lived in the house next door to Rita Ferris, he had spoken to her mother only recently, a fact that

Where is Jason Rayner

was far too coincidental for his liking; it put a whole new perspective on the case. He picked up his mobile and texted Sandy.

THIS TIME WILL GO ALONE - WILL VISIT AUNT AGAIN IN MORNING – DRIVE UP + STAY OVERNIGHT – PLEASE HAVE ANOTHER WORD WITH OLIVER WATTS.

He hated texting but he didn't want to bother Sandy in case she was having an early night. It was an excuse; he knew she wouldn't like the fact he was going alone. He needn't have bothered; his phone rang as soon as the message was sent

"Should I come with you?" she asked hopefully.

"Not this time." He explained about Jennifer Teague's murder and the fact that Jack Robinson was possibly involved. "This changes things. I've thought it over and I need you to hold the fort for a day or two; we can't leave the office to Harry alone, this time. If he still wants to come in, fine, but it will have to be at reduced rates, I'm afraid. As I said, talk to Oliver Watts, see what he has to say."

"Anything you say, Boss, but let me know if there are any developments. Oh and have a safe journey. Bye."

Richie looked at the phone long after the connection had been cut. She was a good kid. The fact that she cared whether he arrived safely or not was like a knife turning in his gut. It was the sort of thing Lucy or Tess would have said but his son would have just grunted but men cared in a different way and Tess had always been the more talkative twin even when they were in their pram. He sighed, closed his eyes for a moment then walked into the bedroom to throw a few things into an overnight bag ready for the next morning. Memories of his family haunted him when he least expected them, turning him into a quivering wreck of a man. Thankfully, as the years went by, the occasions when this happened were less often but their consequences were just as distressing.

The journey to Sheffield was fraught with traffic jams, idiot drivers and heavy showers that obliterated his view and battled for supremacy even with windscreen wipers set on high speed. I must be getting old, Richie thought, then shrugged; forty-five wasn't old by today's standards – he was barely middle-aged. Catching sight of his once-fair hair in the rear view mirror, he saw that it was threaded with fine grey strands. 'Who am I trying to kid?' he asked his reflection.

Taking the slip road from the motorway, he drove into the centre of town and out towards Beaufort Avenue. It was one-thirty and his belly rumbled as he closed the car door. He thrust his hand into his pocket, removed a packet of extra-strong mints, slipped one into his mouth, opened the wrought iron gate and walked up the cracked paving stones to the front door of number 32.

This time the door flew back as soon as his finger left the bell. Rita Ferris stood in the doorway, her face set as if ready for battle. She took a step back. "Oh, it's you. I thought it was one of those blasted reporters hounding the life out of me again."

"Sorry to bother you…" Richie began.

"You'd better come in then, before they all turn up again. I'm about to get some lunch. You eaten?"

Where is Jason Rayner

He was going to say yes but his belly rumbled before he had a chance to reply. "Yes, well, I know the answer to that one, don't I? I'll put some ham in a bread roll for you."

Thanking her for her trouble and confused as to the agreeable welcome he was receiving, Richie followed her into the kitchen. There had been some sort of transformation, surely. The room had been newly decorated and the kettle and appliances shone with a showroom-new gleam. Watching her making his lunch, he began to think he'd been wrong – she wasn't that old at all – probably mid sixties.

"I hope you don't mind me asking, but your sister – Catherine's mother – how much older than you did you say she was?"

"Why do you ask?" She looked up, the knife poised over the bread roll.

"I thought Cathy's mother had her late in life and you don't seem that old." He wasn't sure whether it had come out right but he needn't have worried; she was flattered, she almost preened.

"I can see you don't miss much. I thought I told you, Norma was two years older than me and was nearly forty-eight when she had Catherine. It was tragic, her dying of cancer and her Jim following her six weeks after – stroke they said but our poor Cathy, being in that room with him for two days." She sighed, seemed to collect her thoughts and said, "Go on into the front room now and I'll make us both a cup of tea. Here, take this with you." She handed him a plate on which sat a large bread roll cut in two and filled with ham.

"This is very kind. You're sure you don't mind me asking a few questions?"

Where is Jason Rayner

"If it will help, you can ask as many as you like," she replied filling the shiny new kettle.

In the front room overlooking the garden and the road where reporters seemed to be gathering once more, Richie asked, "This is obviously all because of these latest developments in the murder of Jennifer Teague, I presume. They'll soon get fed up and leave you in peace.

"Been there ever since last night's news. It was like this when it first happened months ago, I thought they'd got fed up."

"I understand Catherine has been staying with you for a while, whilst you were ill?"

"Catherine? No, what made you think that? I saw her a couple of weeks ago but it was a flying visit. She doesn't stay long. Never has the time, she says. That job of hers, I expect, she's always been the conscientious type."

Richie was surprised. Tracy Golding had given him the impression his client had been staying with her aunt before suddenly turning up in Lockford as if nothing had happened. Watching Rita Ferris pouring another cup of tea from a china teapot, he said, as she handed him his cup, "How well did you know the young woman who was murdered?"

"Jennifer? I've known her since we moved in; she'd have been about twelve then. And after Bill died and Catherine left, she'd pop in to see me most days." She sniffed. "She was a good kid. I don't know who would do such a thing. I'm really going to miss her."

"Were Catherine and she good friends?"

Where is Jason Rayner

She screwed her eyes into slits, bit her bottom lip and as the silence grew she poured him another cup of tea.

"Mrs Ferris?"

"Catherine wasn't one to make friends. Not whilst my Bill was alive. Later, yes, I think she and Jennifer used to go out together occasionally but I wouldn't go so far as to say they were close friends. I would say though that it was not for want of trying on Jennifer's part. My Catherine likes to keep herself to herself." She blew her nose loudly. "Mr Stevens, have the police told you who they think did it? Who killed Jennifer?"

"No. I gather they're still completing their enquiries. Has someone been to see you?"

"A young woman police officer asked me a few questions but I couldn't help her. I'm as much in the dark as anyone."

Richie stood up. "Did Catherine say where she was going when she left you, after her last visit?"

She looked confused. "Of course; didn't I say? She's working in Lockford, down on the south coast."

Later, ignoring the few remaining reporters who half-heartedly tried to question him, as he opened his car door, Richie drove out of the avenue in the direction of the house Jack Robinson had once shared with his wife. He wondered where Cathy Barton had been during the weeks she'd said she was looking after her sick aunt.

At first Vanessa tried to slam the door in his face. He couldn't blame her, if the response to Jennifer

Where is Jason Rayner

Teague's murder had been that experienced by Rita Ferris, Richie might have been tempted to do the same thing. He tried to explain, in the short time it took for her to close the door in his face, but something must have stayed her hand because she spoke to him through what remained of the open doorway. "I told you before, he's with his mistress."

"I don't believe he is, Mrs Robinson. At least he isn't with her now."

She opened the door wider. "You'd better come in. The neighbours have enough to gossip about without me adding to their supply of titbits."

The inside of the house was as neat as the front garden and driveway. She showed him into a room at the back the house overlooking a narrow lawn bordered by flowering shrubs. It looked as if someone had trimmed the lawn with precision, not a blade of grass was out of place.

"Please, sit down, Mr Stevens."

Richie sat on a well-upholstered leather armchair. "I've come to see you because, in the course of my investigation into the disappearance of my client's husband, some issues have arisen which I think you may be able to help unravel. By the way, it's Richie."

"Me?" She frowned. "I don't see how. I thought you'd come to speak to me about Jack."

"I have. You see, my client's name is Kate Rayner but she was formerly known as Cathy Barton." All colour left her face and she plucked at the hem of her cotton cardigan. "You told Sandy about your husband's involvement with Cathy when she was a pupil at your school and I understand you and he became close at that traumatic time."

Where is Jason Rayner

He was choosing his words very carefully, "I wonder if you could tell me about the letter your husband left which made you so sure he'd left you for another woman. Do you still have it?"

"No, I ripped it into small pieces and threw it in the waste bin. But I'll never forget it, if only I could remove the words from my brain so easily. He wrote all the usual platitudes about still loving me. He said he couldn't carry on because, when he was with me, he couldn't forget what he'd done. He apologised but said he'd met an old flame from his college days and they'd fallen in love…Huh!"

Richie could see it was still raw. "And that's the last you saw of him?"

She nodded.

He came straight to the point. "I have reason to suspect that my client's husband Jason Rayner and Jack Robinson might be one in the same. But, as yet, it's only a hunch, I have no real evidence to support my theory."

He'd expected an immediate response but silence filled the space between them. "I'm not really surprised, I knew he'd be with her." She looked down at her hands, which were folded in her lap. "She was always like a drug to him. How could he be so foolish?"

Richie hesitated; her question didn't require a direct answer. "The problem is twofold – on the one hand we believe we know the true identity of the man who has been living in Lockford as Jason Rayner – on the other hand, I can find no one who has actually seen him and I only have his wife's word that he ever existed."

Where is Jason Rayner

Chapter 52

Leaving the house Jack Robinson once shared with his wife, Richie drove in the direction of the city centre. The ham roll he'd eaten earlier had done nothing to alleviate his hunger. Pulling into the car park of The Wheatsheaf, Richie noticed its proximity to the building where Cathy Barton had spent her schooldays. He looked at his watch; it was nearly four o'clock. The Wheatsheaf served meals between midday and ten pm, mostly of the chips with everything variety.

He ordered a meal of beer-battered haddock and chips and bought a glass of lemonade at the bar. He was in the middle of eating his meal when the door opened and three men and two women entered. Their voices were loud and from their conversation Richie gathered they were teachers at Westbank. He finished his meal and went up to the bar.

"Excuse me," he said to the tallest of the three men. "I wonder if you could help me. I couldn't avoid overhearing – I understand you all teach at the school down the road? I'm trying to trace an acquaintance of mine, Jack Robinson. The last I heard of him he was on your staff but I rang the headmaster and he said he'd left. Do any of you know where he might be living?"

A swift glance was exchanged between the three men. "What are you, a reporter is it?"

"Reporter? No, I'm a writer, Bernard Smith." He hoped Sandy's father would forgive him for assuming his identity, and held out his hand. "I met Jack a while ago when I was working on research for my new book and when I finished he said to look him up if I was ever in Sheffield again."

"He left some time ago. Not sure where he went – no one is, not even his wife." One of the women, in her twenties with hair curling around an elfin face, introduced herself. "I'm Imogen Green, a friend of Vanessa Robinson's. We were all shocked when those two broke up."

Richie recognised a talker when he saw one. "Really?" he said, "Take it badly, did she?" He tried to look sympathetic.

"Furious, and I for one don't blame her. She had no idea he was seeing someone else. But I can't say I was surprised – I never did like the way he was so friendly with the year eleven girls."

"Hang on a minute, Imogen, you're making Jack sound like a paedo," a short thickset man intervened.

"Well, if the cap fits," she replied with a shrug.

The taller man moved closer, "Look, if you don't mind, we've all had a busy week, we'd like to have a chat and unwind, if it's all the same to you."

Richie nodded. "Fair enough, sorry to have bothered you." His shoulders drooped and he started to walk away but Imogen took a step towards him. "Whatever the others say," she lowered her voice, "I know Jack Robinson was capable of almost anything. Try looking up some of his old college mates; perhaps they'll know where he is. Oh and by the way, I can smell a reporter a mile off." She grinned and turned back to the group of friends at the bar.

Where is Jason Rayner

It wasn't is if he hadn't thought of trying to contact college friends of Jack Robinson's before, just he wasn't sure how significant it would be. What could they tell him that would make it easier to find him? He supposed it was worth a try. He rang Vanessa Robinson and asked if she knew of any friends her husband had made in college.

"Apart from the one he's supposed to have run off with? Let me see," she hesitated. "I never met any of them but a while back he did say he was going to meet Ben Jennings for a reunion in Bristol, if that's any good."

Thanking her for her time, Richie turned on the ignition and drove away from Sheffield and back towards the south coast. There was nothing more he could do for the moment. He wasn't even sure it was worthwhile trying to contact this Ben Jennings. Beginning to feel uncertain how to continue with his search for the elusive Jason Rayner, Richie switched on the car radio and took a deep breath. He hated driving long distances; they were both tiring and boring. It was almost midnight when he returned to his flat.

Stars shone like diamonds thrown onto black velvet and the warmth of a summer evening wrapped around him as he entered the building. He nodded to the night watchman who was watching an old black and white film on his laptop. He raised his hand to Richie. "Night Mr Stevens," he said, his eyes never leaving the screen.

Richie yawned as he opened the front door to his flat and saw the message light flashing on his answering machine.

Where is Jason Rayner

Catherine's story

Chapter 53

So it is finished. I've fulfilled my commitment to everyone's satisfaction. The therapist will make his report and it will be filed away by the police authorities. I can imagine the summation – *Mrs Rayner was suffering from a paranoid delusion from which I am satisfied she has recovered* or words to that effect.

Of course, it's not the end of my story; the true story that is. To understand the truth I have to take you back to the day of Mason Trent's birthday. I was carrying a tray of doughnuts across the road to the office when I tripped and was rescued by a stranger.

"Steady," he said, "Don't want to drop those, now do we?" His accent wasn't bad, I'd have to give him that. He smiled and I saw blue eyes twinkling down at me. I wasn't fooled, not even for a second but I let him believe I was, at least at the start. The rest of the week unfolded much as I'd told my therapist. As I said, it made sense to stick as near to the truth as possible to avoid pitfalls.

He told me his name was John Rice; it wasn't inventive enough, I could have done much better, I thought. We went to the cinema, dined out, fell into bed together and later bought bicycles. The holiday in Amsterdam was a fabrication. We never went near the place, but spent the time in my flat, mostly in bed and eating take-away food. I made up the story of a holiday to keep the gossips in work off my

Where is Jason Rayner

back; there would be too many questions, what did I do, where did I go, wasn't I lonely on my own, or did my 'boyfriend' stay with me?

As for Jack, he'd abandoned his Welsh accent, some time ago, after an evening of drinking wine in my flat, when I told him I'd known all along.

"So it wasn't that good?"

"No. It was perfect, I doubt if your best friend would have known you." I didn't add 'but I know every line on you face, every touch of your hand and the scent of your skin'. I kept that to myself.

The year passed. I invented an imaginary boyfriend but the name I chose was Jason Rayner, John Rice was far too insignificant, too easy to forget. I liked to think Rayner was unusual but still in keeping with his former identity. Perhaps part of me was already thinking of it as a sort of insurance for the future. It was a name you couldn't easily forget, especially if I mentioned it often enough.

We made certain we were never seen together at the office, just in case, and when we went out we chose out of town restaurants and cinema complexes. It was added security, he said. Nevertheless, it seemed to work. We even had a holiday together but it was in Cornwall, not Devon and we didn't take our bikes, we went by train and stayed in a small B&B off the beaten track, not far from St Ives.

During our second year together, he said he wanted us to get married. I did point out he was still married to Vanessa but he said Jack Robinson was married to her, not John Rice. He'd refused to accept my preference, Jason Rayner, but there was no way I was going to change it.

Where is Jason Rayner

It would be difficult but we could go away, somewhere where we wouldn't be known, somewhere like an island in the back of beyond. We talked about it endlessly but then thought the logistics would be far too complicated and decided we'd perform the ceremony ourselves, in my flat. It was romantic, he said, as he kissed my finger before putting on the ring.

Getting married in Las Vegas was also an invention but one which seemed to satisfy Tracy and the rest of them. Lying to them was beginning to become a habit. Ollie congratulated me but I could see he was hurt and upset.

Life went on, I went to work, my husband continued tutoring his pupils in his flat during the winter and working in the fields in the summer months. He kept his flat, the rent of which I covered when he was short of cash. It was a bolthole, he said, should he ever need it. He was being careful. Both us knew the danger of him being discovered as Jack Robinson. He made as little contact with his landlord as possible and paid his rent by slipping an envelope under his door every month. His pupils knew him as Mr Rice and as the months passed he said Jack Robinson no longer existed and I could see he believed it. That was until Jennifer Teague, who was visiting a friend in Brighton, stopped off in Lockford, on her way home, to look me up.

It was Saturday. A cold wind buffeted the windows of my flat and howled down the street. My husband was in the shower. I could hear him singing as I made our breakfast.

Where is Jason Rayner

"You should have stayed in bed," he said, kissing the back of my neck and I felt his hair, still wet from the shower, against my skin. "Just because, I've a pupil at ten, it doesn't mean you have to get up and make my breakfast."

"No problem. I'm awake, no point in wasting the day."

"You know I won't be back until this evening?"

"You said."

"It's a bit of a pain, having to wait for George to finish his shift at Burger King before I can open his mind to the wonders of Shakespeare." He sat down and picking up his knife and fork began to make short work of his favourite breakfast, a full English, his Saturday treat. "Anyway, it's money and that's the important thing."

Later, after he'd gone, I was in the middle of filling the washing machine when I heard the buzzer and went to look at the viewing screen to see who was waiting outside my door. It was Jennifer Teague. I let her in.

"Cathy, your aunt gave me your address and I thought I'd come to see you on my way home. How are you?"

"Jennifer, come in. This is a surprise. I'm fine; you look well."

She sat on our couch, I made us coffee and we ate some of the cakes I'd baked the day before, whilst we caught up on news of each other's lives. At least that's not quite true, I didn't tell her everything, not about my marriage. If she noticed the ring, she didn't comment.

"Your hair suits you," she said. "And you're happy living in Lockford? We all miss you."

"Perfectly." It wasn't a lie. "I've a good job and I like it here."

"So you won't be coming back soon then?" I thought she looked a bit downcast at this and didn't know how to react.

"I'll visit Rita sometime soon, and you, of course. I'll come, when I have some time off work."

At lunchtime, I suggested we pop to the café around the corner and have lunch before she started on her journey back to Sheffield. However, she said, "I've some shopping to do in town first, sorry. But I'll be in touch. Who knows, I might come down and see you again before long." She scribbled a note on a piece of paper. "My new mobile number, give me a ring, let me know how things are with you."

"I will, thanks."

At the doorway, we hugged awkwardly and I watched as she opened the door of her car, waved, and drove away. Something kept me standing there long after she had driven away from the flat and the road was filled with other people's cars. A cold wind blew through my hair and I shivered, unaware that we'd exchanged empty promises as I was never to see Jennifer Teague again.

Jack's story
via his laptop

Chapter 54

At first, I wondered how long I could keep it up without her recognising me? It seemed impossible; a disguise is just that, surely I wouldn't be able to maintain the deception without being discovered? In the event, I decided to play it by ear, but resolutions are meant to be broken, I suppose, and mine were woefully inadequate.

We met the day I saw her with the tray of doughnuts; we dated, we slept together and still I thought she didn't recognise me but I was never quite sure whether she was playing me along or not. You could never tell with Cathy, it was one of the first things I'd noticed about her. You could never tell what she was thinking. As it turned out she told me she'd known from the beginning.

Weeks turned into months and the first year disappeared like smoke on a windy day; soon I felt confident enough to take the extra step. We were unofficially married in a ceremony in her flat, but as far as we were both concerned, it was merely a formality – she was now my wife, in all but name.

Although we considered ourselves to be a couple, we decided it would be better not to introduce me to her work colleagues. It was important that I still kept a low profile; I had what I wanted and was content. I retained my flat for tutoring purposes, whilst summer fruit picking jobs helped with our funds. It wasn't really necessary as she had enough money for

Where is Jason Rayner

us both but I still had my pride. I looked upon my flat as a safeguard, an escape if anything went wrong and I needed to hide away for a bit.

Life followed a calm, relaxed, pattern until the day I saw Jennifer Teague walking towards me. I was on my way to Cathy's flat after tutoring George when I decided to stop off in the town centre to buy her some flowers

"I thought so," she said. "I knew you'd be with her."

I contemplated telling her she had mistaken me for someone else but could see it wouldn't wash. She knew who I was. I attempted to bluff it out but it was a weak attempt; it was no good pretending I was someone else, she'd recognised me. "You're wrong, I live on my own. I wanted to get away from people like you."

"Hard luck. Weak story. Time to pay up, Jack; we'll discuss how much over a coffee, shall we?" she said, leading me towards a café in a side street.

Afterwards, I had no illusion that she would ever leave me alone. She'd bleed me dry. I was a cash cow as far as she was concerned and there was nothing I could do about it. So I went along with it for a while but after Christmas I decided to take matters into my own hands. I made an excuse to Cathy about having to go away for a day or two and took the train to Sheffield, safe in the knowledge that even my own mother wouldn't recognise me. My hair was almost non-existent, I'd had it shaved, my eyes were now blue and a thick beard covered the lower half of my face. Although it hadn't taken Jennifer Teague long to recognise me before, I

Where is Jason Rayner

considered the beard changed my appearance considerably and wished I'd thought of it earlier. With my coat collar turned up and a knitted beanie hat pulled down to my eyebrows, I went to pay an unexpected visit to my tormentor.

Waiting in the cold was the worst bit. I shivered at the bus stop opposite her house aware that the property next door belonged to Cathy's aunt. The wind was blowing the trees in the Ferris's garden and I saw them tapping against the windows as if begging to be admitted. I thought I saw a curtain move in an upstairs window and imagined Rita Ferris watching my every move. I hung my head trying to make it look as if I was searching the Internet on my mobile phone whilst waiting for a bus.

It seemed an age before she opened the door, the dog snapping at her heels. I turned away pretending to look at the bus timetable on the wall just as snow was beginning to fall in earnest. The wind swept down the avenue lifting the snowflakes into a swirling eddy around my legs as I risked turning around to watch her progress. She walked along the pavement, the small dog trotting beside her, passing the Ferris's house until she reached a pathway between the houses. I knew it led to a wooded area at the back of the avenue, which was surrounded by fields.

I picked up the bag at my feet; it felt heavier than it had done when I'd packed it earlier. Unzipping a side pocket, I removed the thin leather thong and then slung the bag over my shoulder, hoping I'd have the guts to go through with it.

Where is Jason Rayner

Chapter 55

Following her at a safe distance, I saw her entering the wood. She took a ball from her pocket and threw it amongst the trees as the dog barked excitedly and ran off. Stamping her feet on the frozen ground, she wrapped her arms around her body, and I saw snowflakes clinging to her short spiky hair, turning it as white as an old woman's. Taking cover behind a large tree trunk, I watched as she removed a packet of cigarettes from her pocket, cupped her hands to the flame from a match, and lit up as she waited for the dog to return.

She didn't hear my approach; the howling wind, the dog barking and a low flying plane overhead masked the sound of my feet padding over the frozen ground. I was standing behind her when I heard a sharp intake of break. The leather thong bit into my skin, as I tightened it around her neck, the sound of her last breath sighing like the wind in the trees.

To say it was easy would be an overstatement but I was amazed she didn't put up more of a fight; I had the element of surprise in my favour, of course, which was an advantage. Did blackmailers ever consider they were playing a dangerous game and normal rules of behaviour didn't apply? This one didn't. I could see the shock in her eyes as I strangled the life out of her.

Afterwards, I walked back the way I'd come and was sure, this time, the curtains definitely twitched in the upstairs window of number 32. I wasn't

Where is Jason Rayner

bothered. What would she see? A man she didn't recognise taking a walk on a cold winter's day. She'd have forgotten about it by the time she settled down to watch Coronation Street.

Deciding there was little point in booking into an hotel, I slept overnight in the waiting room of Sheffield's busiest railway station, one of many who'd been caught out by train cancellations and bad weather and then caught the first train back to Lockford the following morning. I'd thought it all out; security cameras would see a man whose features were indistinct. I'd made sure to turn away at the first sight of a camera and besides the clothes I was wearing, together with my beard, meant little of my face would be visible. The beard would be a casualty of the day's events and would disappear as soon as I returned to my flat, which was a shame because Cathy had said she liked it. She said it made me look like a spy and the name Jason Rayner suited me so much better than John Rice.

My future plans were unclear. We'd probably have a holiday, when Cathy was able to take the time off from work. We could start planning it now. It would be something to look forward to. Spring was just around the corner and the future was looking bright. I wouldn't be looking over my shoulder for Jennifer Teague to bleed me dry at the first opportunity and my past would be just that – a thing of the past.

I started to hum tunelessly as the train pulled into Lockford station some hours later. Even the icy rain didn't dampen my spirits. In the small supermarket on the corner, I bought a bottle of merlot, and let myself into my flat. It was beginning to smell musty, so I opened the windows and let in the icy air for a while. However, the flat was cold enough without me adding to it. The smell would soon wear off, I thought, switching on the electric fire and closing the windows. After making a cup of strong black coffee, I went into the bathroom and shaved off my beard. I couldn't wait to get rid of the image of a bearded man following a young girl along a path into a frost-coated wood. Then I picked up the bottle of wine and headed for Cathy's flat, the events of the previous day almost forgotten.

Cathy didn't ask too many questions about where I'd been but I had a funny sort of feeling she knew. Perhaps paranoia was a side effect of my actions, I thought, unwilling to let the events of the past few days lessen my optimism about the future.

"Shall I order a take-away for tonight - save us bothering to cook?" I asked, as she dressed for work the next day.

"Yes, that would be nice," she replied but I definitely detected a coolness towards me. Perhaps she was waiting for me to tell her where I'd been in detail. Perhaps she suspected I was having an affair? Yes that would be it. As she was leaving, I caught up with her in the hallway and turned her to face me.

"You know I love you, don't you?"

She nodded.

"I'm mad about you. Don't ever forget it. We've been through such a lot to be together, remember." I bent forward and kissed her mouth, tasting youth on her lips.

She sighed, kissed me back, and said, "You shaved it off then," and I knew I'd been worrying for nothing.

Where is Jason Rayner

The following day, it was on the local news in Sheffield. Rita told Cathy that every time she switched on the TV, there was a report of a young girl's body being found in woods at the back of the houses on Beaufort Avenue. It took a day or two before it was headline news in the Daily Mail; it had travelled to Lockford; there was no escaping it.

Cathy wouldn't leave it alone.

"I can't believe it," she said, sitting down at the kitchen table. "Jennifer? Who would want to kill Jennifer?"

"She was a friend of yours?" I asked, switching on the kettle as if it was just a normal day and my pulse wasn't drumming in my neck.

"She was so kind. Who would do such a dreadful thing?"

I made the tea, hot and sweet for her, put my arm around her shoulders, sympathised, made all the right moves, until she went to bed before me.

There was a small item on the ten o'clock news and from the safety of Cathy's flat, I watched the unfolding story. The police were on the lookout for a man, approximately six foot tall, slim build who had been walking down the short-cut to the field at the rear of the properties on Beaufort Avenue at approximately two thirty on the afternoon of …etc…etc..anyone with any information please contact etc….etc..It was the usual news report when such an event occurred, nothing specific enough to warn off the perpetrator but enough to encourage witnesses to ring the police. I felt secure enough to pour another glass of wine and watch a chat show until midnight, knowing that Cathy would be asleep

Where is Jason Rayner

by then and not asking me unanswerable questions about Jennifer Teague.

The following morning, I switched to another channel but there it was again. I couldn't get away from it. Cathy constantly asked the question, 'who would do such a thing?' until I knew I had to spend a day or two alone. I made an excuse about having to catch up with some work at my flat, before I put it on the market but I was beginning to think she didn't believe a single word I said.

Catherine's story

Chapter 56

Somehow, I managed to get up, go to work and behave as if everything was normal but the news had shocked me to the core. When Rita phoned to tell me about what happened, she was distraught. I said, "I'd come up, aunt, but it's a bit difficult for me at the moment, we are busy in work."

"There are reporters everywhere – morning, noon, and night. What am I going to do now? She used to see to things for me."

I wasn't sure exactly what she meant by this but a shiver crept down my spine. "See to things?" I asked, dreading the answer.

"Yes, you know, she bought me all those new things for the kitchen, got the decorators in, paid for a gardener."

I was stunned. "You let her pay for doing up the house?"

She didn't seem surprised. "Yes, and my make-over – that's what she called it – my make-over. I couldn't get over the difference it made, everyone said so, Brenda Cox said she would never have recognised me, even Charlie Bates from number 12 passed comment, said we should go to the cinema some time. He's been lonely since Vera passed away."

"But where did Jennifer get the money from, she's a student, she was always short of cash? And why would she do such a thing?" I was confused.

"What? Oh Jennifer, yes," she hesitated, no doubt still thinking of the effect her 'new look' had on the neighbours. "Well, I asked her that once, after she'd got Bert Hicks in to paint the kitchen.

"And?"

"And, she said, not to worry about the money, there was plenty more where that came from and it was owed to me."

"That's strange, surely she didn't owe you anything did she?"

"Yes, well, it struck me as strange too, so I asked her how, and she said a funny thing."

"Funny?"

"Mmm…she said, 'if it wasn't for me, Cathy would never have met him'."

"But a few days later, I found your diary and then I understood. I know I shouldn't have read it, I just wanted to read about the days before you went away."

My hand began to shake.

"Catherine?"

It took all my will power to answer as I did. "Diary?"

"I read all about you and him, see, your teacher, the one who talked to us in the Mall."

"I'm just shocked that Jennifer would do such a thing." I muttered trying not to think about the diary. But Rita didn't seem to notice.

"I expect she had her reasons and she was a very kind girl, you know that, don't you dear?"

I mumbled a suitable reply then added, "It makes it so odd. Why would anyone want to murder a girl like Jennifer? I don't understand."

Where is Jason Rayner

The answer died on my lips. It was becoming clearer by the minute – she was blackmailing him.

"It's those druggies, I expect, they hang around the streets, like they own them It's the government's fault of course, I said to Brenda Cox, only the other day…"

Rita's voice bemoaning the state of the country filtered into my ear, and although I heard the words, I ignored them. My head was thumping. Jennifer had been blackmailing him and, buying things for Rita with the proceeds. In addition to which Rita knew about what happened between Jack and me when I was in Westbank. I couldn't believe my aunt had gone along with it; she must have thought, in some twisted way, that it was due to her. The answer to who had a motive for killing my only friend was staring me in the face.

After I put the phone down, I slumped in the chair, as memories, begging to be let in, refused to stay put. I could feel the weight of my father's dead body pinning me to the floor, hear the sound of Bill's heavy breathing outside my bedroom door and see Jack's face as he kissed me and promised to love me forever.

Where is Jason Rayner

Jack's last story
Via his laptop

Chapter 57

Leaving her flat, I felt the clouds lift and could forget Jennifer Teague's face for the first time in days. I told Catherine I needed to spend some time at my place, made up some excuse, whilst all the time feeling she could see right thought me. Perhaps the time had come for me to get away from Lockford, disappear, go to Manchester and pretend I'd had a life there since leaving Vanessa. What if Cathy decided to call the police? She wouldn't, would she? I felt sweat breaking out on my forehead as I inserted my key in the lock, not sure about the answers to the questions which refused to go away. I had to think.

Closing the door behind me, I sighed, walked over to the window and looked down into the dingy street. A disused office block, gradually falling into decay, stood opposite, sightless windows staring at me, each one with a question. Closing my eyes, I tried to remove the images that were creeping back. Her face as I'd tightened the thong around her neck, the choking sound that I was sure could be heard a mile away, the dog barking at my heels.

Perhaps I was worrying for nothing. Cathy loved me, she would understand, I had to do it to save us. We were together at last; I was no longer Jack Robinson and Jennifer Teague had been the only threat to our life together. Rita Ferris no longer had Cathy's diary, apparently my blackmailer had persuaded her to destroy it, for Cathy's sake. I don't know how she managed it but she told me the old lady didn't want a fuss and seemed happy that I was being made to pay. So now I'd made sure we were safe and I had to make her see that if we stuck together, we'd survive.

The air smelled stale, a small stack of mail had collected behind the door since my last visit. I picked up the letters, mostly advertisements and offers of insurance cover. There was nothing for me; they were all addressed to the previous owner, a Miss N. Childs. I sat in the chair behind the small desk where I sat when I coached my pupils and opened my laptop to continue with my story.

I've been writing this ever since I first met Cathy Barton. It's been a catharsis and no one knows it exists, except me; it's in a file named Shakespeare's Romeo and Juliet. Time becomes a nebulous concept and, as I write, I relax and let it flow over me; so I'm not exactly sure how long I've been sitting here when I hear the sound of someone knocking on the front door.

"It's me, open the door." So she's followed me - she does know - she wants an explanation. Pasting on an expression of innocence, I go to let her in, still wondering if she's worked it all out, whilst knowing that she has……………………………….

Where is Jason Rayner

Catherine's story

Chapter 58

I couldn't stop thinking about Jennifer. The more I thought about it the more convinced I became. I hadn't seen my husband since he left yesterday, he said he wanted to spend some time at his flat, there were things he had to do, pupils he had to see.

The newspaper reports said that Jennifer had been killed on the 15th and I remembered he had been away from the 14th to the 16th and that when he came home he was jumpy. I thought he'd been afraid someone had recognised him and had taken himself off to avoid discovery. He'd shaved off his beard even though he knew I liked it.

Nevertheless, I was scared. The two had to be linked, his absence and her death. I'd worked it out after Rita's phone call; Jennifer was blackmailing him. In some ways, I couldn't blame her; in some ways, he deserved what he got. But love got in the way and I wasn't used to dealing with such strong emotions as I'd buried them along with parents when I was nine years old.

Thoughts spun around in my head until I felt dizzy, I was getting nowhere. Did I trust him? Had it been an accident? Was I imagining it all? When I could stand it no longer, I decided to drive to his flat. I wanted to confront him, ask him to explain where he'd been that day and what he had done.

The air was cold but nothing like the weather they'd had in Sheffield. Rita said Jennifer's father had dug a path to her front door so that she could go

Where is Jason Rayner

shopping. I shivered, remembering the photo of the woods where the body had been found. It was where she liked to walk with Jessie; it was covered in frost and a fine layer of snow. Tears pricked my eyelids as I wondered if she'd put up a fight, if she'd marked him in any way and what had happened to Jessie?

I stood trembling outside his flat until I could put off the moment of confrontation no longer. There was a light on in the main room; I could see it from the street. The shabby front door with the numbers indicating 12a, 12b, 12c, had long since given up the ghost where the accompanying names of their occupants were concerned. I pushed the outer door and it opened with a creak. Inside, there was a dim light in the entrance hall that flickered as if about to expire. There were no signs of occupation on the lower floor and I knew from my husband that the rest of the building was also unoccupied. There was a threadbare carpet covering the staircase, which snagged on the rubber soles of my shoes as I climbed the stairs to number 12b.

Standing outside his flat, I hesitated. I could go home and wait for him to come back and explain or I could face him. My hand was poised to knock, when I heard the sound of a crash followed by a curse from within. I started to turn away but my feet wouldn't move, so now I had no choice. I knocked. "It's me, open the door," I called out.

His hand was bleeding from a small cut and broken glass was strewn across the kitchen floor, "What are you doing here?" he asked and I noticed that his hand was shaking.

Where is Jason Rayner

"You did it, didn't you?" the words fell out unbidden. I hadn't intended them to spill out quite so soon but it was like a dam bursting and it was too late to take them back.

"Did what, for heaven's sake? Break a glass?"

"Kill Jennifer Teague."

"You're not serious?" It was a waste of time him denying it, I could tell he was lying. There was a time when I would have believed his lies but no longer. He did this thing with his shoulder whenever he was lying, a tell, I think it's called – some poker players use it, apparently – it's a sort of clue that they're bluffing. Anyway he raised his shoulder a fraction then dropped it almost immediately.

"She was blackmailing you, wasn't she?"

He sat down. "It was an accident." I could see him frantically clutching at straws, finding an excuse for me to believe him.

"Not according to the police report in the papers."

"You know you can't believe all you read in the papers. It was an accident, I tell you." His voice was raised and for the first time in my life, I thought he looked ugly.

"She was my friend." I accused him, angry now. "How could you do such a thing? How could you murder her?" The word murder is ugly, the act even uglier, I know how it feels.

"If she told, I'd go to prison, our lives would never be the same again, the publicity, reporters, you wouldn't like it. They'd want to know all about you."

It was a threat. He was warning me about what I could expect our future to be like if he hadn't silenced her. He thought he could twist me around his little finger. Bill Ferris's face swam before me, 'Don't tell, Cathy, or they'll take you away from us and put you in a children's home.'

I turned away from him. "You can do as you like, we're finished. I'm leaving and if they ask me I'll tell them the truth." I'd reached the door when I felt his hand grab my arm. I tried to wriggle free but he pulled me towards him.

"I can't let you do that, Cathy. You do realise why, don't you?" His hand was firmly clamped over my mouth. I was terrified, thinking that this was what it must have been like for Jennifer. Blind fury swept through me and I struggled, managing to bring my knee up into his groin. He winced, cried out in pain, his hand leaving my mouth. Then with my free arm, I spun around and circled his neck before the pain could wear off. We toppled forward, both of us in a heap on the floor. He was underneath me and I felt his grip on my arm loosen.

I wrenched my body away from his and stood up, ready to run but then I saw the blood.

Where is Jason Rayner

Chapter 59

Afraid to touch him, I crouched over his prone body. "I'll call for an ambulance," I said, in the silence. "Open your eyes, please, I'm scared." My nine-year-old self appeared and spoke the words, I'd said before. I was trapped, but this time I could move, and do something about it.

I opened my bag, found my make-up mirror and slid it towards his mouth. When I inspected it, the surface was clear. I stood up. What should I do? There was no doubt that my husband was dead; calling an ambulance would be useless. I had to get away from him; I had to get away from the shabby flat, with its peeling wallpaper and ghastly contents. I wanted to run as far away from this as possible.

I hardly remember running down the stairs and walking back to my car. I prayed that I could stop my hands from shaking long enough to turn the key in the ignition and drive home without causing an accident.

"Cold one, should snow later," the caretaker of my block of flats, said, as I parked my car in my allocated space.

With my head down, I mumbled, "Yes, looks like it." and moved quickly, as far away from him as I could, in case he could read the terror in my eyes.

When I reached my flat, I opened the door, leaned against it and gradually sank to the floor. It was as if my whole life had slid backwards and I was a child again. I could smell the rancid scent of a body whose life had left it; my father's lifeless form pinning me to the ground, a weight from which I would never escape.

My phone began to ring and in my confused state, I thought for one moment that it might be him and I'd been mistaken and he'd woken up. Rushing to pick it up, I heard Ollie say, "Kate? How are you feeling?"

He was worried, I hadn't turned up for work and there had been no explanatory phone call from me. I swallowed and tried to think up an excuse but all rational thought escaped me and I started to sob, "Ollie, I've done a terrible thing."

He didn't ask what, just replied, "I'm coming; I'll be with you in ten minutes."

When I opened the door to him he still didn't ask any questions. He made me sit down, found a bottle in the cupboard and poured a large measure of brandy into a glass and handed it to me. I clutched the glass with both hands to stop them from shaking then spluttered as I gulped the amber liquid.

"Steady now, take your time and when you're ready you can tell me all about it."

Looking back, I expect he thought I'd had a row with my husband, a lover's tiff, nothing too dreadful. But when I felt able to tell him what had happened, he bit his bottom lip, poured a small measure of brandy into a glass for himself and another for me, then said, "We'll have to go back to the flat. We must make sure he's actually dead. You might have been mistaken, he might just be concussed."

Where is Jason Rayner

The fact that Ollie was now saying we and not you gave me an enormous feeling of relief. I was no longer alone.

When we arrived at the flat, I opened the door with the keys I'd taken earlier from the table near the door. There was no way I was going to risk someone walking in on him; somehow I'd had enough sense to lock the door before I'd fled down the stairs.

Ollie walked into the room ahead of me and I heard him gasp as he bent down.

"There's no doubt?"

"None." He leaned forward and peered at the gash that had stopped oozing blood into the threadbare rug.

It was dark outside, and the overhead light cast a yellowish glow over the body.

"What am I going to do, Ollie? They'll think I've killed him, especially when they discover his true identity."

Still he didn't ask any awkward questions.

"We have to get rid of the body and clean this place - your flat as well. It's important that we remove all traces of him."

"I shouldn't have involved you in this. I know I should tell the police what happened but I don't think I could bear it to come out and have to live through it all again." My voice was rising in panic. During the drive to the flat, I'd given him a brief outline of my sham marriage to Jack Robinson. I didn't tell Ollie everything of course but just enough to make sure he knew there was no way I could ring the police. "They'd never believe me, they'd arrest me for his murder, I'd be locked away," my voice sounded odd, as if it didn't belong to me.

Where is Jason Rayner

"Steady now. I'll help." He thought for a moment. "I know a place. They'll never find him. Leave it to me."

I wanted to let him take charge, I wanted to be led by the hand like a child and told it would all be OK. I wanted an end to it at last, to be free.

It seems so unreal now, impossible to believe that we actually did it. At the time I felt as if I was in a dream and now even more so. How could two people such as Oliver Watts and myself have carried out such a plan so efficiently?

We began by Ollie rolling the body in the blood-stained rug and securing each end with a ball of string he'd found in a kitchen drawer. I don't think I've mentioned it before but Ollie used to play squash in the Leisure Centre on Thursday evenings with a friend of his, and, although he was thin, his muscles were firm and strong. I helped him to pick up the rug but with difficulty as he staggered under the weight of the body.

"You'll need his car keys," Ollie said.

On the landing, I watched him struggle down the stairs then followed him into the street. The four by four with the number plate A1 JR was parked outside. I clicked the remote as instructed then watched, unable to move, as my husband slid into the boot of his own car.

"Right, first things first. I'll go over to the supermarket in the next street and pick up some bleach and two pairs of thin latex gloves and then we'll clean the flat and staircase. Go back inside and wait for me."

Where is Jason Rayner

I nodded and, like an automaton which had been programmed to complete a task, walked up the stairs leading to the second floor and, closing my eyes, leaned against the wall outside the flat.

When he returned, he made me go inside and sit in a chair whilst he cleaned every surface, using the ancient cleaner stored in the cupboard to vacuum the floor before emptying the contents into a plastic carrier. The laptop, phone, degree certificates and other personal items he tipped into a black bin bag telling me we'd go through it all later.

"Wait, there's a safe," I said, suddenly snapping out of my inertia. It's in the cupboard at the side of the sink. There's a false back to it."

Ollie stopped what he was doing and moved towards the sink, bent down and removed the back panel. "Combination?"

My mind went blank. All I could see was my husband lying on the floor in a pool of blood. I started to shake.

"Take it easy, deep breaths, forget what's happened, and think," Ollie's instructions filled the space between us and, as my heart rate slowed, my mind cleared.

"2108." It was the date we first met – our blind date – the twenty first of August.

Emptying the contents of the safe into the bin liner and replacing the false back to the cupboard, Ollie stood up. "We're done here."

He was satisfied he'd removed all traces of us both and after I'd locked up behind us, he told me to go ahead and wait for him in the car, whilst he found a dustbin in a side street in which to place the rubbish in the plastic carrier.

Where is Jason Rayner

I sat in the car in the darkness and waited for Ollie, hardly daring to think about the contents of the boot and what we were going to do about it. As the night closed in around me, I shut my eyes and tried to believe none of it had happened. I'd done it before and saw no reason why I shouldn't be able to do it again.

Where is Jason Rayner

Chapter 60

It seemed an age before Ollie returned and sat alongside me.

"I know this is going to be difficult for you but you have to drive his car and follow me," he said, turning to face me.

"I.. I can't"

"You must. Trust me, it's the only way. We'll drive to the common on the edge of town and I'll tell you what we are going to do next. You can do it ,Kate."

I nodded unable to speak.

"Good. Remove all but his car keys from the key ring and hand the rest to me then follow me out of town.

I swallowed, "I'll try," my voice came out as a croak.

"Good girl."

Looking back, I don't know how I managed to start the car without stalling. I'd driven it several times before of course but never with my head full of the events of that evening. I tried to think of something else but it was impossible. Switching on the music system, I accessed the downloads and let the melodies take me to another place as I followed Ollie's car out of town and on to the common.

Luckily there was no moon that night; a thick blanket of cloud protected us from any prying eyes. I drew up behind Ollie and waited as he closed his car

Where is Jason Rayner

door and, without a sound, slid into the passenger seat beside me.

"Well done, the next bit is easy, as long as you don't focus on what went on before. Just follow me. It's going to be a long journey but the night is closing in, and if we take care not to exceed the speed limit on the motorways, we'll be OK. You've got this far, you can do it, Kate."

"Where are we going?" I asked, my voice barely above a whisper. In the darkness, I could hear Ollie's breathing, slow and measured. He was taking charge of the situation.

"Don't worry. I know a place." He was no longer the shy young man who blushed when I spoke to him.

"Ollie, stop. Tell me where are we going?" I was afraid he was leading us into more trouble.

"I said, don't worry. We'll be sitting at our desks in the morning, just as if nothing had happened. You must say you tried ringing the office to say you had an upset stomach but your phone was playing up and the landline was being repaired."

He'd thought of everything, down to the last detail. An image of him, working on an itemized computer spread sheet came into my mind and I thought about how everyone underestimated him, myself included.

I waited until he started up his car then followed him, my heart pounding like a jackhammer. We were heading miles away from Lockford and I still had no idea where we were going. Gradually my pulse rate slowed as his car hit the motorway slip road and I followed him on to the M25 until we eventually joined the M4 leading to South Wales.

Where is Jason Rayner

I still can't think about that night without shaking but eventually Ollie turned the car off the road and into a lane, which was little more than a track and I followed him for another mile or so until we reached a quarry. It was in the middle of nowhere, disused and, I hoped, abandoned long ago. We hadn't passed a house for miles.

Somehow between us we managed to lift the body out of the boot, still rolled up in the carpet.

Ollie had parked on the edge of the quarry. I'd parked alongside him. In the moonlight I could see the water gleaming like polished glass far below us. It had stopped raining but the ground underfoot was damp. I saw him bend down, and, using a folded up penknife he'd taken from his pocket, cut the string binding the carpet ends. "We'll have to burn the carpet," he said. "I'll see to it, you don't have to worry. We must do this right."

He stood up. "OK, come on, help me to carry him to his car," Ollie instructed.

"What are you going to do?"

"Leave the keys in the ignition, I'll put him in the driver's seat. I can't see anyone finding him here, the quarry has been flooded for years and it's almost bottomless but just in case, we'll make it look like suicide."

I stood and watched Ollie arrange the body in the front seat, then turn the keys in the ignition and release the handbrake.

"Kate, help me to push it over," he said, his breath coming in short gasps.

I closed my eyes and followed instructions but should have covered my ears, as, after what seemed

Where is Jason Rayner

like an eternity, I heard the splash as the four by four entered the water, a sound I was to hear again and again in my dreams. Then Ollie took Jack's house keys from his pocket and threw them over the side.

"What if they find him, what if he comes back to the surface? " My voice was showing signs of hysteria, the pitch high and disjointed. Ollie wrapped me to him in a bear hug.

"They won't, I promise you. No one comes here anymore. This quarry is deep and this is the last anyone will see of him. Trust me. You're quite safe. We have plenty of time to cover our tracks, no one comes here - I told you."

"How can you be so sure?"

"When we were teenagers I used to visit a great uncle, who lived in a village five or six miles away, with my cousin. We found this place one day when we were on our bikes and were told not to go near it, as it was dangerous. That was years ago and I understand they stopped quarrying in this part of South Wales in the middle of the last century."

I clung to him, afraid to let go. "How am I going to pretend none of this has happened?" I asked.

"You will, with my help. At the weekend we'll make a start on cleaning your flat. I've an idea but I have to think it out properly first. Now come on, we must get back if we're to make it in time for work in the morning. Besides you look frozen stiff."

We hardly spoke to each other on the return journey. "Try and rest," Ollie said, once we reached the motorway.

It was an impossible request; I didn't believe I'd ever be able to rest again. I kept thinking about whether the plan Ollie was formulating would succeed but I wasn't aware then that Ollie was one step ahead of me.

It had taken us five hours to reach the quarry and it took four and a half to drive back, the traffic in the early hours being almost non-existent.

We arrived at the office separately and on time the next morning. Fortunately Mason Trent was on a skiing holiday with his family in the French Alps, Tracy was off on the sick and Larry Arbuthnot left the rest of us to get on with our work, except for the odd appearance when he vaguely asked us if we were OK and if there were any problems to let him know.

It was all I could do not to laugh hysterically at this. How would he respond if I told him of my problems? Mechanically, I worked through the hours until it was time to finish for the day.

"I could give you a lift home if you like, Kate," Ollie suggested. "I'm going your way."

We had driven out of the centre of Lockford, before either of us spoke. We have to clean your place now, Kate. It must be as if he'd never existed. I've been thinking of a way out of this. And I think I've found the answer."

So that was how we came up with the idea. No, it was always Ollie's idea really. My husband would disappear on a cycling holiday. We'd wait until the weather got a bit warmer. I think I suggested Devon; I'd booked my spring holiday off work some time ago. It was only four weeks away. Ollie said there would be no problem as he'd already booked a week off at the same time as me, anyway.

Where is Jason Rayner

"There's no hurry, Kate. If this is to work, we mustn't rush it. We've got all the time in the world to think things out properly."

Tears pricked behind my eyelids. Was I looking at the one man in my life I could trust? He was risking prison for someone he worked with and he'd asked for nothing in return, he hadn't even asked for an explanation since that night.

I made up my mind. "Before we do, there's something I think you should know, Ollie."

He reached over and patted my hand. "OK but let's clean your place first, then we can sit down and talk. I won't be happy until we've made sure every trace of him is gone."

We arrived at the allocated parking area for my flat and he parked in the visitors' space. As I slid my key into the lock of my front door, I turned towards him. "Oh, and it's not Kate, Ollie, my name is Cathy Barton."

The rest of it came out, and to my surprise, this time I didn't hold back. He led me to the sofa and kept hold of my hand as I told him the story and when I finished he kissed me; a reassuring peck on the cheek, nothing more, nothing too scary. I began to sob.

He didn't speak just handed me his handkerchief and waited until the worst was over.

"Go and dry your face, Kate and I'll get started on the cleaning, then tomorrow we'll check the contents of the bin liner from his flat," he said, walking towards the kitchen.

"It's Cathy," I said, through my tears, but he didn't answer.

Where is Jason Rayner

Chapter 61

It was fortunate that I'd already explained about my past to Ollie because the next day was Saturday and we had time to look at the contents of my husband's flat. The framed phony degree certificates were easily destroyed. Ollie shredded them in the small shredder he'd brought with him from his house.

"You think of everything," I said, but he just smiled and carried on sliding the paper into the machine.

Jack Robinson's wallet contained a small amount of cash but we also had the money from the safe, which was considerable.

"You take it. I don't need it," I said.

"I couldn't, it's yours. He was your husband."

"Please Ollie. I've enough; I don't want any of it. It would only remind me."

He hesitated, saw the look on my face then put the money to one side. "Thanks," he muttered, opening up the laptop.

There were emails from pupils wanting to make arrangements for further appointments. "I'll deal with these," Ollie said. "Put the kettle on, Kate, whilst I sent a blanket reply saying he's moving on and wishes them well for their exams."

I'd finished brewing a pot of tea for us both when Ollie said, "Look at this!" He turned the laptop towards me and my pulse began to race. "He's written it all down. It's in one of his files. It's like a diary, everything that happened since his mother died and he first met you, as far as I can make out at first glance."

There was no way I was going to let Ollie look at it without me so we spent the rest of the day reading about Jack's version of events up until the moment he opened the door of his flat to me and it all spun out of control.

"I'll kill the hard drive and put the shell out for the gypsies with the rest of the scrap from my mother's back yard."

"Kill the hard drive?"

He smiled. "Nothing as gruesome as the past few days I assure you, a hammer should do the trick."

Laughter threatened to spill out of my mouth in a waterfall of hysteria so I stood up and went to find a large envelope in which to place the money for Oliver.

The weeks passed during which we were biding our time until our holidays arrived when we could begin the next stage of our plan.

Eventually, we finished work and began our fortnight's holiday break. In work, I told them I was going to Devon and Ollie said he was visiting a friend in France. The weather had been steadily improving and we left Lockford on the Saturday morning in bright sunshine, stopping off for lunch in a restaurant along the way. Ollie drove my car and we reached Devon in time for afternoon tea at our hotel. We decided that he would stay in the car whilst I checked us in then he would go straight up to the room with our bags. I waited until the reception area became busy then headed for the desk.

Our room was large with a view over a landscaped back garden, the bed was a double but Ollie insisted on sleeping on the couch until the day arrived when my 'husband' would disappear.

For two days, Ollie hid from view until the day when I drove to the river path, unloaded my bicycle and rode off; Ollie stayed in our room with a *Do not Disturb* notice placed on the outside of the door.

I had been cycling for about ten minutes when I decided this was the place to stop. Standing at the side of my bike, I waited until someone came along. I suppose I'd been standing there about five minutes or so when Sandy found me.

It was as Ollie had anticipated – wait until someone arrives – there'll be someone able to back up your story with the police, when you report Jason Rayner as missing, he'd said. However, there was a slight problem. It turned out that Sandy Smith worked for a Private Investigator and later wanted him to help me find my missing spouse. She was kind and only trying to help, I wanted to say no, I preferred to leave it to the police but Ollie said it would look odd and anyway they'd never find out what had happened. He was so sure of it that I agreed, even though I felt bad at involving Sandy in the deception.

I hadn't forgotten about Jennifer. The police were still looking for her murderer but there had been no mention of Jack Robinson being involved in any way so I felt safe enough to allow Richard Stevens and Sandy to continue looking for Jason Rayner. However, it was Rita who threatened to rock the foundations of the story Ollie and I had devised. Rita, who risked toppling the insubstantial house of cards I'd erected where my 'husband' was concerned.

"I have to go to Sheffield to see her." I told Oliver, after I'd spoken to Rita on the phone the previous evening.

He wasn't sure. "Could be dangerous; Richie Stevens is no fool."

"I have to see her." I was adamant. "I don't know what she is going to say, she's a bit of a loose cannon, you know."

"Right, well, I'll cover your back here. You ring Trent, say your aunt is ill and I'll keep tabs on Richie Stevens at this end."

"So we are agreed?"

"It might be a good idea to disappear as far as the police and Stevens are concerned, at least for a while, anyway. You haven't told them about Sheffield, about Rita?"

"No, they think I'm Kate Newson, all they know in the office is I have a relative living somewhere in the north of England."

"Right, that will give you time to sort things out with Rita then."

It seemed so simple, another plan, another shared conspiracy, but the very fact that I wasn't going through this alone gave me hope for the future. I was beginning to think nothing could go wrong.

The problem of whether I should drive or take the train was solved by Ollie, who said, "If you go by train and they come looking for you, there are CCTV cameras in operation, and if you take your car it's traceable, so I suggest you take mine. If anyone asks, I'll say I'm using my bike to get some exercise."

He'd covered every eventuality, I thought, as I hit the motorway heading north.

I noticed the change in the house immediately. The garden was neat, the trees having been trimmed and the lawn at a manageable length. When she opened the door, I gasped, she looked years younger. It wasn't until the next day, when she'd stopped fussing over whether I'd had enough to eat, had a good night's rest and was wearing enough clothes, that we talked about her sudden transformation.

"As I told you on the phone, it was Jennifer, dear," she said, wiping away a tear. "She said I was owed it."

"What did you do with my diary?" I asked

"Let me see now, Jennifer came around to pick up some shopping for me as I had a cold and she could see I was upset so I showed her the diary. She didn't seem surprised, which I thought was a bit odd but she said she'd make him pay. And afterwards, she said I was due the money. She never kept any of it herself, well just a bit for her student fees, she said."

Rita was rambling again, going over old ground but I didn't want to stop the flow in case she said something new. However, after a while, she began to get angry about Jack Robinson, saying she knew he'd killed Jennifer, it stood to reason, they had to find him. So I said, "And you've told this to the police?"

"Not yet. You said on the phone, I should wait. Why was that, dear?"

Where is Jason Rayner

I sighed and hung my head. "I didn't want it all dragged up again. It would be in all the papers, aunt. My name would be headline news, TV, reporters waiting outside the gate."

"Not again! I've only just got rid of them. Those first few weeks after Jennifer died were a nightmare, I don't mind telling you."

"Well, there you are then. It would be like that, only much, much, worse."

"But if I don't say anything, he might get away with it. I'm certain he did it. I've seen enough detective programmes on the box to know that he'd have a motive."

If only it was as easy as that, I thought, with a wry smile.

"He won't get away with it, aunt, you can rest assured. I'll make sure of it. By the way, what did you do with my diary?"

"Jennifer said it was best if she took it and destroyed it, otherwise you could be in trouble and she didn't think you'd want people to know."

At that moment I felt justified in my actions regarding Jack Robinson, Jennifer had been looking out for me until the day he murdered her – rotting in a quarry in the back of beyond was too good for him.

"Jennifer was right. Now, put it all out of your mind and tell me what you've been up to lately," I said, swallowing my anger and sorrow in one gulp.

"Well, if you're sure he won't get off scot-free, Catherine. Another cuppa?"

"Yes, but I'll make it. You go on into the front room."

In the kitchen, I picked up the new kettle, glanced around at the changes Jennifer had made and for the

Where is Jason Rayner

first time since I'd seen the blood spreading across the rug under his head, I realised that some good had come out of this mess. His face as he'd fallen to the floor, after I'd struck him, held such disbelief, such shock at my actions, although I didn't tell Ollie that bit, naturally; there were still some things he didn't know about me. I had to be careful in case he turned out to be just like all the rest. It was time my husband was made to pay, as I'd told my aunt, Jennifer was right after all.

Later, when Rita was falling asleep in front of the TV, the nine o'clock news reported that the Devon police force were looking for Mrs Catherine Rayner, and were advising Mr Rayner to contact them immediately. It was followed by a report of an unidentified body, which had been found in a tributary of the river Dart.

My heart began to pound as I watched the programme. For a fraction of a second, I forgot my previous visit by the police in Lockford, just before I left, whereby they informed me about the body in the river and thought 'how could they have found him?' However, reason drifted through my fogged mind and made me realise that there was no way it could be Jason Rayner, he was in another place altogether.

However, it was time I moved on, I couldn't risk them finding me just yet, it was too soon; Oliver would let me know when it was safe to return. It was part of the plan.

Rita snorted and opened her eyes. "Have I missed Coronation Street?"

"It's just finished. I'm bushed, would you mind if I had an early night? I have to drive back to Lockford tomorrow."

"Aw, so soon?"

"I'm afraid so, I have to work and we are very busy at the moment. I'll give you a ring in a day or two."

I left her watching an old black and white film and went to bed. The room smelled different but looked much the same. After I'd washed and put on an old nightdress of mine that I found in the back of the airing cupboard, I pulled the duvet up over my head and closed my eyes. There was nothing to be afraid of, my uncle was buried in the cemetery and Jason Rayner had disappeared for good. Tomorrow I would disappear for a while, let them look for me, just like we'd discussed it, Ollie and I, on a night when the wind howled around the walls of my flat and summer seemed such a long way off. They had to spend time looking for me because how else could I be charged with wasting police time?

The investigation

Chapter 62

There was a distinct feeling of thunder in the air, Richie thought, taking a painkiller; the night had been fraught with dreams, night sweats and insomnia. They happened less often now but still had the ability to shock him into wakefulness. He stood at his open bedroom window and looked down at the river, the level of which was low. The BBC weather forecasters didn't seem to know the reason why temperatures had suddenly risen but kept wittering on about the Jet stream, always a safe bet when all else failed, it seemed.

Dawn was breaking over the town. In the distance he could see the cluster of buildings known as The Cuttings, the new estate, which had sprung up where the refuse tip had once been located. Seagulls drifted on the still area, unwilling to accept the fact that rich pickings were no longer to be had, as the inhabitants of the estate diligently re-cycled their food in green lockable plastic bins.

The painkillers having kicked in, Richie yawned. It was going to be hard going today. They had very little to go on where the Rayner/Barton case was concerned and he was beginning to think he should call it a day. If he'd been busy with another case he might well have done but business was slow and there were no other clients on his books begging for his attention.

Where is Jason Rayner

He was getting into his car outside his flat when his mobile rang. It was Sandy, "Sorry, couldn't keep it to myself a moment longer. I had to leave you a message because I was afraid you'd still be sleeping."

"No chance. I'd only just got back last night, when I picked up your message. So, Cathy Barton is back."

"Apparently, she just waltzed into the office as if she'd never been away, or so Tracy told me." He could hear the excitement in her voice. Her enthusiasm lifted his mood; she was worth a thousand painkillers.

"Put the kettle on, Miss Smith," he said, closing his car door with a flourish and driving in the direction of Hastings buildings.

Sandy was waiting for him, two cups of coffee on her desk, another clutched in the fist of Mick Parsons, a reporter from the Lockford Heath Courier who was standing near the window looking into the street, alternately drinking coffee and puffing on an electronic cigarette.

"Richie, my old son! What's new?" he said turning to face him.

Careful not to upset the local press in the event of them becoming useful to his business at some point in the future, he replied, "Mick, haven't seen you in a while. What brings you to our door?"

Effectively turning the question around, Richie waited as the reporter walked towards him and placed his mug on the end of Sandy's desk. "A little bird told me the police have been interested in one of your clients."

Where is Jason Rayner

"A little bird with long legs, blonde hair and false boobs, by any chance?"

"The same."

So much for Tracy Golding's loyalty, thought Richie, picking up his mug from Sandy's desk.

"Ex-client."

Sandy raised her eyebrows.

"Come on now, Richie, you must have something for me."

Richie stroked his chin. "Nothing much, I'm afraid. The police were looking for her as a body required identification, but you already know that from Tracy. There's no mystery, she's been to see her sick relative and said she will contact the police as soon as possible – that's all I know. Now if you don't mind, Mick, Miss Smith and I have work to do, so if you take your butt and your electronic cigarette out of my office I'd be grateful."

When they were sure Mick Parsons had left the building, Sandy said, "How do we go about this? If we're not supposed to be working for her, we can't talk to her officially." She was standing at the window, the small fan on her desk being ineffectual in the rising temperature.

Richie walked into his inner office, placed his laptop on his desk, noted the woefully minute stack of mail in his in-tray then walked back to join her, picking up his coffee mug on the way.

"Chance meetings are all very well but Catherine Barton is no fool, she'd smell a rat, straight away."

"So it's Tracy then?"

Where is Jason Rayner

"One step ahead of me as usual, Miss Smith," he replied, looking at his watch. "She should be arriving about now."

"It's the Sweet Pea café for breakfast? You or me?"

"Umm, me this time, I think. I could do with a fry up. See you later."

Tracy perked up no end when he asked if she'd mind him joining her. "I don't come in here often, good is it?" He pointed to the plate of food she was devouring, wondering where on earth she put it.

"The best."

They discussed the merits of the Sweet Pea's Mega Breakfast until, running true to type, Tracy said, " I suppose you know that Kate turned up yesterday, like nothing has happened."

"Really?"

"Didn't you know?"

He shook his head. "Mrs Rayner is no longer our client."

"Why's that then?" Tracy put down her knife and fork with a clatter.

"She's accepted the police's account that he might have left her to be with a lover."

"Yeah typical, so a bit pointless you looking for him, I suppose?" She looked downcast as if a great topic of conversation had been snatched from within her grasp.

"As you say, no point at all…" He hesitated.

"But?"

It had worked. He was trying to put doubt in her mind and had succeeded. He mentally congratulated himself. "Nothing really, except I'd like to know how she's getting on. She must be a very worried young lady."

Tracy leaned forward. "What if I kept an eye on her? I could let you know if there is anything funny going on."

"Oh, I couldn't ask you to do that, Miss Golding, even though it would be good to have someone intelligent on the inside, so to speak. Miss Smith and I are concerned that Mrs Rayner may need someone looking out for her."

She was impressed. He could see that.

"Right, well, if I'm going to keep an eye on things, I'd better get a move on. Pop in to your office, shall I?

"Sorry?"

"Pop in, keep you in the loop – update you on things. Oh and it's Tracy." She was bending towards him, the top buttons of her blouse opened to reveal her ample cleavage.

Richie said, "Excellent. Er, you do realise that this is unpaid work, Tracy? Although I could stretch to the odd drink in the wine bar on the corner occasionally."

"Of course, no probs."

"Thank you, I appreciate it."

"You're welcome, Richie." The glint in her eye was hard to ignore. He hoped he hadn't just opened up a can of worms where young Tracy was concerned.

Two days after Richie's conversation with Tracy Golding, he left the office at ten o'clock telling Sandy he was going up to London to see DCI Freeman and would be away for a day or two.

Where is Jason Rayner

"Is it business or pleasure?" Sandy asked, filing her nails to perfection.

"Bit of both," Richie replied, tapping the side of his nose. "Be good. I'm on the mobile, if you need me, although it's as quiet as the grave, to coin a phrase. Plenty of time to put on a coat of varnish as well, I should think."

"Have a good time and drive carefully."

There it was again, Richie thought, echoes of Tess following him down the stairwell.

The drive took less time than he'd anticipated, the hot weather no doubt contributing to a general exodus from the city centre. Richie parked in a small parking area attached to his cheap but cheerful hotel, and after dropping his overnight bag in his room, had a quick beer in the bar then took an underground train to Scotland Yard.

He'd put the fear of entering the building, where he'd once worked, far behind him. Most of his contemporaries had moved on, their replacements thankfully not aware of the reason why he'd left the Met and started up in business on his own. So there were no sympathetic glances to contend with as he asked to speak to DCI Norman Freeman.

"Richie, my good man, nice to see you again; come in," Norm called across the office as Richie raised his hand in greeting.

"Still busy, I see."

"You know how it is – never enough hours in the day. But how are the inhabitants of Lockford treating you these days?"

Where is Jason Rayner

"Good. Could be more people beating a path to my door but I can't grumble. The winter was busy so we made enough to keep our heads above water."

"Sandy still with you then?"

Richie crossed his fingers in the air.

"You sounded on the phone as if you needed some help." Norm said and Richie sensed that he should keep it short. He remembered the pressure of working in the city and it was a million miles away from the calm and relatively peaceful days spent working in Hastings Buildings.

"Just a small thing." He went on to explain about Cathy Barton and Jack Robinson and how he was sure there was a connection to the death of Jennifer Teague. "Is there any way you could find out how that investigation is progressing without stepping on too many toes? I need to know whether the police believe that Jack Robinson could have anything to do with the case."

"It's possible. Funny really, you know Nobby Clarke?"

Richie nodded.

"Well, he was transferred to South Yorkshire only six months since. He'll give me the heads up, no problem."

Richie breathed a sigh of relief. "You're a star, Norm. I can't thank you enough, especially as I can see you've got enough to do here." He stood up and reached across the desk to shake his friend's hand. "I'll find my own way out, and thanks again."

"How long are you in town?"

"A day or two. Give me a ring if you find out anything, you've got my number, otherwise, I'll be back in Lockford the day after tomorrow."

Where is Jason Rayner

Leaving Scotland Yard Richie took the underground to Covent Garden. He wanted to buy a gift for Sandy and decided he could kill two birds with one stone. Sandy had loved the necklace he'd bought her a while back and it was an excuse to see Angie Peters again. She no longer had a market stall selling her unique hand crafted jewellery but had joined forces with her boyfriend who made pottery, and they'd opened a small shop near the market. They'd been married for a year or so now; Richie had gone to the small ceremony on Hampstead Heath with a few of their friends.

The shop was busy with holidaymakers, mostly Americans by the sound of it. Angie was wearing a kaftan that did little to hide the fact that she was pregnant. As soon as she saw him she called out to him. "Richie, as I live and breathe!"

"Still got the accent, Sport?" He grinned.

"What makes you think that my old Pommy friend?" She kissed his cheek and he smelled rosebuds.

"Congratulations, I had no idea; when are you due?" Richie raised his hand to Grant, who was dealing with a customer.

"Got just over two months to go. It's twins."

"Great, ready made family, good luck to you. Now I can see you're busy, just point me in the direction of a gift for Sandy and I'll leave you to it."

"No fear you don't. You are not going anywhere until you join Grant and me in a bite to eat after work, in our favourite café."

"The Italian around the corner – Nikki's?"

Where is Jason Rayner

"The same - you remembered." She looked at her watch. "See you there at six. Oh by the way, take a look at that bracelet on the stand, there."

"Perfect," he said handing her the cash and waiting whilst she wrapped it and placed it in a cardboard carrier. "Thanks. See you both later then."

When Richie arrived at the pizzeria it was to see Angie and Grant already sitting at a table outside the restaurant. The sun was lowering in the sky casting lengthening shadows across the cobbles. Shoppers were making their way to cabs and tube trains and the after-work drinkers were making the most of the warm unseasonably sunny evening by spilling out from bars clutching drinks which would prove to be the first of many.

Grant stood up, "What will it be, Richie? I'm drinking the red, Angie's on water, do you fancy a beer or will you share a bottle with me?"

"A glass of red would slip down nicely, Grant. You two are looking well, prospective parenthood obviously agrees with you both."

Meals were ordered, eaten and as the shadows merged into one and stars began to appear in the night sky, Grant said, "Why don't we finish off at our place? I'm bushed, I had an early start this morning to let the wife linger on in bed."

"Don't you start feeling sorry for him now, Richie," Angie said with a grin. "Say you'll come, stay the night, we've a spare room and we've lots of catching up to do."

Richie hesitated, "I'd certainly like to finish the evening at yours but as for staying the night – you two have to get up for work tomorrow, I'll get a cab back to my hotel later, but thanks for the invite."

Amid protests, he followed them to their flat in a block a short walk away from their shop. It was nothing like the cramped accommodation Angie had previously shared with her student friends when Richie first met her. Grant's parents had money, although you'd never have guessed it from his unassuming demeanour.

The concierge acknowledged them in the foyer and they went up in the lift to the second floor where Grant opened the door and let them into the flat. The rooms, although minimalist in design, had benefited from their owners' artistic skills; items of pottery stood on shelves and a glass table set near the window and paintings in vibrant colours, which Richie guessed were originals and not prints, brought a dash of colour to the pale painted walls. The whole atmosphere of the place was relaxing and elegant. He wondered briefly how twins would fit in whilst remembering the chaos his two had created.

"Great place you've got here; couldn't be better situated for your shop. How is business by the way?" Richie asked Grant, as Angie turned on the kettle in the space-age kitchen.

"It's good, people seem to like our stuff. Brandy?"

"Brandy's fine, thanks, small one though."

They chatted about London and the changes since Richie had lived and worked there and when Angie joined them, the conversation turned to how Richie was doing in Lockford. After a short while, Grant yawned. "Would you mind very much, if I get some shut eye, Richie? I've an early start."

Where is Jason Rayner

"No, of course not," Richie stood up.

"Hey, I don't mean for you to leave," Grant said. "My wife doesn't saunter in until midday and I know she'd really like to dig the dirt with you. Stay as long as you like, mate."

When they were alone, Richie said, "Dig the dirt? Mate? What have you done to our fine upstanding Englishman?"

Angie laughed, "Guess some of it's rubbed off on him, my old cobber. Anyway, let's get down to it."

"I'm sure I don't know what you mean."

"Course you do."

Angie had been the first stranger he had told about losing his family. The first person he had told what it felt like. It had been the turning point in his grieving process and he'd never forgotten it. She'd not drowned him in sympathy but had let him talk until he'd got it out of his system. He'd always found her so easy to talk to. Angie never judged, and over the years since the Lawson case, he often found the occasion to seek her wisdom if something was bothering him or he just needed to hear her voice. She reminded him not only of his daughter Tess but also of Sandy. In his mind they were inextricably linked and he found the thought a great comfort.

When he'd finished telling her about Cathy Barton, Angie frowned, sighed and sat in silence for a while. Grant had opened the French doors, leading to the small balcony earlier, and the sounds of a London evening drifted up towards them. Laughter, conversation, and in the distance the low hum of traffic, competed with the intoxicating mix of a night spent in a pulsating, cosmopolitan city

Angie sat back, eased her growing belly into a comfortable position and with her feet resting on a footstool, she said, "What happened to the uncle?"

"Bill Ferris? He died."

"Yeah, you said. But what of?"

Richie thought for a moment. "Er, do you know, I'm not sure. I think it was a stroke, or something similar. Why?"

Angie rubbed her belly. "Nothing." She shook her head and her pre-Raphaelite curls bounced on her shoulders.

"Angie?"

"OK, well I just thought it a bit coincidental that Bill Ferris died at roughly the same time as his niece did a runner."

Richie struck his forehead with the heel of his hand. "Now why didn't I think of that?"

"'Cos you're too busy being a detective."

Richie ran his fingers through his hair, it was no excuse but he noticed she'd smiled to ease his conscience.

Catherine's story

Chapter 63

When I considered enough time had passed and the news reports of my disappearance were more frequent, I returned to work as if nothing had happened, saying that my aunt was much better.

During my lunch hour, in the card shop opposite the office, I chose a card with red roses and the words To a Special Aunty entwined with the petals. As I did so, the memory of my uncle hit me like a slap in the face. Rita never knew, did she? She wouldn't have let him, if she'd known, would she?

I replaced the card and picked up another with a picture of a thatched cottage and the words Happy Birthday written above it, just in case.

Ollie was waiting for me in the cafe and he still blushed a bit as I sat down beside him. We ordered our food and ate our omelettes in virtual silence. Then over coffee, he said, "Don't take any notice of them, Kate. If you want to talk, I'll listen; you know I will. We've done the right thing, remember." He was embarrassed, kept looking down at the tablecloth. I patted his hand,

"Thank you Ollie."

Later that afternoon, I thought about Ollie's words. I could never tell him all of it but he knew enough to make it a burden shared, but would it be halved and not duplicated if I told him the rest? Secrets were better kept in my opinion. How could you trust a person not to tell?

Where is Jason Rayner

I was waiting at the bus stop, having finished work for the day, when I saw Sandy leaving Hastings Buildings. It was too late to avoid speaking to her; she'd already seen me.

"Hi," she said with a smile.

"Er, hello."

"How are you?" she asked. It seemed an innocent enough question but I was waiting for the crunch to come – why didn't I want Richie Stevens to continue with the investigation – where had I been during these past few weeks? Instead she looked at her watch and said, "Nice to see you again, Cathy, I'm afraid I must dash."

She rushed away without looking back and it was only as I stepped on to the bus that I realised she had called me Cathy and not Kate. I began to shake; all the way home I couldn't get it out of my head. How much had Richard Stevens and Sandy discovered about my past? Although there was a cold wind blowing through the open window above my head, I was beginning to sweat.

Inside my flat, I opened the windows, made a cup of coffee and sat at the kitchen table to drink it. I wouldn't think about Jason Rayner. I had admitted to the therapist that there was no one of that name – he had been a figment of my disturbed mind. But it wasn't true; he was my husband. His name was my only invention.

My mobile was still in my handbag. I finished my drink and walked into the hallway, removed my handbag from the hook and carried it into the room. Even then I couldn't summon up the courage to pick up my mobile and access the message menu. I sat

Where is Jason Rayner

looking at the cream leather bag I'd bought in Meadowhall, the one with a pocket for a mobile phone attached to the strap. I could see the bulge in the leather.

I stood up, went into the bedroom, removed my clothes and headed for the bathroom. In the shower, I closed my eyes and wondered if lies could catch up with you and drown you, as a vision of his body floating up from the depths appeared before me.

Where is Jason Rayner

The investigation

Chapter 64

The letter was waiting on the mat when he arrived home. It was written in Sandy's hasty scrawl – *called earlier but could see you were still away – thought you might like to take a look at this before we meet tomorrow. I searched the local newspaper archives again and found the enclosed. I think you'll agree it's interesting! S*

Richie carried the letter and its contents into the kitchen and switched on the kettle. After drinking a fortifying mixture of hot black coffee liberally laced with sugar, he inspected the photocopy.

It was a small item she'd found in a local paper. He was surprised Sandy had been able to find the piece at all, as it was tucked in between a report of a DIY store, which had burned down, and the proposed building of a new Leisure centre on the outskirts of Sheffield. The heading read – **Young child found with father's dead body.**

The body of James Barton was found yesterday in the family home on Beaufort Avenue. His daughter, nine-year-old Catherine, was discovered in the room with her deceased father; she was suffering from shock. It appears Mr Barton died from a cerebral haemorrhage and his traumatised daughter, unable to contact the emergency services, stayed in the same room as her father for three days before she was found. Apparently Mrs Laura Teague, a neighbour, became concerned when she

Where is Jason Rayner

hadn't seen Catherine for some time and had alerted the police. When officers entered the property, they found the young girl wedged beneath the body of her father and the wall, her leg, which was later found to be broken, having been trapped underneath Mr Barton's body. James Barton had, in his youth, played rugby, as a blind-side prop forward, for the Sheffield Tigers.

Richie walked across the room to the window and looked out. The river, meandering through the trees opposite, shone in the moonlight. It was a night that promised a spell of dry warm weather, a night when you could believe it felt good to be alive. He thought about his client, the trauma of her father's death, the possibility that her uncle had been abusing her, her infatuation with Jack Robinson and her subsequent marriage, events any one of which would be enough to traumatise a young person. But to what extent had she been affected? Was it enough to make her invent a marriage and the disappearance of Jason Rayner and if so why?

The following day, Richie slept late, having been awake half the night thinking about the case and the rest dreaming unconnected rubbish. He was in the shower when the phone rang. Dripping water across the floor, he picked up the connection in the bedroom.

"You OK?" It was Sandy.

"Yeah, sorry, I should have rung. Slept late, couldn't stop thinking about your letter. I'll be over, once I'm dressed."

"Right."

Where is Jason Rayner

"What is it?"

"Flintlock just phoned. He said the police have advised our ex-client that she is to undergo treatment by a clinical psychologist or be charged with wasting police time on two occasions."

"I see. And she accepted the former?"

"Apparently so. She's already had her first appointment and begun therapy, which is an intensive course over the next few weeks. I wonder what Tracy will make of that?"

"I'm sure we'll soon find out. Well what do you think? Do we continue?" Sandy asked.

"You think we should?"

"I'm not sure, it's just something doesn't feel right and you've always taught me not to ignore such feelings."

Richie smiled, "In that case, it's business as usual where our client is concerned, Miss Smith, regardless of the fact that we are working for nothing. But I suppose it's better than sitting around staring at the ceiling. As I said before, have another word with Oliver Watts, unofficially. He's carrying such a massive torch for Cathy Barton, I wonder if he's got his fingers burned?

It was several days later, after arriving at the office somewhat later than usual, that he found Sandy waiting for him. She was standing at the side of his desk, with a smile of satisfaction. "We were right. Dan sent his report over this morning."

Sandy's brother Dan worked in the archaeological research department of a college on the outskirts of Lockford and was an expert dealing in facial recognition software. Sandy thought that

Where is Jason Rayner

he'd be able to compare the photo of Jack Robinson with the CCTV image of the man walking down the lane at the side of the Ferris's house on the day Jennifer Teague was murdered and had emailed him copies of both prints.

"So, it *was* Jack Robinson," Richie said, looking at the printout on his desk.

Sandy sat down opposite him. "Possibly. Dan said there are enough identification markers to say that both images could be of the same person, but obviously, unless the CCTV image was clearer, he couldn't say with complete certainty that both photographs are of Jack Robinson."

"I understand but it's enough for us, don't you think?"

"I do. So now we are definitely looking for Jack Robinson."

"Without a doubt, if not for reincarnating himself as Jason Rayner then for the murder of Jennifer Teague." Richie stood up and walked to the window. The sun was shining, promising a warm day, even though it was still March. He saw shoppers hurrying down the High Street in order to take advantage of the spring sales and latecomers hurrying towards their offices before their bosses could discover their tardiness.

"Where to begin, is the problem. He obviously thinks he's invincible," Sandy said thoughtfully. "I'll have that chat with Oliver Watts. What if Jason Rayner is not a figment of Cathy's imagination? Either way we are still looking for the same person. And if so, Oliver, in my opinion, is the man most likely to have seen the elusive husband."

Where is Jason Rayner

Turning away from the window, Richie said, "It can do no harm, in view of the fact that the man has disappeared into thin air."

The Sweet Pea café was busy at lunchtime. Sandy waited for a table but to her dismay saw Cathy Barton was already sitting opposite Oliver at a table situated in a small alcove. Deciding whether to abandon all thoughts of talking to him or wait until a table was free, she hesitated then saw a couple standing up and leaving a table free. As the waitress showed Sandy to a seat, she passed their table. "Hullo, this place is busy today," she said. "How are you both?"

"Fine, thanks," Oliver replied, but his companion just nodded.

Sensing she felt awkward about seeing her again, after dispensing with their services, Sandy asked, "Would you have any idea whether Mr Trent could see me sometime today? I don't want to talk shop whilst you're on your lunch hour but I need some legal advice in a hurry and…"

Cathy Barton, taking the initiative, spoke then, her voice strong and decisive. "He's free most of the afternoon, actually. Why not come over after you finish your lunch?"

"Er, thanks, I will," Sandy replied, leaving them to finish eating their lunch. Sitting at a nearby table, she picked up the menu and wondered why she had never realised before that Cathy Barton was no pushover. It had taken strength of will to leave her home and set up a decent life for herself where no one knew her, and she had survived, in spite of her past, or perhaps because of it.

Where is Jason Rayner

Later, in pensive mood, she left the café and headed back to the office having made an appointment to see Mason Trent later that afternoon.

However, her visit to the offices of Arbuthnot and Trent proved to be unfruitful. She'd discussed with Richie the possibility that Mason Trent might have noticed something during the time before Kate Newson's relationship with Jason Rayner began.

"Nothing, I'm afraid, Miss Smith. I wish I could help you. I know you've had a word with Tracy about this and she is the one who would be most likely to have seen her husband – Jason Rayner – funny sort of name, I always thought. I understand, she had some personal problems at the time, sort of breakdown, I gather. She seems OK now though; right as rain." As his gaze focused on her chest, Sandy realised she was wasting her time. The man had only one thing on his mind, his powers of observation were nil.

Sandy still hadn't managed to speak to Oliver Watts alone, so the following day, she waited until the lunchtime rush in the Sweet Pea café was over but there was still no sign of Oliver. She'd wanted to make it appear as if they were meeting by chance so his guard would be down. But it looked as if he were breaking the habits of a lifetime and giving the café a wide berth. She stood up and made for the door. It wasn't her intention to go to the office of Arbuthnot and Trent and make an official request to talk to him; she'd have to think of another way.

She was considering what to do next when she heard, "Hello there, you work with Richie, the private detective, don't you?" Tracy Golding

Where is Jason Rayner

emerged from the dress shop next to the café carrying a large cardboard carrier.

"Yes, it's Miss Golding from Arbuthnot and Trent, isn't it?" Sandy asked falling into step alongside her. "On your way back to work? Lunchtimes eh? Never enough time to do what you want to. I'm a bit late going back myself actually."

"Yeah, but I can soon get around Mason Trent, and Larry Arbuthnot's taken his family to Brussels so I can more or less do what I like."

"Lucky you, my boss watches me like a hawk." It wasn't true, of course, but Sandy decided a white lie, to gain her confidence, was fine. "I didn't see Oliver in the café today, he's often there when I'm having my lunch." Subterfuge was becoming a habit, it seemed.

"Our Oliver? No, he's on holiday too, and Kate; a bit much if you ask me, she's only just got back from visiting her aunt and she's off again. Anyway, things are always quiet at this time of the year – everyone off enjoying themselves, I expect."

They were nearly outside the office when Sandy said, "Has Oliver gone anywhere nice?"

"Not sure, wouldn't think so, he never goes too far, bit of a home bird our Oliver. Although he did go to France a while back, which was a surprise."

"Well, nice to see you again, I have to dash," Sandy said, rushing in the direction of Hastings buildings.

"So," Richie said, "Cathy Barton is supposedly on holiday, Tracy obviously doesn't know about the therapist or that her name was Cathy Barton and now Oliver Watts is unavailable."

Where is Jason Rayner

"He's just on holiday, people do, surely?" Sandy said pouring hot water over a tea bag.

"You think I'm looking for trouble where none exists?"

"Got it in one."

Richie sighed. "When you've finished making that foul smelling brew, I think we should put our heads together. This case is unravelling before our eyes."

"It's camomile."

"What is?"

"This foul smelling brew. It's supposed to be calming. I could always make you a cup if you want?"

"I'll take your word for that, Miss Smith. Open the window a fraction wider before you bring your laptop into my office and we go over some details. I have the distinct feeling we're missing something that is right under our noses."

It was after lunch; Richie was in the middle of the Telegraph crossword – Sandy completing most of it as his frequent questions, requiring an answer to the anagram puzzles, were supplied by her. The ringing of the phone disturbed the relative peace in the office. Richie reached out an arm to pick it up.

"I see. Thanks for letting us know, Inspector. Good, I understand. I'm sure you are."

Replacing the handset, he sighed, "Well now, that's a turn up for the books."

"What?" Sandy looked up from the puzzle.

"Flintlock's informed me that the therapist's report concerning Kate Rayner concludes that his patient was suffering for a paranoid delusion when she invented Jason Rayner and his subsequent disappearance. Apparently the paranoia occurred as a result of traumatic childhood, the details of which are, of course, confidential.

Sandy raised an eyebrow. "And we believe it?"

"As you're so good at puzzles, Miss Smith, maybe you have the answer to that one?"

Where is Jason Rayner

Catherine's story

Chapter 65

Everyone at the office was treating me with kid gloves, since they'd heard the news that I'd invented Jason Rayner, even Mason Trent didn't seem quite as obnoxious as usual. The only person who hadn't changed was Ollie, which was just as well under the circumstances. I needed Ollie to be the same.

"Fancy lunch in the Sweet Pea?" he asked. I thought about saying no but it was only for a fleeting second; as I said, I needed Ollie.

"Of course, I'd like that. See you inside at a quarter past, I've to do some shopping first," I replied, and saw a slow smile creep across his innocent face.

The café was busy. Sitting opposite him, I studied his face; I felt sorry for involving him in this mess and noticed he looked pale as he toyed with his meal, without eating much of it. When Sandy spoke to us, I thought he was going to faint right there into his plate of fish and chips. But he managed to speak to her and when I saw how much of an effort it was for him, I did the talking and she soon left to sit down. Ollie breathed a sigh of relief when she eventually finished her meal and left the café. I realised how awful this must have been for him, not knowing how I was, whilst playing his part with the police and Richie Stevens, not to mention the office staff.

Where is Jason Rayner

"It's OK," I said touching his hand. "They can't know what we did. You said so yourself."

Later, when I was sitting in bed watching the ten o'clock news, the reassuring words I'd said to Ollie earlier, came back to haunt me. I picked up the phone.

"We need to speak. Not now, not on the phone, " I said. "Meet me here before work tomorrow."

"Do you think….?" His voice shook.

"Not now, tomorrow. Try and sleep, I'll see you in the morning."

I was trying to be the strong one, afraid he would crack and spoil things for us but I knew there was no way I was going to get any sleep that night.

At half past six the next morning, Ollie pressed the intercom and I let him in. I could see by his face, he had spent the night in much the same manner as I. "They'll think it's suicide," I said, handing him a mug of black coffee. "You said they wouldn't know we had anything to do with it." At this point I wasn't sure whom I was trying to comfort, Ollie or myself.

"That was before they found the body." His hand started to shake.

"Ollie get a grip, please. You'll give yourself away. You could mess this up for both of us. Take a deep breath and relax. No one can possibly tie him to us. We made sure of it. They've identified the body in Devon remember, and this has nothing to do with us."

"Sorry, I don't know what's got into me. I've missed you these last few weeks. I'll be OK now you're back."

Where is Jason Rayner

I suppose it helped to go back to work. I saw him talking to a customer at the desk and thought - no one would know he'd helped to get rid of a body. And when Sandy arrived to speak to Mason Trent, I saw him give her a nervous smile. He was acting normally. It was normal for Ollie to be diffident. Nevertheless, I couldn't rest until we'd finished work for the day and he was driving me home. The rest of the office staff were used to us spending time together now, Tracy had even got fed up of passing remarks aimed at us.

It was all over the television news and newspapers. I awoke next morning, after finally drifting into sleep, exhaustion having taken its toll, switched on the TV and saw the quarry where we'd thrown my husband's body on a newsflash report. The phone was ringing before I could take in most of the details. It was Ollie.

"You watching the news?" he asked.

"Yes," my voice was barely above a whisper.

"I'll come over straight away."

I'd barely had time to close the door behind him, when he said, "They'd begun in the quarry again and it must have disturbed the rocks somehow, and I'm not sure exactly how it happened but the car rose to the surface." His voice was rising.

"We knew yesterday that this was going to haunt us. We have to be strong, sit it out. Switch off the TV, don't watch the news or read the papers, if that will help."

I don't know how we got through that day. I can only remember acting as if every simple task took more effort than I could imagine to complete it as I waited for the police to come looking for me.

"You OK, Kate? You look as if you've seen a ghost," Mason Trent said as I handed him the last letters of the day for him to sign.

"I'm fine, Mr Trent, just a bit tired," I replied, which seemed to satisfy him, although he'd never know how true his words were; a ghost was exactly what I was seeing every time I heard a news report about the discovery of the body or opened a newspaper. Unlike Ollie I needed to know, I couldn't hide away from it. I needed to know every last bit of it.

Later, when Ollie and I were watching the nine o'clock news, the full story was beginning to emerge. In the soft light shed by the table lamp, I watched Ollie's face for signs of weakness. I couldn't afford for him to crack up now. It would spoil everything.

"They think he murdered that girl in Sheffield," he said. "It's just like you said at the time. He killed her - Jennifer Teague - he killed her and they think he couldn't live with it and drove his car over the edge of the quarry."

"It was fortunate we got rid of the rug," I replied. "You're mother didn't think it was odd? I often wondered if she did."

"Nah, all mother is interested in is EastEnders and Bingo. She was only too pleased when I said I was clearing up some of the rubbish she'd collected in the back garden. All she said, at the time, was 'it's like Bonfire night, when you were a kid, Oliver.'

"Good."

Where is Jason Rayner

"So you think we are in the clear?" He was looking at me for reassurance.

"Of course, no one will be able to link John Rice, the man, who lived for a short time in a flat in Lockford, paid his rent on time and left after notifying his landlord by letter and enclosing his remaining payment, with Jack Robinson. The police will close the case. It will be yesterday's news in a day or two, once everyone's stopped talking about it."

He gave a sigh and I saw him relax at my comforting words but they were just words, how could I know if they were true or not?

Where is Jason Rayner

The investigation

Chapter 66

Richie had to admit to failure. He closed his laptop and walked into the outer office.

"This is the first time I've not been able to solve a case, Miss Smith. There's no link between Jack Robinson and Jason Rayner that I can find. We have to assume the therapist treating our ex-client is correct - Jason Rayner never existed and we should forget the whole business. I can't afford to spend any more time on it. Life has moved on."

The following morning Richie switched on the TV and was in the middle of eating a slice of toast when he saw a newsflash – a body had been found in a quarry in a remote part of South Wales. Blasting had been resumed in the Pant-y-Glas quarry and the bloated body of an, as yet, unidentified male had been discovered in his car.

Richie glanced at his watch, it was half-eight; Norm would be at his desk, drinking his second black coffee of the day by now. He picked up the phone and rang his old friend.

"DCI Freeman, please," he asked the operator.

"Richie? And what can I do for you at this early hour. I thought you'd be still getting some beauty sleep, being your own boss."

Where is Jason Rayner

"I wish. Have you seen this morning's news flash about a body being found......"

"In a quarry in South Wales?" Freeman finished his sentence for him.

"Any idea who they think it is?"

"Bit early to say officially but I've just spoken to Nobby Clarke; he rang about some do or other they're arranging for Brian Timson, and he told me, unofficially, they think it might be Jack Robinson. Didn't you ask me about the Barton case a while back?"

"I did. Why does he think it's Robinson?"

"The body was found a day or two ago and it's only just been released to the press. They sent a forensic chappy down yesterday and everything points to it being him and it's his car."

"Car?"

"Nobby said, they think he took his own life by driving his car over the edge of the quarry. The number plate was A1 JR, and I understand it's registered in the name of Jack Robinson."

"I see."

"He also said that a park keeper has identified Jack Robinson as the man meeting a girl fitting Jennifer Teague's description, at the bandstand in the park, on more than one occasion. He remembered the girl's spiky hair and thought they looked odd together, furtive was the word he used. It sounds like an open and shut case, to me."

"Right. Thanks, Norm. I appreciate it."

"Unofficial, Richie."

"Of course, you don't have to worry about me."

"Didn't think so for a minute. Now tell me when you are coming up to see us?"

Where is Jason Rayner

Sandy phoned in sick; she'd eaten something that had upset her but promised to be in bright and early the next day. There was nothing doing in the office so Richie closed up at four and drove home. He watched TV without engaging with the detective drama unfolding on the screen until the ten o'clock news began. The camera panned in on the quarry and Robinson's car then focused on the reporter. Next Vanessa Robinson was interviewed who said that her husband had left her to be with a former girlfriend. She didn't mention his involvement with Catherine Barton but said that he was a man who liked younger women. The impression she gave of Robinson seemed to suggest that he was an unstable individual.

Richie couldn't settle, took a sleeping pill and tried to get his head down for the night. But his dreams were of his client's elusive husband and despite the sleeping pill he awoke at five with the distinct feeling that at last Jason Rayner had a face, and one which he recognised. What if Cathy Barton had created the perfect murder? It was the question he asked himself over and over again as he ate his breakfast, showered, and dressed for work. He wondered if it were possible. Surely someone had seen him with Cathy? But unless they had a clear image of the man Jack Robinson had evolved into, there was no way they could prove it.

Driving towards Hastings Building, the sun's morning rays spreading across his dashboard, he pondered how a man could exist without leaving a metaphorical footprint behind. How did he live? What work did he do? They'd drawn a blank with the identity Cathy Barton had created for her absent husband. Perhaps it had all been a ploy to keep them away from the truth. Perhaps she'd planned it all along.

Arriving at the office before Sandy, Richie looked down on the High Street and waited for his ex-client to arrive at her office. At five minutes before nine, he heard Sandy's footsteps climbing the stairs at the same time as he saw Cathy and Oliver arriving at Arbuthnot and Trent's together. He frowned; had she murdered her non-existent husband and covered it up so completely that there was no trace of him or was that non-existent husband Jack Robinson? If so she couldn't have done it alone – it would be a physical impossibility – she must have had help. As Sandy opened the door to the outer office, he saw Oliver Watts place a proprietary arm around the young woman's shoulders. It didn't take a gigantic leap of the imagination to realise who her accomplice might be.

Sitting at her desk finishing off updating the Cathy Barton file, Sandy called through to Richie who was catnapping having had a disturbed night. "Can I get you a drink?"

"I'll get it, you carry on with what you're doing." He ambled into the outer office and walked towards the kitchen area.

"I wonder?"

Richie looked over his shoulder. He knew what to expect from her tone of voice. "It's just, when the photo of Jack Robinson was circulated on the initial news report, it was the one

Where is Jason Rayner

Vanessa Robinson gave to the police and it would have shown him as he was."

"I'm not with you," Richie left filling the kettle and walked towards her.

"The one I sent to Dan for comparison purposes was the same one as on the news report regarding Jennifer Teague's murder, the CCTV photo of the man coming out of the lane at the side of the houses. And, even though they looked different, Dan's report showed that there were enough identifying features for it to be Jack Robinson. What if he was also Jason Rayner, Cathy's missing husband."

"I know, I should be following this, but I'm not sure that I am."

"Well, no one is going to recognise Jason Rayner from the photograph of Jack Robinson ...."

"I've been thinking along the same lines but there is no evidence to support it so it remains just a theory. Best to shut the file and forget about it."

Sandy nodded.

But the thought, once implanted in his brain, grew and grew until the next day, it was all Richie could think about.

He sat at his breakfast table munching his way through a bowl of cereal, thinking of how she could have got away with it. When he reached his office, he desperately needed to bounce some ideas around with Sandy.

She arrived, looking neat in a black skirt and white blouse, her hair tied in a knot at the back of neck. Sandy took one look at him and asked, "Coffee?"

"Strong and black." He couldn't wait to tell her. " I think I've got the answer to the question, 'Where

Where is Jason Rayner

is Jason Rayner?'," Richie said, walking towards the window.

The morning rush hour was in full swing but he couldn't concentrate on the scene unfolding below him. He picked up the mug of coffee Sandy handed him and began to explain. When he'd finished, Sandy drummed the back of her left hand with the fingers of her right. "What are you going to do about it?" she asked.

"Not sure. What can we do? The problem is twofold as far as I can see. Firstly there is no evidence to support my supposition, if, as I suspect the two of them made sure that every trace of Jack Robinson was removed from her flat. And even if they didn't, Cathy Barton could explain it away by saying that he visited her on several occasions, thus covering her back." He ran his fingers through his hair distractedly. "So, there is still nothing to suggest she was ever linked to his murder. Secondly, the police have been looking for Jack Robinson in connection with the murder of Jennifer Teague and as his body shows no signs of foul play other than a crack on the head which wouldn't be out of the way considering the nature of his demise, it seems to suggest he couldn't live with what he'd done and took matters into his own hands."

Sandy stopped finger tapping. "So she gets away with murder? Or should I say both of them do, Oliver Watts would be an accessory at the very least."

Richie sighed. "In some respects. However, I don't think either of them will rest easy again. Cathy Barton is a troubled young woman with a past, the depths of which have yet to be reached, in my opinion."

"And Oliver Watts?" Sandy asked.

"Oliver is a horse of a different colour entirely. His conscience is the cross he has to carry. I wouldn't be surprised if it all came spilling out at some time in the future. So for now it's case closed, Miss Smith."

Later that day, as Richie prepared to lock up the office having sent Sandy home early, he heard footsteps on the stairs. The sound of high heels clacking on the treads gave him an indication of who it might be before Tracy opened the door.

"Mr Stevens, I've some news," she said breathlessly.

"It's Richie, Tracy, sit down, catch your breath and tell me all." He smiled and she hitched up her skirt a fraction higher as she crossed her legs.

"I thought you should know; Kate and Oliver are getting married."

Richie smiled. "Really? That's good news, isn't it?"

Tracy looked crestfallen. "Is it? Don't you think it's a bit odd, her having lost her husband so soon and now she'd getting married again?"

"Ah, but you've forgotten that Jason Rayner never existed."

Tracy bit her lip. "No, not forgotten exactly. I know what her shrink said, it was all around the office, but I can't believe that there was no such person."

"What makes you think that there was?" Richie sat forward.

Where is Jason Rayner

"The flowers, for a start. Who in their right mind sends flowers to themselves and pretends they are from someone who doesn't exist? Then there's Trent's birthday. She bought the doughnuts as usual and when she was carrying them back to the office she met him."

Richie's pulse began to race. "You saw him?"

"Not saw, no. I heard her speaking to someone as the door opened and her face was flushed when she handed the tray to Mason Trent."

"I see. Well, thanks for that, Tracy. I appreciate your help in this case and your valued assistance in bringing it to a close."

"That's it?"

"It is. But I will certainly keep you in mind should I require your invaluable expertise in the future."

Tracy brightened and stood up, smoothing down her skirt to a respectable length, as Richie showed her to the door.

"When is the wedding, by the way?" he asked.

"A week on Saturday, at Lockford Registry Office – eleven o'clock – we've all been invited, even Trent."

He heard Tracy close the door at the bottom of the staircase and sighed. Part of him felt there had been no satisfactory conclusion to this case and part of him wished a damaged girl a happy married life; only time would tell whether it would be so.

Where is Jason Rayner

Catherine's last story

Chapter 67

In the office of Arbuthnot and Trent there is a new topic of conversation. Oliver and I are getting married next Saturday and we've invited Tracy to be one of our witnesses. It's not going to be a big wedding; just a few of Oliver's friends, his mother and my aunt Rita, oh and Mason Trent and Larry Arbuthnot. This time everyone will see my husband and know that I'm not making it up should he suddenly disappear.

There are times, when I think back to the men in my life and how they've treated me, I'm thankful that I've found someone I can trust at last. The psychiatric therapist reported I was traumatised by what happened to my father, I was so young, a horrific event in anyone's estimation and if that wasn't bad enough, afterwards, there was my uncle Bill's sudden death, but even he didn't know the truth about Bill.

There is some truth in the report but it's not the whole story, as, no doubt, you have guessed. I try not to think about it but he deserved what happened to him, my dad did not. As for Jack Robinson, he was a user. He used both Vanessa and myself; I might have forgiven him though, if it hadn't been for what he did to Jennifer. He had to pay, you see, just like Bill Ferris. I imagined I could become a new person but like Jack Robinson, reality has a way of fracturing our dreams.

Where is Jason Rayner

No one can link Jack Robinson with Jason Rayner - after all he doesn't exist, he never did and I have a psychiatrist's report to verify the fact.
And Ollie? Ollie's OK; I can handle Ollie.

The End

Where is Jason Rayner

If you have enjoyed reading this book please pass on the word. If you are looking for more, visit www.kjrabane.co.uk
Many thanks, K.J.Rabane

Where is Jason Rayner

K.J.Rabane has written for local newspapers, had short stories published in magazines and an anthology of crime fiction, in addition to which she's written television scripts for an on-going drama series, which is ready for submission. She is also a commissioned contributor to the Food & Drink Guide and works as a freelance 'extra' for film and television productions. Her main interest is in writing crime fiction and psychological thrillers but her novel According to Olwen falls into neither category. All her books are full of idiosyncratic characters and her crime fiction novels are plot driven. Her poem Luminous socks was a finalist in the 2012 All Wales Poetry Competition and Who is Sarah Lawson? reached the Amazon Breakthrough Novel Award 2013 Competition Quarter Finals. To check out a comprehensive list of reviews on all of K.J.Rabane's books visit www.amazon.co.uk.

Follow on Facebook and Twitter.

Printed in Great Britain
by Amazon.co.uk, Ltd.,
Marston Gate.